FINDING
KATE

Also By Pamela Humphrey

In This Series

Finding Claire

Other Books

The Blue Rebozo: A Novella

Researching Ramirez: On the Trail of the Jesus Ramirez Family

FINDING KATE

PAMELA HUMPHREY

For my boys

CHAPTER ONE

January 18, 2016 – 10:21 pm

Stars twinkled in the West Texas sky as my crazy, life-altering Monday sped to a close. I glanced at Alex, visible only by the lights of the dashboard. When he'd proposed a road trip to Denver, I jumped on his impulsive idea with both feet. Spending uninterrupted time together on the open road stirred my romantic notions. Only hours before, we'd acknowledged our mutual interest, sending our relationship in a whole new direction.

The truck, with Alex behind the wheel, acted as a bubble, a quiet space in my world turned upside down. After being kidnapped, escaping, then learning I'd grown up under a false name, with people who weren't my parents, I was a raw, emotional wreck. Alex probably suggested the road trip knowing I needed time to acclimate to the idea of my new identity. The cab of his truck, a quiet place to talk it out, served that purpose well.

Finding him was the best part of all that happened. My heart bubbled with anticipation, thinking about living in Texas and dating Alejandro Ramirez.

In the hours since we'd left the cabin, we'd talked and laughed, the in-between interspersed with comfortable silence. His permanently etched smile marked a drastic change from the sullen man I'd met less than two weeks before. With big life changes looming outside my bubble, inside, I splashed in a pool of happiness and contentment; that is, until he mentioned stopping for the night.

"We're getting close to Raton. I think that's a good place to shut it down. We'll find a hotel, then something for dinner." Alex laid his hand on mine.

Warm and strong, his hand—which all last week had been such an anchor of safety—caressed my fingers, a reminder of the tenderness I'd learned lay buried underneath his protective exterior. When he'd suggested the road trip, stopping for the night hadn't registered as a concern. No thought of sleeping arrangements had crossed my mind, at all. Everything about him set my heart fluttering, but I couldn't sleep with him.

I wouldn't.

I had my reasons—reasons I'd never shared with anyone. Besides, there'd been no mention of the L word, and that, at least in my book, was a definite prerequisite. The only reference to love was a red heart on the tee shirt he'd given me. If my reservations weren't enough, letters my mom wrote heaped reasons on top of all mine.

Given the emotional roller coaster of the past few days and the deep connection Alex and I shared, one far deeper than expected for the short time we'd known each other—fueled by his willingness to take me in and protect me with little regard for himself, but even more so by his honesty—anyway, that connection convinced me that one hotel room was a bad idea, a seriously bad idea.

His sideways glance pulled me out of my thoughts. *I need to answer him.*

"Raton? Sure. I'll see if I can find a hotel." Once I regained a cell signal, I Googled and found a suitable stopping place near our route. I entered the address into the map app on my phone, and a woman's voice spouted directions every few minutes. I stared out the window, mustering the courage to set boundaries. I didn't doubt that he'd respect my wishes, but my heart pounded, anticipating his disappointment. I didn't want to be the reason the clouds returned to those green eyes.

After ten minutes of quiet, Alex's smooth voice spilled over my thoughts. "What did your dad say? Or Travis? I'm not sure what to call him."

"I'm not ready to call him Dad. I think Travis works."

"Was he disappointed you left without stopping in to see him again?"

"If he was, he hid it." I smiled at Alex's profile. "He just sounded excited when I told him you and I were driving to Denver to get my stuff."

"I bet he was."

"When he offered me the house, he hesitated. Not sure why."

"How do you mean?" Alex laid his open hand on the center console, inviting me to hold it.

I skimmed my fingertip along the length of each of his fingers. "He asked where I planned to live, then before I could answer, he said, 'never mind.' After a short, awkward silence, he told me The Castle was mine if I wanted it."

Alex closed his hand around mine. "Hmm. Maybe he didn't want to seem too pushy?"

"Could be. I'm stunned at the offer but very happy about it."

"Having you back in Schatzenburg is a dream come true for him."

"And I hope that living in that house, maybe I can feel Emma? I know that sounds stupid. One of the hardest parts of all this is that she's gone. I'll never know her—my mom. It still feels so odd to call her that."

"That's not stupid."

"I'm moving into a house and adopting it as home just because the woman who birthed me loved it. Pretty sure that's not exactly normal."

"Normal is overrated." He pulled my hand to his lips.

"Travis also said there's more family for me to meet when I'm ready. I have an Aunt Beth living in Schatzenburg, apparently."

"That's exciting, right?"

"Yeah. Having extended family will be a whole new adventure."

"Have I mentioned how happy I am that you're moving?"

"Not for the last thirty miles." I tilted my head back against the headrest, thoughts and emotions still spinning from the day's revelations. "I get a whole house. It looked so cute when we stopped that day."

"Absolutely adorable." He didn't need to wink for me to understand his teasing tone. "He's taking care of all the moving arrangements, you said?"

"Yep. Everything." I smiled into the darkness, picturing the bungalow on the corner.

Alex squeezed my hand before letting go and turning into the hotel parking lot. "Sit tight." He stopped near the double doors, then slid out of the driver's seat and bounded around the truck.

Despite being tired and emotionally drained, I smiled. I climbed down, using his extended hand for balance, glad to stretch my legs. He grabbed our luggage, and, with his free hand, reached for mine.

As the first set of double doors opened, I stopped. Alex glanced back over his shoulder, a question knitted in his brow. I shook my head.

"What?" He tugged me to the side. "What's wrong?"

I stared at my feet and let the words tumble out. "I want separate hotel rooms."

He dropped the duffle bags near his feet and folded me into his arms.

I buried my face in his chest. Remembering my past came with its own price. People I knew long before meeting him shaped my view of the world, but I couldn't tell him about all of that.

Not yet.

Somewhere buried in my tangled mess of memories, hopefully still locked in a remote closet, lurked a memory that, if it seeped out, would darken everything, like an oil spill in the gulf. I needed to avoid triggering the latch on the door that kept it hidden.

"Please look at me, Kate."

I lifted my gaze, steeling my emotions against what I expected to see. Instead of disappointment, relief softened the lines in his face.

"I planned to get two rooms." He pulled my head to his chest and kissed my hair. "Wanting you to stay doesn't mean I expect you to sleep with me." Soft and matter-of-fact, his words eased my tension.

Relief outweighed the embarrassment of my foolish assumption. I sighed, and he brushed his thumb across my lips before picking up the bags.

"I think you've been dating the wrong kind of guys."

"The non-perfect kind?"

He chuckled as the sliding doors opened. "Just wait 'til you know me better."

The brightly lit lobby, decked out in loud splotches of color, sat empty, yet the news still spewed from the television mounted to the wall. He dropped the bags near the front desk. After looking around a moment, he tapped the little silver bell on the counter. "After we get our rooms, I'll find us some dinner."

The clerk stepped out from the back, smiling. "Good evening. Y'all need one room?"

"Two, please. Adjoining if you have them." Alex looked at me and raised his eyebrows, requesting my approval.

"That'd be great." Grateful for a separate room, I liked the idea of having him close by. It wrapped me in a promise of safety. Not enough time had elapsed, and though my attackers were in either the morgue or a jail cell, I caught myself looking over my shoulder, wondering who was around the corner, fearful they'd find me. I desperately hoped time would erase that paranoia.

The blonde behind the desk tapped on the keyboard. "I have two kings, adjoining, on the third floor. Will that work?"

"Perfectly." To me, Alex added as he squeezed my hand, "Not far away."

As promised, once we were settled, he hurried off to get dinner. I headed for the shower. An unending stream of hot water was just what I needed after the day I'd had. I expected to emerge relaxed and rejuvenated. But after way too long under the hot water, I reluctantly stepped out of the warmth onto the cold tile floor, tired and hungry.

I dried off, dug clothes out of my bag, and put on yoga pants and the *Someone in Texas Loves Me* tee shirt Alex had given me earlier that day, only in place of the word *love* was a red heart. As I toweled off my hair, he knocked. I unlocked the door between our adjoining rooms, and he stepped in carrying Chinese take-out and drinks.

He set the food on the desk. "Cashew chicken and a Cherry Coke."

"Mmm. Thanks." I picked up my fancy little box and a fork before crawling onto the bed.

He dropped into the desk chair and spun to face me. "Have you called your sister?"

"I texted Meg. Told her we were driving to Denver instead of flying." I stared into my food container, the buzzing in my ears and heat rising on my skin evidence of my irritation at the thought of talking to her.

"And?" Alex didn't want to let it go.

"She's called about twenty times, left several voice messages—which I haven't listened to—and texted at least ten times."

"She's worried about you."

"I know she is. I'm just not sure how to tell her about everything. It's not that I'm mad about how she talked about you." I stabbed my fork into the food. "Well, I might be a little mad about that. But really, I just don't know what to say to her right now. How do you tell your sister that biologically she's not and that her dad is a kidnapper?"

"I get it. It's not a conversation you want to have over the phone."

"I don't want to talk about Meg. Can we just drop the subject?" My sharp tone surprised even me. I focused on my food, the sounds of munching and chewing keeping silence at bay.

As I popped the last bite in my mouth, the bed jostled slightly when Alex kicked his stocking feet onto the corner and wiggled his toes.

I glanced at his feet, and he kept still. As soon as I looked away, he wiggled them again.

It was silly. I laughed. "I'm sorry I snapped at you."

Sparkles danced in his green eyes. "You're beautiful. I don't think I've said that out loud."

A warmth washed over my face and neck, whether prompted by his compliment or his gaze, I wasn't sure. My reaction drew an even bigger smile from him.

"You really are."

I uncapped the bottle and sipped my Cherry Coke, waiting for the heat to evaporate from my cheeks. "Becca's texted me at least thirty times. They picked up Bureau, by the way."

"Yeah, DJ let me know."

"When I texted her a picture of the tee shirt, she said to extend her apologies to you."

A deep, robust laugh poured out of Alex before he covered his mouth. "It's late. I should be quiet." He set down his empty container. "I surprised a lot of people, it seems."

I slid off the bed and tossed my container in the trash. As I stepped up in front of him, he rested his hands on my hips and pulled me between his knees.

My heart thumped a hundred miles a minute. "Thank you."

"For what?" Warm and husky, his voice increased my flutters.

"Coming with me. Calling me beautiful, letting me know you've been thinking it."

That wonderfully boyish grin spread across his face as he stood up. He cradled my face in his hands. "I've been thinking it a lot." Sliding his hands down over my shoulders, his fingertips danced down my arms. He circled my waist with those strong arms. Softly and slowly, he brushed his lips along mine, then traced them with the tip of his tongue.

I gathered his tee shirt in my fists and pulled him closer. His hands roamed my back as he covered my mouth with his. I returned his kisses with fervor until breathing became necessary. I felt more than heard his chuckle when my knees buckled slightly. His arm tightened around me. I pressed into him, and he tangled his fingers in my wet curls. *Please let him be my happily ever after.*

He pulled away, leaving me breathless. "Night, Kate. Knock if you need me." After planting one last kiss on my forehead, he strode out if the room.

Knock, knock. Need is most definitely the word I'd use.

CHAPTER TWO

January 19, 2016 – 12:03 am

Alex closed the adjoining door but didn't lock it. He picked up his phone and clicked a number in his favorites. It rang several times before a sleepy but familiar female voice answered. He'd woken her up.

"Alex? Is everything okay?" Her last word cut off with a yawn.

"Better than okay. Sorry for calling so late." He sat on the edge of the bed. "Just wanted to let you know I'm on my way to Denver. I'll be gone a few days."

"Denver? What's going on?" She didn't have to be a mind reader to know something was afoot.

"I met someone." He glanced at the door, wondering how much Kate could hear through the wall.

Dead silence echoed on the other end of the line. If it weren't for the soft rhythm of breathing, barely audible, he'd have thought the line had disconnected.

"Marisa?" He hadn't quite expected that reaction.

"Who is she?"

"Her name is Kate Westfall."

"You sound happy." Her voice cracked. "It's been a long time."

"I'd almost forgotten how it feels."

"Tell me about her." His little sister sounded like she might cry.

Alex laid back on the bed and recounted the events since Kate had shown up at his door. His sister followed that with many, many questions, and they talked until almost one.

"I should go. I need to get some sleep before driving tomorrow."

"When do I get to meet her?"

"Not yet." He hoped his sister understood. "It's too soon for that."

"I'll wait . . . for now. And, Alex,"—Marisa's voice softened—"I'm happy for you."

He ended the call, dropped the phone onto the bedside table, and stripped off his clothes as he made his way to the shower.

Relaxed and clean, he slid under the covers, happy to sleep in a bed again. Too many nights in the recliner made for lackluster sleep. Finally able to fully relax, knowing Kate was safe, he closed his eyes and snored.

He awoke with a start when his phone vibrated across the bedside table. Rubbing sleep from his eyes, he focused them enough to recognize sunlight peeking around the edge of the blackout curtains. *Morning already.* He picked up his phone and read the text from DJ: *Kate's on the news.*

He reread the message three times. *How? Who told the news?* He hadn't even considered the possibility that the news would cover her reappearance, but it wasn't a surprise that someone considered a kidnapped child resurfacing after nearly thirty years newsworthy. He ached thinking of all the upheaval in her life.

Fully awake, raking his fingers through his hair, Alex scrolled through the messages he'd missed. Travis had texted a couple hours earlier, but Alex had been too sound asleep. Two other messages from Travis, one from Becca, and another from DJ had all come in while he slept. *I need to tell Kate.* She'd want to call her sister to tell her before she caught wind of the news. That's when he heard Kate in the next room.

He jumped out of bed and knocked on the door. "Kate?"

"It's unlocked."

He pushed open the door. Wearing only flannel pajama bottoms, he hadn't given his attire a second thought until she looked at him. Her eyes widened before she focused on her phone. She glanced up again, her eyes red and puffy. When her phone lit up, she tossed it across the bed.

He didn't have to ask what was wrong. Crossing to the bed in two long strides, he sat down, and she fell against him. He scooped her into his lap.

She melted into his arms. Hot tears wet his chest. "I'm more mad than upset. But when I get really angry, I cry."

He filed that tidbit away for future reference and opted not to make an attempt at humor to lighten the mood.

After a minute, she sniffled. "Meg heard it on the news." She breathed in deep, her breath stuttered as she inhaled. "We were on the phone for a while, but all she does is cry and yell." Kate teased her fingers through the dark curls on his chest as she spoke, making it hard for him to focus on her words. "Meg says Travis is lying, that the story is all made up." A new stream of tears chased out the last half of the sentence.

"Shhh. I'm sorry it hit the news. Travis messaged me early this morning, but I slept through it. I'm so sorry." Alex hugged her close. "Meg is dealing with the shock. She's upset. Lashing out isn't unexpected."

"Don't defend her. Just don't." Kate shook her head. "It's everywhere. LeAnn called me. My friends are texting. The whole world knows I was stolen from my parents. The news even has a picture of me." She wiped her face. "I can handle all that, but Meg pushes my buttons. At least the more recent kidnapping didn't hit the news."

He kissed the top of her head. "Hand me your phone."

She pulled away long enough to pick it up and unlock it.

"I'm going to change your privacy settings on social media. I can't do anything about the photo they already grabbed." With Kate still snuggled against him, he limited who could see her posts and information. Having something to do, a focus besides the feel of her fingers brushing his skin helped. "I think I got everything locked down. I wish I could make it all go away. Maybe a celebrity couple will get engaged or break up, then your life will get bumped from the news cycle."

She gave a half-hearted laugh. "Thank you. Between phone calls and texts, I hadn't done that, yet. I never expected to be so popular." Tears started anew, and she cried into his chest. Alex did the only thing he knew to do. He held her.

When her phone lit up, he recognized the number. "Travis is calling you."

"Answer it, please. It'll give me a minute to pull myself together."

He swiped the screen. "Hello."

"Alex? I was calling to check on Kate. Has she heard?"

"Her sister called. Friends are texting." He rubbed her back. "But she's okay. Just a bit rattled."

Kate held out her hand for the phone. "Hi, Travis. . . . Yeah, I'm okay. . . . Don't blame yourself. It's not your fault."

Alex ran his fingers through her hair as she leaned on him and talked to Travis about the leaked news. As the conversation moved on to arrangements for the move, she relaxed even more.

Alex's pragmatic side warned him to take it slow, let the relationship grow unhurried. *Don't rush it. She's still reeling from all the craziness.* A whole other part of him ignored that bit of wisdom.

Beth-

Having you as a roommate made my first semester at school better than I could have imagined. I'm so glad I met you. I think—and I hope you feel the same—that we'll be friends for a long time.

Sorry I ran out in such a hurry. The last part of the semester was hard. Even Christmas break hasn't been great. There's something I should've told you in person, but I was too embarrassed. Remember how you thought I had the flu? It's definitely not that. I'm pregnant.

I broke the news to my parents tonight during dinner. My mom screamed and yelled, then nothing. My dad hasn't spoken a word to me. I guess I should be glad they haven't asked me to leave the house.

I haven't even told the father yet. He'll be as happy as my parents are, I'm sure. Remember that guy I met at the Broken Spoke that night—the night I got home so late, the night you met Patrick. That's the guy. I haven't talked about him because I'm not even sure if we're dating. I feel like a fool.

Dropping out of school is really my only option. I don't want to leave you without a roommate, but I have to get a job. I refuse to raise this baby here in the small town where I grew up, not that my parents want me moving in, anyway. Too many wagging tongues. I'm going to find a job, make things work.

I promise to write.

-M

CHAPTER THREE

January 19, 2016 – 9:21 am

I dropped the phone on the bed. "We should hit the road. It's still a long way to Denver. I'll tell you what Travis said in the truck."

"Whenever you're ready." Alex tugged me back to his chest. "We'll get there when we get there."

I didn't resist but tilted my head to meet his gaze. "I'm ready to get packed and go back to Texas."

"When you put it that way . . ."

I ran my finger down the center of his chest indulging in a long look. "I assume you aren't driving dressed like that."

"I'd be cold, but . . ." He winked. "I should probably wear a shirt."

Clothes lay over and around my bag, a reminder that I needed to pack. I shifted out of his lap. "Give me about five minutes."

He stopped in the doorway before disappearing into his room. "Just knock when you're ready."

I closed the adjoining door, threw on jeans and a clean tee shirt, and made a mad dash around the room, gathering my belongings.

Thirty minutes later, we were back on the highway.

"What did Travis say?" Alex tucked his coffee in the cup holder.

"He was pretty upset, the angry kind of upset. Apparently, someone at the office saw me when I was up there yesterday." After finishing the last bite of my taco, I wiped off my chin. "Whoever it was put the pieces together with Travis's long-lost missing daughter and called in a news tip. A clever reporter stopped in at The Drugstore in Schatzenburg." I tossed the foil wrapper from my breakfast taco into the trash bag.

"And Maggie happily shared all she knew?"

"If you talk to the waitress in the know, you get all the information you want. She meant well." I swallowed back my frustration with the talkative waitress.

"I'm glad you called Gram yesterday." Alex had taken an instant liking to his friend's grandmother, Gram, who seemed to be the heart of Schatzenburg.

"I am too. I think she had a pretty good idea of who I was before I was willing to admit it. Did DJ go see her?"

"Uh-huh. But I get the distinct impression she is not as fragile as people assume."

I laughed, knowing full well what Alex meant.

We rode along in silence for a while, the pavement whooshing by like floodwaters down a gully. "Alex . . ."

"Yes?" Reacting to the tone of my voice, he dragged out the word into a long question, his eyebrows raised.

"Thank you for this morning. I promise I'm not always such a mess."

He winked, brandished a satisfied smirk, and touched his hand to his chest. I sighed remembering how it felt to do the same.

"Meg thinks you've brainwashed me, made me think I'm a different person. She even went so far as to accuse you and Travis of being in cahoots and planning the whole thing."

"No wonder you're mad at her."

"The worst part is I've convinced myself that her words should devastate me, make me feel cut-off and alone, but they don't. And then guilt sets in."

He reached over and interlaced his fingers with mine. "You aren't alone."

"All of a sudden, I have this whole other family—Travis, even Becca and DJ, and you."

"Please don't say I'm like a brother to you."

I rolled my eyes. "Parts of it seem too good to be true. But enjoying it makes me feel like I'm somehow wronging Meg. It sounds stupid, I know."

"I get it, Kate. I get how enjoying one person makes you feel like you're betraying another." He shot me a sideways glance. "You aren't betraying anyone."

I barely choked out, "Neither are you." Understanding his reference to his late wife, I wanted to hug him, but since he was behind the wheel, driving, I didn't. "Are you and Travis in cahoots? Did you orchestrate it so that I'd wander in the dark for hours and end up at your door?"

"Yep. Every step, except the fall."

"I honestly don't know why she doesn't like you." No sooner were the words out of my mouth, a realization dawned. "Okay, well, maybe I have one idea."

His eyebrows shot up. "Now I'm curious."

"It didn't really occur to me until now, but it's the only thing that makes sense."

"You're stalling."

"When Meg and Tom flew out to Denver at Christmas, Tom's brother came with them. Jerry asked me out to dinner."

Alex guffawed and slapped the steering wheel.

Confused, I asked, "What's so funny?" Sipping my Cherry Coke, I waited for an answer.

He caught his breath. "Seriously? Tom and Jerry?"

I clapped a hand over my mouth trying not to spit soda all over the cab of the truck. Finally, when I stopped laughing long enough to speak, I answered, "Yep. Technically, it's Thomas and Gerald, but yeah." Funny that I'd never noticed it before.

"Sorry to interrupt. You were saying." His grin didn't fade.

"Jerry and I went to dinner."

"You already said that."

"That's all that happened. I didn't think much of it, but . . ." I shifted to face him.

Alex kept his eyes on the road and let silence hang in the cab.

"Meg mentioned over and over how much Jerry enjoyed our date. According to her, he thought that was part of the reason I was moving to San Antonio." I touched Alex's arm. "It wasn't at all. But Meg brought him up again at the hospital."

"And I messed that all up?" His quick sideways look made me laugh.

"Jerry isn't my type at all."

"What's your type?"

I ran my finger down his arm and ogled him. "My type? Hispanic, green eyes, broad chest, Six foot one or two, warm hands, great smile. Protective."

"Six even." His ego had been stroked, and his smile reflected it.

"You feel taller than that."

"And your type before I orchestrated our meeting?"

I shrugged. "Don't know."

"What kind of non-perfect guys did you go out with?"

"For a while, mostly whoever Meg set me up with. It took me a few years, but I finally learned that if Meg liked them, I probably wouldn't."

"So I've got a chance."

My phone rang before I could think of a quip to toss back.

"Hello?"

"Hello. My name is Jonathon Milton. I'm a lawyer with—" Crackling on the line cut out the name. "You there?"

"I'm here."

"Yes, well, sorry. May I speak with Claire Bentley?"

Besides Travis, no one had called me that name, the name on my actual birth certificate. It sounded foreign.

"Hello?" The gentleman at the other end of the line didn't sound agitated, only nervous.

"Sorry. This is she."

"Now that you've been located, I need you to come into our office. We have paperwork that needs to be signed."

I shrugged at Alex's questioning look. "Travis said that I could take care of that when I returned from Denver."

"Absolutely, ma'am. Sorry to bother you on your trip. Have a nice day." The phone beeped as the call ended.

"What was that about?" Alex asked.

"A lawyer wanting me to sign papers."

"They must really be in a hurry to give away money."

My phone rang again as soon as I laid it down. "Hello?"

"Claire? Or maybe you want to be called Kate? Sorry. I'm just so excited that you've been located."

"Who is this?" I put the call on speaker.

"Forgive me. My name is Justin Carson. I'm your uncle." Half of the word uncle cut out as we hit a spotty cell signal.

"Oh." I should've been thrilled, but something in his tone set my suspicions humming. "You can call me Kate. If I don't respond, it's because I'm losing my cell signal."

"If we get disconnected, I'll call back at another time. Just wanted to welcome you back to the family."

"Thank you. Carson? You're Emma's brother?"

"Yes. Your mom was my little sister."

That was the last I heard of his conversation. The signal dropped out completely.

"He seemed excited." Alex picked up on my hesitation.

I tapped out a text to Travis: *Justin called me.* But I waited until bars reappeared before hitting send. "As soon as I get time, I want to research Emma's family tree. I have a branch to add already."

As we neared Denver, I texted friends and arranged to see them during the few days we'd be in town. I'd pushed all thoughts of saying goodbye out of my head, but the closer we got to the city, the harder that reality was to ignore.

"You okay?" Alex didn't take his eyes off the road. "After that flurry of texts, you got really quiet."

"Just thinking about saying goodbye to friends, one especially."

He made no comment. I'd made the decision to move to Texas at Meg's insistence. I could thank her for that. Given all that had changed, my reasons for moving far outweighed any reasons for staying. The reason sitting beside me was enough.

As he navigated Denver traffic, I told him in great detail all about my friends: Lindsey, Ashley, Sarah, Mona, and, of course, LeAnn. She'd been my friend since high school, and although we had very little in common, she was my closest friend. Of all my friends in Denver, only she knew about Alex, and she'd sworn not to breathe a word.

"They don't know you're coming. They don't even know you exist."

"Oh?"

"You're a surprise." I giggled at his bemused look. "And believe me, they'll be *very* surprised."

We arrived at my apartment building just before sunset. Vivid oranges and blues painted the skies behind snowcapped peaks. I'd miss the beauty of the city, of the mountains. Eager to be among my own things, I leaned forward, drinking in familiar sights. "Just pull in there next to my blue car."

Alex parked and grabbed my hand as I reached for my door handle. "Kate, thanks for letting me tag along."

I stretched across the cab and gave him a quick peck. "It means a lot to have you here in Denver with me."

He tucked a strand of hair behind my ear. "What do you say, after we get unloaded, we grab dinner somewhere that doesn't serve food in disposable containers."

"Like a date?" I ran my finger down the cleft in his chin.

He kissed me again. "A second first date. This time, without trouble."

"How can I say no to that?"

He grabbed our bags as I fished keys out of my purse. After a half second of panic, I found them buried deep in the bottom under receipts and other odds and ends.

"My apartment is on the second floor."

He put down the handle of the rolling case and picked it up. "Lead the way." He followed me up the stairs.

I tried to hide the concern that nibbled at me as I unlocked my door. So much had happened while I was away, I couldn't remember the state of my apartment. I didn't usually leave it trashed, but I'd been packing before leaving for San Antonio. I opened the door and smiled. It was picked up but lived in. Boxes were stacked against one wall of the living room. Being among my own things offered a certain comfort and assurance.

Alex stepped inside and dropped the bags near the door. "Nice place."

I picked up the carry-on bag. "I'm going to change really quick. I'll only be a few minutes."

"Sure. I'll get the rest of the stuff out of the truck."

I left him standing in my living room and darted back to the bedroom. *My bedroom.* The eclectic blend of furnishings and décor somehow made me feel more myself.

The weather was considerably colder in Denver, so I slipped out of my tee shirt and jeans in favor of something warmer and cuter. After pulling on a warm sweater and my skinny jeans, I dug my knee-high boots out of my closet. I hurried into the bathroom to run a comb through my hair. During the last week, Alex had seen me in yoga pants and an oversized sweatshirt most of the time, but for our dinner out, I wanted to dress like it was a date. A touch of lipstick finished off my cleaned-up look.

I hurried toward the living room, but halfway across the bedroom, I spotted my bunny, the stuffed animal I'd dragged around with me as a kid, the one that appeared in the pictures of a two-year-old Claire in someone else's arms. "Alex, come see."

That little bunny had convinced me to believe the photos and the DNA test. Emblazoned with the initials CB, the floppy stuffed animal had been my constant companion. I told it my secrets growing up, and just the day before, it had whispered its secret to me, almost a thousand miles away.

Alex wandered into the room, his eyes fixed on me. "Wow. You look amazing."

"I meant this." I held up my tattered, stuffed friend. "Cuddle Bunny."

Alex slipped his phone out of his pocket. "May I?"

I nodded and held the bunny close to my face, smiling. After he snapped the picture, I stepped up beside him to take a peek.

"I know who'd like to see this."

"Send it to him." I kissed him on the cheek and ran back into my closet to dig out my heavy coat.

When I walked back into the bedroom, Alex caught me around the waist. "Travis says to hurry home." He pulled me up against him. "Where do you want to eat? You'll need to tell me what's good."

I traced the plaid on his flannel shirt. "You changed your shirt."

"I wanted to look nice for our *date*." He winked.

Tucked in a corner booth, snuggled side to side, Alex and I shared the last few bites of dessert. Reminiscent of a sappy time sequence in a Saturday afternoon romance, the evening unfolded as all kinds of wonderful.

"You want to sleep on my couch tonight?"

"I can get a hotel room."

"I'm sorry I don't have a second bedroom. I know the couch isn't very comfortable."

His coffee cup clinked as he set it on the saucer. "You want me to stay?"

"On the couch, yeah." As hard as it was to admit to myself, I wasn't ready to stay alone. In the hotel, he was in the next room. *How do I explain it to him without sounding weak and needy?*

"Then I will." He leaned down and whispered in my ear. "And I promise to keep my shirt on." He laughed, presumably at the color that washed over my face.

Back in the apartment, Alex dropped onto the couch and pulled me into his lap.

"Alex, when I asked you to stay here . . . I wasn't trying to be a tease. It's just that staying alone still scares me a little."

"Leaving you alone still concerns me." He shook his head. "But I'm trying not to be overly protective."

I snuggled in closer, content. "Travis texted me pictures of The Castle. Want to see?" I fished my phone out of my pocket.

He nodded. "You keep referring to *The Castle* like it should mean something to me."

"It's the house at the corner of Fourth and Main in Schatzenburg. Emma, my mom, called it The Castle in her letters." I swiped through the photos.

"This is the main room. It looks like one big space: the living room, dining room, and kitchen. I love the open plan. And there are three bedrooms." After I swiped past the last picture, I jumped up. "You haven't seen the letters. She wrote me a letter every year on my birthday. Dear Claire—over and over again. Want to read them?"

"I don't want to intrude."

I pulled the manila envelope out of my bag and handed it to him. "I'd like for you to read them."

The white envelopes spilled out onto the coffee table, and I arranged them so he could read them in order, then snuggled up next to him and leaned my head on his shoulder.

One envelope at a time, he read through the letters, handing them to me as he finished each one. As he read the last letter, he wiped his eyes. "Kate. I knew they'd been searching for you, but I didn't realize . . ."

"After reading those, it's hard not to hate the people I thought were my parents." It scared me to say it without tears.

He put his arm around me. "I don't have wise words of advice, but I'm here. I'll listen."

I ran my finger through the cleft in his chin. "Next to your eyes, this is my favorite part."

He beamed as I kissed my second favorite spot.

When I awoke early the next morning, Alex was awake and packing. I shuffled to the bathroom, made myself presentable, and walked out wondering what there was to eat for breakfast.

"Good morning." He laid the tape gun on the counter before wrapping his arms around me. "I've been packing the kitchen."

"How long have you been up?"

"You don't want to know." He tightened his embrace and said good morning with a sweet, tender kiss. "Now that you're up, I'll run and get us breakfast. Donuts okay?"

"Yeah, I think I have coffee around here."

"Already made some." He pulled on a coat. As soon as he opened the door, he closed it again. "There are reporters and cameramen out there."

The air whooshed out of me. "I really hate this."

"Lock the door behind me. I'll be back soon. And do not open the door for anyone, except me."

"What are you going to say to them?"

"Nothing. I'm actually pretty good at that." He winked before slipping out the door.

He'd only been gone a few minutes when someone knocked. I froze. The press hadn't yet left to chase other stories. I had no intention of answering questions about my past so I didn't answer.

After a minute, whoever it was knocked again. "Miss Bentley?"

Sitting quietly on the couch, I waited for Alex. The knob rattled as someone checked that it was locked. *Alex, please hurry back.*

I let out the breath I'd been holding as footsteps sounded on the stairs. Either the reporter retreated, or Alex had arrived.

Tired of sitting and waiting, I started packing to pass the time.

Another knock startled me as I added another box to the stack.

"Kate? It's me. Open up." My scraggly, keep-to-himself neighbor surprised me.

"Hey, Keith," I called through the door. "Can you come back later?"

"Sure, okay. Just wanted to ask about the hubbub . . . and see you."

See me? My phone lit up with a text from Alex: *In the parking lot. Who's the guy at your door?*

I tapped out a quick reply, grateful my bodyguard was back: *My neighbor.*

With my ear to the door, I listened trying to make out the conversation on the landing. Keith didn't sound pleased when Alex told him later would be a better time to stop by. Keith's door slammed shut just before Alex texted: *I'm at the door.*

I ducked behind the door as I pulled it open, avoiding any cameras. As soon as Alex cleared the door, I snapped it closed and flipped the bolt.

"Close friends with your neighbor?" Alex set the donuts on the coffee table.

I handed him a mug. "Not really. He's not very sociable." I pulled one of the lemon-filled yummies out of the box. "I invited him to a party here once. He stayed maybe fifteen minutes."

"He looked very unhappy about my arrival. Jealous, maybe?" Alex licked powdered sugar off his fingers.

"I doubt it. He's a kid. I don't know why he'd be upset about you."

"He's older than a kid, Kate."

"I guess, but he's like eight years younger than I am. I doubt he's jealous." I shook my head. "How long do you think the reporters will stay? I feel like a zoo animal on display."

"Which one?"

"Does it matter?"

"Sure." He tore a glazed donut in half.

"You're silly."

He chuckled. "Eventually they'll move on to the next cage, either get bored or leave to chase a lead on another story."

Hands on my hips, I swung my hair over my shoulder. "Are you calling me boring?"

He shook his head, laughing. "If only."

By lunchtime, the kitchen cabinets were completely empty, the contents of the hall closet had been packed, and only furniture remained in the living room—well, furniture and a large stack of boxes. I was about to clear off my bookshelves when someone knocked.

Alex stepped to the door. "Expecting anyone?"

"No, but my friends know I'm back." I stepped back as Alex reached for the knob.

"Kate?" Keith seemed determined to talk to me.

I nodded. Alex yanked open the door and lingered in the doorway a second before stepping aside. Easily four inches shorter, Keith, hesitated, intimidated.

"Excuse the mess. I'm packing." I pointed to the wall of boxes.

"You're leaving?" Keith stepped up next to me casting sideways glances at Alex.

"Moving to Texas." I sat at the edge of the sofa.

"Oh." He sat next to me. "What's with all the people?"

Alex brushed his knuckles against my hand. "Should I finish packing up the books?"

"Thanks. That'd be great." I watched as he strolled out of the room.

Keith relaxed a little as soon as Alex disappeared into the hall.

"Reporters." I shrugged. "While I was on vacation, I learned that the people I thought were my parents, weren't. I met my dad. Now the long-lost-child-returns story is all over the news."

"Ouch. Sorry. Must be rough."

"Yeah. I'm adjusting."

"Who's your friend?" He nodded toward the hall. "I didn't think . . ."

A knock sounded, and Alex strode across the room. "You're Miss Popular today."

He opened the door a crack, and my friend LeAnn squealed.

"You must be the bodyguard!" She was so loud that the reporters outside probably heard her.

"A bodyguard?" Keith pointed at Alex.

Alex glanced back over his shoulder for verification of what he already knew. I answered by jumping up. LeAnn's full, curvy figure greeted me when I stepped toward the door. Jeff, her boyfriend, stood behind her, holding a bag from a burger joint.

"Thought you might want lunch." She enveloped me in a bear hug, her blonde hair whapping me in the face. "What's with all the paparazzi?"

"Let's not talk about it. Thanks for bringing lunch." After all that happened, I missed my friend even more than the few weeks away warranted.

"Lunch? I'm really just here to meet the new boyfriend." Her eyes glinted as she grinned at Alex.

I hugged her again, laughing.

Keith mumbled something unintelligible as he hurried to the

door. He slipped past Jeff and around the corner faster than a lightning bolt in a mountain storm.

Jeff stepped into the apartment, kicking the door closed behind him. "I'm Jeff."

"Alex. Nice to meet you."

LeAnn raised her eyebrows. "Now I get why you are moving." She hugged me again before beelining back toward Alex. "I'm LeAnn. I can't tell you how excited I am to meet you." She threw her arms around him.

His eyes went wide, and he stiffened. I giggled at the surprised expression on his face.

"Thank you for taking care of Kate." LeAnn released him but kept her hand on his arm.

"Glad I could help." He stepped back from her and shot a help-me look my direction.

His discomfort both amused and interested me. I slipped up next to him and rubbed his back. "Let's eat. I'm hungry." I pointed to the kitchen.

Alex clutched my hand and followed me to the table. As he pulled out a chair, LeAnn grabbed my arm.

"I need to talk to you *alone* for a minute." She nodded toward the bedroom.

"You guys eat. We'll be back in a minute." I walked into the bedroom. "What?"

"How serious is it between you two? I ask because his bag is in your apartment."

"I've known him a week and a half. It's not like that." I perched my fists on my hips. "You know me, LeAnn."

"And that why I ask. The bag surprised me. A lot."

"He's sleeping on the couch." I let my exasperation show on my face.

She held her hands up. "Don't be mad. Just asking. He seems great and all, but I don't want to see you hurt."

I appreciated her concern but wasn't interested in divulging more about my relationship with Alex than I already had. "You need to come visit. The house I'm getting is in this quaint little town named Schatzenburg. And I'd love for you to meet Travis."

"Your dad?"

"So not ready to call him that yet, but yes."

"Is it having a new dad or Alex that's prompting you to go through with this move so quickly?"

"I'd have probably moved anyway, but knowing Alex wants me in Texas makes it an easy decision. And family is important to me, so saying it is only Alex or only Travis isn't true."

"I'm just so glad he was there in that cabin, right where you needed him to be."

"He protected me when he didn't have to, and he'd been through a lot. Taking me in wasn't easy on him."

"He seems pretty happy now."

"We're good for each other." I lowered my voice and leaned closer. "When he didn't know my name, he started calling me Rainy because I showed up on a rainy night."

LeAnn clutched her hands to her chest. "That makes me want to cry it's so sweet. Does he still call you that?"

I glanced back over my shoulder toward the door. "Sometimes, and I love it, every time."

"While we stand here swooning, our food is getting cold. Let's go eat." LeAnn trotted back to the kitchen.

The smile that welcomed me back to the table had me turning LeAnn's question over in my mind. *How serious are we?* Trying to divine that answer would only distract from enjoying the moments as they happened. I squeezed his hand as I sat down. "I said not to wait."

"Alex, what do you want to know about Kate? I'll tell you things she won't tell you herself."

He poked my leg under the table, but I kept my eyes focused on LeAnn. She had more secrets to spill than any of my other friends.

"You know how we met, not exactly ordinary. What would I have learned about her if we'd met at work or a party?" Alex picked up his burger but set it down again without taking a bite.

LeAnn studied me for several uncomfortable seconds. "At a party, you'd have found Kate out of the way, people-watching and maybe sipping a glass of wine—something sweet. She loves to dance, but rarely does." She popped a fry in her mouth, keeping us all waiting. "Some people think she's really sweet. They don't know her well."

He squeezed my knee.

"When she invites you in—and I don't mean into her apartment—you'll know, but very few get that invitation. Some of us had to hang around a long time."

Alex slipped his hand in mine.

I hadn't exactly been my hesitant, untrusting self with him. My emotions were running at full tilt when we'd met, which didn't allow for my normal filtering. "Eat, you guys. That's enough talking about me."

"I'm not done getting answers." Alex focused on me as he asked his next question. "What will you miss most when she moves away?"

LeAnn teared up. "Dang. You don't ask easy questions."

Jeff rubbed her back. "LeAnn was really unhappy about the move until she learned about you." He avoided my gaze, focused on Alex. "She's going to miss her best friend."

LeAnn wiped her eyes. "Kate's baking. That's what I'll miss most."

Alex chuckled. "I've tasted her baking. That makes perfect sense." He nodded at Jeff.

I blinked, refusing to cry. "When you come visit, I'll bake you whatever you want."

"Then we definitely have to visit soon." Jeff looked at LeAnn. "What do you think?"

She clapped her hands. "I'd love that."

I picked the tomato off my burger. "So would I. I'll let you know when I'm all moved in."

After LeAnn and Jeff left, ignoring the reporters as they dashed to their car, Alex and I continued packing. Books, towels, sheets—all got shoved into boxes. Slowly, closets and cabinets emptied.

After hours of work, Alex peeked out the front window. "Looks like all the reporters left."

"I can thank this crazy election year. The primary race is nuts. My story can't compete with that."

"Where did you get these boxes?" He restacked the piles, sorting so that the heaviest boxes were at the bottom of the stacks.

"I bought them at a storage place." I pulled the elastic band out of my hair and released tangles with my fingers before sweeping it back into a ponytail.

"Oh." His tone invited more questions.

"Why?"

"I thought you'd gotten them used. There are twelve boxes labeled Christmas."

"Is that a problem?" I put my hands on my hips and raised my eyebrows, pretending to be offended. "I like Christmas, *a lot.*"

Alex held up his hands in defense, chuckling. "Just asking. I happen to like Christmas too. At least, I used to."

"Used to?"

"Memories make the season difficult." The teasing disappeared from his voice.

"I didn't realize."

"Ellie and I were married a few days before Christmas. I was widowed only weeks before the Christmas after that." He was somber but didn't shed a tear.

"I'm so sorry."

"The Christmas lights blinked across the front of our house that night—all white—as I pulled up and noticed the door hanging open."

"As someone else once said to me . . . I don't have wise words, but I'm here. I'll listen."

He crossed the room in three strides and drew me to his chest. His heartbeat pounded in my ear and almost drowned out his whisper. "Rainy."

That name, what he called me before I remembered who I was, or thought I was, had become more than a silly nickname. Forever it would be a memory of protection and vulnerability. Every time he called me that, I melted inside.

We might've stayed wrapped in each other's arms for a long while, but my sister texted at that very moment. Alex handed me my phone.

Meg texted words that, while true, were more hurtful than I ever expected: *We aren't sisters.* Her biting tone reached across the miles, punctuating the words of her message.

I dropped onto the sofa and buried my face in my hands. Anger and hurt escaped as bitter, hot tears.

"Inconsiderate, self-centered child." Alex paced, muttering things about my sister I'm pretty sure he didn't intend for me to hear. I choked back sobs. I hated feeling weak and weepy, but the bombardment of emotions had wiped out my ability to control them like I used to.

"Kate." He brushed the hair away from my face and waited for me to look up. "Follow me."

"I need to respond to her. What do I say to that?"

"In a bit." He led me into the bedroom and sprawled out on the bed, his arms open. "Come here."

I crawled up next to him, nestling into the perfect spot, my head resting above his heart.

"Whatever you respond, think about it first. You can't take back what you send." His tone was soft, but knowing, a reminder that there was still much to learn about him.

"Personal experience?"

He nodded. "My siblings. I didn't send anything hurtful, I just quit sending anything." He ran his fingers up and down my back. "Things changed. We'd been pretty close before that."

I listened to the pounding of his heart trying to figure out something to say that didn't sound cliché or cheesy. These windows into the wounded parts of him didn't happen often and could slam shut just as quickly as it had opened. After a few quiet seconds, I whispered, "You could email them tonight."

He covered my hand with his, threading his fingers between mine. "I should." He pulled my palm to his lips.

His soft warm kisses dotted the inside of my hand. Words swirled in my head. "I want to make you happy."

He pressed my fingers closer to his lips. His heart rate increased.

My words came out wrong. I did want him to be happy, but saying it that way made it sound like I meant something else. "What I mean is—"

He rolled me onto my back and shifted so that he hovered over me. I shivered when I glimpsed the hunger in his eyes as his mouth sought my lips. All the tenderness and playfulness from earlier disappeared. His weight rested on his elbows, his arms and back flexed, firm and defined. My fingers danced along his back, exploring each muscle. Citrus and musk danced in the air. The safety I'd felt pressed to his chest mingled with passion. My fingers laced in his dark waves, I rose to deepen our kiss. Breathing ranked second in the list of what I most wanted.

His arms relaxed, his body weight pressing me to the bed. He threaded his arms behind my neck, cocooning me in his embrace. Without warning, images, memories, flashed in my head. *No. Not now. Not with him.* I squeezed my eyes closed and pulled my hands in front of me, bracing them against his chest. He lifted his head. When I opened my eyes, confusion mingled with pain filled his eyes. *He thinks he caused it.*

"Kate?"

I looked away and pushed on him, desperate for the memory to pass. He rolled off, and I scrambled to the head of the bed and hugged a pillow. Tapped out emotionally and angry that the flashback interfered with my relationship with Alex, I shielded myself with the pillow.

He perched at the edge of the bed and reached out to touch my hair. "Hey."

I recoiled and shook my head. From the expression on his face, I might as well have stabbed him.

He pushed off the bed and walked out of the room.

And slam. The worst of it was, I'd shut that window.

Beth-

These last few months have been crazy. Remember Sticks? He likes to show up unexpectedly after long absences. I don't see him for the first two years of Scooter's life, then one day he shows up at the door with an armload of toys. And after that he's a regular visitor but still refuses to call Scooter his son. Yeah, that Sticks.

Well, he showed up late one night a few months ago. His dad died, and he was a mess. Scooter was already in bed, but I let Sticks in, let him cry on my shoulder.

I probably don't have to tell you what happened next. After that night, I didn't see him for two weeks. Which, for him was a bit unusual because he'd been pretty regular about spending time with Scooter. He showed up after work one evening and took Scooter out for pizza, but then dropped him off without even coming to the door. Visits went on that way for the next few weeks.

The night he showed up with a bucket of chicken was different. He asked to stay the night before he even walked inside. Scooter was standing right next to me and jumped up and down cheering that Sticks was having a sleepover. He'd packed a bag. You know what that means? He planned it, knew I'd say yes.

I'm dragging this out way farther than necessary. But, anyway, he stayed a couple days, then one Saturday, he told me he was going home to his wife.

Yes, I knew he was married.

He'd slip his ring off before coming to the door, but the permanent white circle on his tanned finger was a big giveaway. That night was the first time he'd mentioned her.

But he came back to me. At 4 am, he knocked on my door asking to move in for a while. I'd never been able to say no to him. I turned into an insecure eighteen-year-old all over again. But because Scooter loves having Sticks around, it was worth the inevitable heartbreak, I thought.

Anyway, he stayed for a month or more. There was one night after he'd been with me a few weeks when I was sure he was going home, leaving. I'd seen him toss his bag in the truck. That night, after Scooter went to bed, we did, too. It was all I could do not to cry while we made love. Instead of holding me afterward, he slipped out of bed and showered. I knew he was headed home to his wife. And he left.

He showed up again later that night, drunk and madder than I'd ever seen him. I hardly slept. Maybe he was trying to get back at her by being with me, over and over. I twisted it into hope, but only for a little while.

I was wrong to hope that whatever she'd done to make him so mad was enough to make him mine. I waited a few weeks, but then I broached the topic of him leaving his wife. It was the wrong thing to say. He walked out, slammed the door behind him, and drove away. What am I going to tell Scooter?

As you can imagine I'm a mess. When will I learn that Sticks isn't ever going to be mine? I know you've heard all of this before, multiple times. Enough of my whining.

How was your summer? Happy Belated Anniversary. Hard to believe it's been three years already. Married life still treating you well? Write back and give me some good news. Good news would be a nice change.

-M

CHAPTER FOUR

January 20, 2016 – 10:45 pm

What the hell happened? Her reaction reminded him of the first night at the door, when she'd flinched as he reached for her. Someone, at one time, had hurt her. Whatever it was went deeper than the two days in a closet. And Alex had triggered the memory. The notion horrified him.

He closed his eyes. Strong feelings bubbled inside him—feelings that should've taken months, even years, to develop. He couldn't even pretend they were real until they'd been time-tested. And clearly, there were things he didn't know about her.

He yanked his phone out of his pocket and dropped onto the couch. Her advice was pragmatic and wise. But after opening a new email, he only stared at the tiny keyboard on the screen. The oldest of five, after his parents died, he'd kept family connections alive, making sure they gathered at holidays and spoke regularly on the phone. After Ellie died, he'd retreated from the world. Besides his youngest sister, he'd hardly spoken to his siblings. *What do I say after three years?*

Kate sat down at the opposite end of the couch and hugged her knees to her chest. "What would you say if they walked in right now?"

Alex laid his phone down and made eye contact with her. "I'm sorry." He rubbed his face.

She rested her head on her knees. "You didn't do anything wrong." Her voice wavered. "When I was in—"

"Kate, please, you don't need to explain." He shook his head and focused on the phone. He couldn't bear to see the hurt in her eyes again and didn't want her to see his, either.

She took the out. Whatever story she'd started to tell was one she didn't want to talk about. She gestured to the phone. "Tell me what you would say to them."

He patted the cushion beside him, hoping he hadn't created a permanent distance between them. She shifted next to him but didn't touch him. He added his sisters, Lucia and Marisa, and his brothers, Sam and Nico, as recipients on the email. Kate leaned on his arm, her cool cheek offering hope that they could move beyond whatever had happened. She read over his shoulder as he typed a message.

Hey –

I know it's been too long. I hope things are going well for you. Marisa has kept me updated about your lives. Please forgive me for not responding to emails, calls, texts.

–Alex

His finger hovered over the send button a moment before he added another sentence. *I met someone.*

She pressed into his shoulder, her smile evident from the rise in her cheekbone.

"*You* are what I'd talk about if they walked in." He kissed the top of her head. Words, way too soon to say, danced a polka on the tip of his tongue. *You can't say that, not yet.*

Her phone rang, and Meg's picture filled the screen. The quiet intimacy in the room dissipated, replaced with tension.

"Answer it. I'll be outside." He gave Kate a quick peck on the cheek before slipping out the front door.

A text from DJ flashed on the screen just before Lucia's number popped up as an incoming call. Alex answered, bracing for he-wasn't-sure-what. "Hello."

"Alex, I'm so happy for you."

"I'm sorry, Lucia."

"Don't apologize. It only matters that you sent us a message now. She must be special."

"We haven't known each other long. I'm trying not to rush things." He proceeded to explain how he and Kate met. The sighs, sniffles, and occasional giggles from the other end of the line reassured him that his family didn't find it distasteful for him to find love again.

He'd just hung up when the front door opened.

Kate poked her head out, arms wrapped around herself. "You're going to freeze out here."

"How'd your call go?"

She shrugged and teared up.

He stepped inside and pulled her close. "Just keep trying. She'll come around."

"Becca texted. She wants to know why you aren't answering DJ."

Alex shook his head and chuckled. "I haven't even had time to read it."

They both turned as Keith's door opened a crack. Kate tiptoed further back inside as Alex closed the door. She flopped onto the couch, phone in hand.

"Texting Becca?" He fished his phone out of his pocket and read the text DJ'd sent earlier: *Becca's curiosity is eating her alive. She hasn't slept well the last two nights. You know what that means. I've hardly slept the last two nights. Please text and let us know how it's going.*

"Yeah. She keeps dancing around whatever she really wants to ask me, I think. You know her better than I do."

"She worked so hard trying to get me to ask you to stay. What's she possibly worried about?" Alex dropped down next to Kate and winked before tapping out a quick reply, holding the phone so that she couldn't see it: *Better than okay. Just trying not to mess it up.* He stuck his phone in his pocket but yanked it back out a second later. *Tell Becca not to worry.*

Kate yawned. "It's going to be colder tonight. Do you need an extra blanket?"

"Nah. I'm good." He kicked off his boots. "We've got to finish packing tomorrow. You should try and get some sleep."

"You're right." She took a few steps, stopped, and glanced back over her shoulder.

He gazed at her, too tired to mask the depth of his feeling. As if reeled in by his stare, she made her way back to the couch.

He rose to meet her.

She slipped her arms around his neck. "I want this, us. Please know that. Earlier, I enjoyed every second until memories pressed down on me. And you—" She kissed his cheek. "Thank you."

He held her, wondering what he'd done to earn her gratitude. If anything, he thought he'd crossed an invisible line, conjuring up her past. "I'm not sure what for, but you're welcome. And I enjoyed it, too." He chided himself for sounding like a gawking teenager.

She trailed her fingers through his whiskers as she stepped away. Did she know the power and pull she had on him? "Sweet dreams."

Pretty sure that won't be a problem.

When Alex awoke the next morning, Kate was already up. Busy packing the last tidbits in her closet, she glanced up when he leaned on the doorframe. A delighted sparkle in those brown eyes accented her smile.

"Good morning. Looks like you've been busy."

"Did you sleep okay?" She stood up and dusted off her pants. "There's coffee. Want me to get you a cup?"

"I'll get it." His smile widened as she walked up close.

"Mona and LeAnn are bringing lunch at 11:30."

He grinned, coiling one of her curls around his finger. "I can ask more questions."

"And we have dinner plans with Ashley, Lindsey, and Sarah."

He wrapped his arms around her waist. "Full calendar. What about the storage unit and the trailer?"

She stretched up and brushed her lips against his. "Tomorrow morning, and I still have lots to do."

He tightened his embrace and pressed his mouth to hers. When she tilted her head back, he relaxed his arms, freeing her to step away.

She didn't. "When the boxes are all packed, I want to do more of that."

"Let me grab coffee, then you can put me to work. Maybe I can knock the rest out in under an hour." He loved the sound of her laughter. "Any sign of reporters this morning?"

"Haven't seen a one."

Four hours later, Kate ran to the door when someone tapped on it. Alex hung back, watching from the kitchen.

"Kate! You've been all over the news. What a story!" Mona, with LeAnn right behind, hugged Kate as they walked into the apartment. "You're almost done packing, it looks like."

"Yeah. I've had great help." She pointed toward the kitchen. "I'll tell you about it over lunch."

LeAnn held up pizza boxes.

Mona put her hands on her hips. "Help? You could have called us, you know."

Alex retreated closer to the table when they neared the doorway. LeAnn hung back, grinning, as Mona walked into the kitchen.

When she spotted him, she stopped. "Helloooooo, help."

He chuckled. "Nice to meet you. I'm Alex."

"You're a bit of a surprise. Kate didn't mention you." Mona shot Kate a questioning look.

"I'm what you'd call a recent development." He motioned toward the table and pulled drinks from the refrigerator. He stood until the ladies had all taken their seats.

Pizza boxes open, they each piled slices on paper plates.

"That was quite a trip to Texas." LeAnn picked the bell pepper off her pizza.

"*How* did you meet? I've known Kate for what? Five years? She's not really the adventurous type." Mona folded her pizza slice in half before taking a bite.

"She saw my cat, and then one thing led to another." He winked at Kate. His completely truthful answer left out volumes of information. She wanted to share as little information as possible about all the craziness that happened. News of her real parents had already been delivered courtesy of the 24-hour news cycle, but he could at least help her keep the latest kidnapping and amnesia under wraps.

Mona asked about Alex's cat, and Kate told the story of how he got his name. One cat tale led to another, and soon, Bureau sounded like the hero in his own story.

"Oh! We got you something." LeAnn sat a gift bag on the table.

Kate opened the card first. A bouquet made of buttons and trinkets adorned the front. The stems—made of twist ties, maybe—were tied with a blue ribbon. Someone had spent a lot of time trying to make it pretty.

"Did you make this?" She moved the card so that he could read the goodbye message inside. *We're sorry to see you leave, but he sounds like a pretty good reason.*

Mona nodded toward LeAnn. "She's talented, isn't she?"

LeAnn squeezed Alex's arm. "I sort of guessed the pretty-good-reason part from the tone of her voice when you were next to her while we talked."

Mona shot Kate and LeAnn a hurt look. "LeAnn knew?"

Kate's cheeks glowed a bright red. "I wanted you to be surprised."

Alex scooted his plate to the side and rested his elbows on the table. "So, what should I know about Kate?"

The expression on Kate's face drew laughter from the others at the table.

Mona piped up first. "Nothing ever seems to rattle her. I can count the times on one hand that I've seen her cry."

LeAnn stifled a laugh. She'd known Kate since high school and had a different understanding of her.

"What would you add, LeAnn?" Mona reached for another slice of pizza.

"Can I just open my gift now?" Kate derailed the line of questioning and tossed paper in the air behind her, letting it settle in piles on the floor. Bureau would've been in heaven. Hidden beneath the decorative tissue lay a colorful apron with layers of ruffles. "I love it." She held it up in front of her.

Alex fingered the ruffles and hoped his expression didn't give away his thoughts.

Mona pointed at him. "And she bakes better than anyone I know. Her cinnamon muffins will be greatly missed."

"Thanks, you guys." Kate hugged her friends.

"Tell us about the news story." Mona poked Kate in the arm.

"Long story short, I met with a man in San Antonio hoping to help him locate his daughter. It's a complicated story, but she was taken by his brother when she was only two years old."

"How horrible for those poor parents." LeAnn wiped her eyes with a napkin. "I can't believe your dad—or whoever he was—did that. He seemed so nice and charming."

"The daughter would have been my age, and I looked just like the mother, who recently died of cancer. The man bore a strong resemblance to my dad so we had a DNA test run."

Mona grabbed another slice. "You knew her parents?"

LeAnn ran a napkin across her mouth. "Our senior year, I spent almost every Saturday at Kate's house."

"How are you not going crazy, Kate? I can't even imagine." Mona shook her head.

"I'm not sure I'm not crazy." Kate laughed. "It's a bit discombobulating, but I'm looking forward to building a relationship with Travis, my dad."

After Kate's friends left, she showed Alex what still needed to be done, and he set to work. Four and a half hours later, he taped the last box closed. "Except for what you need tomorrow, everything's in boxes. Know what that means?"

She laughed. "It means we have just enough time to get cleaned up before we have to leave for dinner."

"I think you look great, just as you are."

"Nice try. Mind if I take the first shower?"

"I wasn't just feeding you a line." He pointed to the hall. "Better hurry. We don't want to be late for dinner."

Beth-

When I read your letter, I screamed so loud it startled Scooter. I'm so excited for you. Six months without talking to you and I miss all the big news.

You and Patrick will be fabulous parents. It's obvious that you both love each other. That's the best ingredient for a happy family. When I lived in Austin, you were so good with Scooter. The way you and your friends helped me when he was a baby was amazing. And if you have a boy, you'll be prepared for the fast diaper swap so as not to get sprayed.

There must be something in the water in Schatzenburg because Sticks mentioned his wife was expecting. He came by last Saturday to take Scooter fishing. I hope a new baby doesn't interfere too much in that relationship. Scooter loves spending time with Sticks.

He's not staying the night anymore, and I'm okay with that. I have to move on. He's married to someone else. I've been very careful not to use his name, but if you ever figure it out, please don't say anything. He's very private, and we were so young when Scooter happened. I need to keep that secret. Besides Sticks and I, only some clerk in the records office knows Scooter's dad's name. Scooter doesn't even know.

He thinks Sticks is just a friend of mine that likes to hang out with him. I worry that I made the wrong decision about not telling him from the very beginning. One day Scooter will ask, and I'll have to tell him the truth. But little boys aren't great at keeping secrets, so I'll wait until he's older.

Keep me posted about the baby on the way. How are you decorating the nursery?

-M

Beth-

Congratulations. Dad called me when he heard about it. His Wednesday lunches at The Drugstore keep him up to date on Schatzenburg news.

Boys are so much fun! I bet Patrick is over the moon, not that he wouldn't have been just as thrilled with a girl. But imagine how cute a little Patrick will be running around your house. Better get him a cowboy hat soon!

I'll try and stop over the next time I get a chance. Maybe I'll let Scooter visit his grandpa while I run over and hold that new little bundle.

-M

February 1984

Beth-

You know, don't you? I saw you glance toward his house when I mentioned Sticks during our visit. Something in your look said you knew more than just that, but I can't rightly ask you to keep secrets and spill them in the same letter.

Does everyone know he is the father? I am trying to shield them both from the judgment of your small town. Sticks deserves whatever judgment he gets, but Scooter doesn't, not for my bad decisions. It's good that I left Schatzenburg when I did.

Because of my secret, it's hard to go home. Even when I'm there for a visit, I rarely take Scooter all the way into town for fear that we'll bump into Sticks. If it weren't for the whispers about my little boy, I'd just shoe polish the truth on the back windshield of my car and drive around town. If I stopped in front of The Drugstore, I might not even have to drive down every street.

Sad part is, I love that little town. I miss living there.

It was great to see you. Your baby boy is adorable. He looks like a mini Patrick. I'm not sure I've ever seen you so happy. Seeing you that way makes me happy.

I'm glad you liked the latch hook pillow. That Noah's ark pattern was too cute, and I thought it would fit your animal theme nicely.

-M

May 1984

Beth-

I understand that it's asking a lot for you to keep that information to yourself, but thank you for keeping my secret. Living in Kerrville keeps enough distance that not all my activities are discussed over the counter at The Drugstore, but we get back to town occasionally. I don't want people whispering about my boy.

You made a good point about being honest with Scooter. I'll talk to Sticks about it.

He mentioned his wife had a baby girl. He glows when he talks about her—the baby, not his wife. Don't get me wrong. I'm happy for them. I just don't want Scooter to miss out on time with his dad and get relegated to second fiddle. This isn't what I pictured my life would be like.

-M

CHAPTER FIVE

January 21, 2016 – 6:30 pm

Alex clutched my hand a little too tightly as we neared the door of the restaurant. His nervousness amused me, but I didn't understand what had him on edge.

"You okay?"

In his plaid flannel shirt, he set my heart racing in several directions at once. "Mostly." He chuckled. "I'm just not sure what I'm in for."

"You'll be a big hit."

My friends waved from inside the door, their eyes wide with surprise.

"They're gonna hug me, aren't they?" He shot me a sideways glance.

"Is that okay?"

"Just stay close."

I bumped my shoulder against him, laughing. "Tonight, I'll be *your* bodyguard."

A delighted smirk tugged at the side of his mouth. "Promise?"

As we stepped through the glass doors, we were met with a flurry of squeals and cheers. Ashley wagged her finger at me. "You kept a secret from us!"

Sarah hugged him, twice. Before she grabbed him a third time, I stepped between them and wrapped my arms around him.

She clapped. "Did Meg get it right finally?"

Alex poked me in the ribs, a boyish playfulness in his eyes.

"No. Meg didn't introduce us." I chose my words carefully.

Lindsey waited until we were all seated to ask about the news story, and I filled them in on my new identity.

Dinner was a flurry of chatter and memories. In turn, my friends shared stories, feeling it their duty to offer Alex as much information about me as they could pack into the evening.

"We got you something so you won't forget us." Lindsey handed me a wrapped package.

Ashley and Sarah eyed me as I tore open the paper.

"I could never forget any of you." I uncovered a maroon scrapbook emblazoned with the word *Friends* in silver foil. "Wow." I flipped through the pages and laughed at the silly photos and funny caption stickers they'd added to the pages. They had no idea about my episode of memory loss and would never know how deeply I'd treasure a book of memories. "You included pictures from our Halloween party."

"Of course. That night was such a blast." Ashley wiped her eyes. "Did Mona and LeAnn make it by to see you?"

"They came by for lunch."

"No wonder neither one answered their phone today." Lindsey shook her head. "They didn't want to spoil our surprise." She pointed at Alex.

"Are you the reason she didn't answer any of our texts while in Texas?" Ashley leveled her gaze at Alex.

"You kind of did drop off the face of the earth." Sarah smoothed hairs that weren't out of place.

"I lost my phone for a while."

"And I occupied a lot of her time." Alex put his arm around me.

In the parking lot, my friends and I exchanged hugs and promises to stay in touch. Goodbyes never became easier.

Alex opened the passenger door for me, a habit that hadn't changed since I'd needed help. When he climbed into the driver's seat, before pulling out of the parking space, he leaned across the cab. "I've enjoyed meeting your friends. Even if they do hug a lot."

"Which surprises me."

"That I like your friends?"

"That the hugging bothers you."

He grinned. "Given our first week, this will sound far from the truth, but I'm not really a touchy-feely kinda guy."

"Now I get why DJ always looked at you the way he did. And I just thought you were being friendly and protective."

"I like hearing their stories about you, too."

"Feel like you know me a little better?" I laid a hand on his cheek.

He bobbed his head slowly and pressed into my hand.

"I'm glad you're still here." I closed the inches between us, answering his silent invitation.

"I'm not going anywhere, Kate." He kissed my fingertips before starting the engine.

Back at the apartment, Alex dropped onto the couch. "The storage box is getting here early, right?"

"It is." I cuddled up next to him, sending cues I wanted to be held.

"Whatever shall we do with the rest of our evening?" With the swiftness and grace of a jewel thief, he swooped me from my sitting position. His eyes sparkled like emeralds in the sunlight.

Laying across his lap, I fluttered my eyelashes. "The boxes are packed."

He hadn't shaved since we'd left San Antonio and the stubble gave him a scruffy, rugged look. "I do recall something you said about wanting to do more of . . ." He brushed his lips on mine.

I ran my fingers through his whiskers. "That night in front of your fireplace . . ."

He hovered so that his mouth felt like a feather dancing on my lips. "We were like this when the phone rang."

"Uh huh." I tugged on his shirt, pulling his mouth to mine. Pushing him back gently I continued, "Except after that call, there was none of this. Which made me think your walls were too well-mortared and had no chance of coming down." I rubbed my hand on his shirt. "And I remembered Ellie's picture and started thinking that . . ." I stopped because I didn't quite know how to finish the sentence. Bringing up his late wife wasn't what I'd meant to do, and I'd already said more than I ever intended to admit to anyone.

He closed his eyes and rested his forehead against mine.

"She wasn't anything like me. I know it sounds stupid."

"You're beautiful, Kate."

"That night after you opened up, I thought it was the beginning of something for us."

"Wasn't it?"

"But then we sat in the kitchen drinking coffee, and you mentioned you dreamt about Ellie. I didn't think I could compete with that." I fought the urge to jump up and run across the room. Saying these things, baring my insecurities, especially while in his lap, left me open and vulnerable. I fiddled with the collar of his shirt.

He pulled my fingers to his lips. "I did dream about her that night, a different one than any other I'd had about her. She waved goodbye."

"I didn't know. I just assumed . . ."

"I dreamt about you, too."

"You did?"

"But I thought 'hey, I dreamt about you' sounded a little too creepy."

"Maybe a little."

He gazed down at me for a long, quiet minute. "Kate, talking about stuff is still hard. Please know that I'm trying."

I ran my finger down the cleft in his chin. "I know. There are things I should . . ."

"When you're ready." He brushed the hair away from my face. "When are you going to start researching your family tree?"

"Soon. I've learned quite a bit about Travis's side, but not very much about Emma's family. That's where I want to start."

"Finding Justin? Wasn't he the one that called? What about him bothered you?"

"You could tell?" I cringed, thinking maybe Justin had picked up on the same vibe. "Not sure. He sounded too eager. I also want to know more about the Aunt Beth, who Travis mentioned."

"Sniffing out a story?"

I shifted to a sitting position. "I hope I don't find a scandal. I think I've reached my limit of secrets for the month, for the year, maybe a lifetime."

"No more scares. No more secrets. I just want to take you home, go out on dates without wondering if we're being followed or hunkering down somewhere waiting for police to catch the bad guy." Alex covered a yawn.

"I like the sound of that." As much as I enjoyed being wrapped in his arms, I needed to let him sleep. "I'm going to get a quick glass of something before bed. Want anything?"

"Any juice left?" He followed me into the kitchen.

I poured him a cup, then filled a plastic tumbler with water. Between sips, I admired that broad chest I was so fond of touching, the deep olive tone of his skin, and those hands.

He glanced at me, a smirk playing on his lips. "Find what you're looking for?"

Startled out of my thoughts, I replayed the question in my head, confused. "What?"

"You're staring at me." He tossed his cup in the trash.

"I was, wasn't I?" I drank down the rest of my water before walking out of the kitchen.

He followed me as far as the hall. Any question about whether he gave any thought to what happened the night before was answered by the way he said goodnight. He stopped far from my bedroom and kissed me on the forehead. "'Night."

"Sleep tight." I pressed my lips into his prickly whiskers.

A noise jarred me awake. I picked up my phone. *2:30 am.* The front door opened, and Alex yelled as he pounded down the stairs. I jumped out of bed and ran out the front door. I was at the top stair when Alex barked, "Get inside, Kate!"

As I hurried back inside, two men jumped into a car and backed out, squealing their tires. Alex ran up the stairs two at a time.

In the apartment, he slammed and bolted the door. "Someone tried to break in."

"What?"

"Did you see them? Recognize them at all?"

I shook my head. "I didn't really see their faces." I dropped down onto the couch. "To think I was glad the reporters left. If they'd been here, stalking my apartment, this wouldn't have happened." My attempt at humor fell flat.

Alex sat next to me, lines etched in his brow, his jaw tight. "What if you'd been alone?"

"I've been gone. Maybe they thought the apartment was empty." I desperately wanted to believe what I told him, but I didn't. A sour gnawing in the pit of my gut said it wasn't random.

"I'm sorry for snapping at you to get back inside." Alex stroked the back of my hand with his thumb.

"You did sound a little bossy." I waited for his reaction but got none. "Apology accepted." I caught a slight rise at the corners of his mouth.

"Is there a Wal-Mart near here? I need something for connecting the trailer."

"Now? But . . ."

"You're coming with me." There was no request in his tone. "I can't sleep. Might as well run to the store."

As much as I hated being told what to do, I wanted to stay in the apartment alone even less. "Give me two minutes to get ready."

He grabbed my hand but remained silent.

"Thank you for staying here, sleeping on my couch."

We were back at the apartment before the sun was even up. Alex sat at the end of the couch, a far-away stare betraying his exhaustion.

I tugged him up off the couch. "Go crawl in my bed."

"What?" He blinked, my words tearing him from his stupor.

"Go sleep. The unit won't be here for at least three hours."

"I'll be fine."

"I didn't ask."

"You're forcing me into your bed?" Without a hint of a smile, he raised one eyebrow.

"Alex, please."

He stepped away from the couch. "A nap will do us both good."

"I won't be able to sleep."

He slid an arm around my shoulder and stared at the floor chewing his bottom lip. "If you want me to sleep, I need you close."

"I think you—"

"Are being irrational? Probably." He let go of me and stuck his hands in his pockets. "I'll stay on my side of the bed."

I shook my head but made sure he caught a glimpse of my smile. It wasn't sides of the bed that concerned me. How could I sleep? I worried I'd keep him awake tossing and turning.

He laid down on the bed and set an alarm. "You can read or whatever." Once he closed his eyes, his breathing changed almost immediately.

I slipped out of bed to pick up my laptop off my desk. When I turned around, he smiled, half sitting up in bed.

"I'm going to work on my family tree." I sat down on the bed, leaning back against the headboard. *I'm going to find Justin.* Learning more could either confirm or dismiss my hesitation. But I didn't breathe a whisper of that to Alex. He needed sleep.

His head hit the pillow and soft snores emanated from his side of the bed. Tapping quietly on the keys, I added Travis and Emma as my parents. Little green leaves showed up almost as soon as I entered the information. Betty and James filled the grandparents' slots on the paternal side. I added my uncle, Scott, but I ignored the leaves that popped up. No part of me wanted to uncover any more about him.

I chased down the little green leaves on Emma's profile. I downloaded Emma's birth certificate and stared at the parents' names. *I'm making progress.* With their names entered into the tree, new leaves popped up. Research confirmed that Emma had siblings. I added a Randall, an Elizabeth, and a Justin to the tree.

My uncle. I wasn't having great luck with uncles. I'd just added Justin's marriage certificate to the tree when the bed shook. Startled by something, Alex picked his head up off the pillow and glanced around the room. After only a second, he sprawled on his stomach. I ran my fingers through his hair, soothing him. He sighed deeply and mumbled something I couldn't understand.

What did he say? My brain had a new puzzle and no longer cared to focus on genealogy. Thirty minutes later, when his alarm beeped, I gave up puzzling through the syllables, trying to piece together what he might've said.

He rolled over and rubbed his eyes. "Did you sleep?"

"Didn't even try. I'll sleep while you drive."

"Thank you for indulging me. Now I won't be grumpy all day."

"Thank goodness." I closed the laptop and slipped off the bed. "Want coffee?"

"Sounds good."

He had just enough time to shake the cobwebs before the portable storage unit arrived, right on time. Unfortunately, the movers were late. Alex paced just outside the door.

When he paused, I wrapped my arms around him from behind. "Keep up the pacing, and you'll be tired before you even start loading."

He patted my hands. "I'm ready to get you home."

As he uttered the word "home," a truck pulled into the lot. Three guys with matching jackets, which had the movers' logo plastered on the back, hopped out and pointed toward the empty container.

Alex hurried down the stairs, barking instructions. I went back inside, happy I didn't have to coordinate packing the unit.

After dragging the cleaning supplies into the bathroom, I closed myself off from the commotion and scrubbed. Once the tile sparkled, I yanked open the door and yelped in surprise.

Keith greeted me with a nervous smile. "Looks like you're really leaving."

"What are you doing in here?"

"Didn't see you outside. Came back here looking for you."

Uncomfortable, I hurried out to the living room. "Need something?"

Movers flipped my couch on its back and maneuvered it out the front door. They stopped just outside, discussing how to get it down the stairs.

"Not really. What was all the commotion last night? I heard your bodyguard shouting in the middle of the night. You guys didn't have a fight or anything?" His last question sounded more hopeful than concerned.

"No. Nothing like that. Someone tried to break in, we think." I sat the bucket on the floor, trying to dismiss the idea that maybe Keith was jealous.

"Can I help you with anything?" His eagerness didn't help shake the notion.

A man walked out of the kitchen. "Oh, you found her." His ball cap pulled low, he hadn't taken off his sunglasses.

"Who are you?" I forced a semi-polite smile.

"This is my friend J—" Keith turned toward the man, eyes wide, mouth open as if he didn't know what to say.

"Jon. Nice to meet you." Jon reached out to shake my hand.

"Hi." I crossed my arms. "You don't want to shake my hand. I've been cleaning the bathroom." I studied what I could see of his face, trying to decide if he was old enough to be Justin. The way Keith hesitated struck me as odd. Behind the sunglasses and beard, the man hid his secret well.

"Hello?" Jon waved a hand in front of my face, pulling me from my conspiracy theories. "Put us to work. What can we do?" Jon patted Keith on the back. "He's tougher than he looks."

I chided myself for my crazy thoughts. *As if Keith would even know Justin.* I glanced around, but other than cleaning, there wasn't much to do. "Ask Alex."

"Ask me what?" Alex squeezed between the couch and the door.

"Keith and his friend want to help." I leaned into him when he stepped up beside me.

"We can stay in here and help you clean." Keith pointed at the bucket of cleansers and supplies, completely ignoring Alex.

"As soon as they get this couch down, grab some boxes. Kate's got everything inside under control." Alex kissed the side of my head. "Am I right?"

"Yep. I'm going to get back to it." I dragged the vacuum into the bedroom and closed the door.

After dusting vents and wiping down walls, I pushed the vacuum, back and forth, around the room, hoping the apartment would glisten enough for me to get at least part of my deposit back.

The vacuum blaring, I jumped when a hand touched my shoulder.

"Kate!" Keith held out a cup. "Thought you might want something to drink."

Without turning off the vacuum, I shook my head and continued. He stared at me another few seconds before walking out of the room. I hated being rude, but with a looming deadline, I needed to finish cleaning. Besides, his seeking me out made me uneasy, probably because Alex planted the seed that Keith was jealous. The thought had never crossed my mind, but after Alex mentioned it, whenever Keith showed up, that thought jumped up and down waving its arms.

When the entire bedroom floor was covered in wide stripes marking the back and forth passes, I opened the door and moved into the hall.

Jon stepped around the corner. Running his fingers through his beard, he leaned against the wall. "Where you moving to?"

"Texas." I dragged the cord out of the bedroom and plugged it into the nearest outlet.

"To be with him?" He nodded toward the living room.

"Lots of reasons." I flipped the switch on the vacuum and drowned out any further conversation.

He disappeared around the corner.

I finished up in the hall and wrapped the cord back onto the handle. *No point in vacuuming the living room until the movers are done.* I grabbed the duster. *Never dust before vacuuming.* My mom's words echoed in my head—well the words of the woman who lied about being my mom. Anger and hurt pounded on my chest. How could she keep such a secret from me? She cared more about protecting her husband than she did about me. I dusted my way through the living room. I wouldn't bend my cleaning to her advice.

Only a small pile of boxes and a couple bookshelves remained in the apartment. *Almost. What's left on my list?* The kitchen still needed to be cleaned. I grabbed the bucket, pulled on gloves, and set to work wiping down walls and counters.

When I'd finished everything except the floor, I peeked out into the living room. Five boxes sat in the middle of the room. *Nearly done.* I grabbed the empty bucket and walked back to the bathroom. After pouring in a little vinegar, I maneuvered the bucket under the tub faucet to fill so I could mop. In a matter of minutes, water crept more than halfway up the sides.

As I leaned down to turn off the water, the door opened behind me. I froze. The water neared the top of the bucket, but I didn't move.

A familiar arm reached around and turned the knob. "Need me to carry this to the kitchen?"

I nodded, recovering from my fright.

"What's wrong? You're pale." Alex sniffed his shirt. "Do I smell *that* bad?"

I sat on the edge of the tub. "I thought you were Keith."

"Your hands are shaking." He squatted in front of me, closing his hands around mine. "I sent Keith and that friend home, but your neighbor wants you to stop and say goodbye before you leave. I came to find you because LeAnn is here."

"She is?"

"Go talk to her. I'll mop."

I hugged him before darting out to the living room.

A teary-eyed LeAnn stood sniffling in the middle of the room. "I promised myself I wouldn't cry, but now . . . in the empty apartment."

I wagged my finger at her. "Not fair. You're making me cry now."

She walked around the empty living room and finally slid down the wall, to sit where my couch used to be. I joined her, and we sat side by side, not saying much. I'd miss my friend.

Alex whistled as he mopped.

"He cleans, too?" LeAnn nudged me.

"He's being extra nice because I'm such an emotional mess."

"Cause of all the crazy?"

"That and I'm skittish still. I hate it, too."

"I'm so glad he came with you."

"If I had a nickel for every time I've thought that, I . . . I could buy you round trip tickets to Texas." The last words sounded squeaky as I choked back tears I refused to shed.

"I really should go. I don't want to leave, but I have to get over to Jeff's. He expected me there an hour ago."

"You promise to write? And come visit?"

"I promise. And tell Mr. Bodyguard I said goodbye." LeAnn hugged me before darting out the door without looking back.

I taped together the last remaining flat box. My new photo album and apron lay on the floor next to my luggage along with a few other stray items I found while cleaning. I tossed them all in the box.

"You okay?" Alex had the mop bucket in one hand and his other arm wrapped around the box of cleaning supplies. "I'm going to toss these in."

"Is there room for this?" I taped the box closed.

"Barely." He winked. "I'll be back up to get it in just a minute."

While he tromped down the stairs, I piled our luggage and bag of snacks near the front door. After he picked up the last box, I ran the sweeper in the living room while he loaded and locked the container. The sparkling, clean apartment sat empty, except for the pile near the door. He carried out the vacuum, and I slid to the floor, exhausted.

Alex nudged me on the shoulder. "They picked up the container, and I hitched the trailer to the truck."

"You already loaded the car onto the trailer?"

"I did."

"I fell asleep."

"You did." He dropped to the floor next to me.

"I couldn't have managed this without you." I leaned in to hug him.

"You might not want to do that just now. I'm sweaty and nasty."

I kissed his cheek. "Take a quick shower before we go."

"I'll be fast. I want to have you back in Texas before midnight." He disappeared around the corner, his duffle bag slung over his shoulder.

Hearing the water come on reminded me that there was nothing in the bathroom for him to use to dry off. The box with the last of the towels was already on its way to Texas. All that was left in the apartment was luggage and snacks. *My suitcase.* Remembering that

I'd packed a beach towel, I dug through the clothes to the bottom and yanked out my large purple towel.

I pushed open the bathroom door and blinked at the clouds of steam.

The quiet penetrated my skull too late. The shower curtain open, Alex leaned out of the tub, shuffling through his bag. Water droplets glistened on his shoulders, back, hips, thighs, and—I squeezed my eyes shut, the image still very visible.

"Whoa! Hello." The shower curtain rustled. "That towel for me?"

I opened one eye and nodded. The bathroom warmed, or at least I did.

He stood with his duffle bag held in front of him.

Mesmerized by the parts still in view—his wet, bronze skin tinted a deep red—I stood and gaped.

"Ahem." His green eyes glinted. "Are you going to hand it to me or just stare?"

My cheeks burned. "Sorry." I slipped out the door.

Alex's robust laugh echoed in the bathroom. "Kate?" His hand poked out the door. "The towel?"

I pushed the purple terry cloth into his hand and dashed back to the living room.

When he strutted into the living room, I buried my head in my arms. I felt his stare as he gathered the luggage.

"I'll be back for the snacks in a minute." He opened the door. "Should I knock before I walk back in?" Chuckling reverberated up the stairs as he carried the bags down to the truck.

My heart pounding on my chest cavity wasn't only because of embarrassment. I ran through the apartment one last time, making sure I wasn't leaving anything important behind, and debated about whether or not to say goodbye to my neighbor. Back in the living room, prepared to deal with more ribbing from Alex, my conundrum was settled when Keith met Alex at the front door.

"Didn't you tell her I wanted to say goodbye?" Keith stepped between Alex and the open door.

I caught Alex's eye and waved my hand, hopefully conveying that he didn't need to run Keith off. "He told me. We haven't left yet." I stood in the doorway.

Alex shifted, not happy with Keith's posturing. "Excuse me. I need to get in there."

Keith moved only enough for Alex to slip past into the apartment. "Oh. Well, I liked having you as a neighbor. When did you decide to move? This is kind of sudden."

"It's not. I'm only leaving a few weeks earlier than I planned." I rubbed my arms as a cold rush of air dropped the temperature in the apartment.

"I guess I'll go so you can leave. Don't want to keep you." He stepped toward me, opening his arms.

I tensed a little as he hugged me, but patted his shoulder, hoping to end it quickly. Before he pulled back, he whispered, "That guy's not forcing you to go or anything, is he?"

I bit my lip, struggling not to laugh out loud at the ridiculous question. "I decided to move before I even met him."

"Good. Okay. You know my address if you want to write or anything." Keith surprised me by reaching to shake Alex's hand. "Have a safe trip."

"Thanks." Alex smiled but, to his credit, not smugly. He seemed to pity the kid crushing on his older neighbor.

Keith slunk back to his apartment and waved before he closed the door.

Now it's time to go.

Alex wrapped his arms around me from behind. "You ready?"

"The snacks?"

"Only thing not in the truck is us." He kissed the top of my head. "I'll be downstairs."

I stood in the doorway of my empty apartment with tears running down my cheeks. There wasn't much I would miss about this apartment, but closing the door represented ending a chapter of my life. I hadn't cried this much in years and didn't like it. The slightest word or emotion set off the mister in my eyes.

Alex waited at the bottom of the stairs. He rubbed my back as I climbed into the truck, then drove around to the office. I ran in and handed my keys to the lady at the desk. I smoothed my unruly hair and wished I'd taken a few extra minutes to apply a tad of makeup or at least wash my face.

"Ma'am, we'll need your forwarding address to send the deposit if the apartment is in good condition."

"Oh, yeah. Just a second." *I wiped vents! I better get my deposit back.* I ran outside to the driver's side window of the truck. It slid down as I approached.

"Can I give them your address since I don't know what mine is yet?"

"Sure." Alex turned off the truck and walked inside with me.

The lady at the desk smiled, clearly making an assumption, but I didn't correct her. Alex scribbled his address on the form.

"Thank you." I slipped my hand in his and waved to the woman, who grinned ear to ear as Alex and I walked out the door.

We climbed into the truck, and Alex wasted no time. As soon as I buckled in, he backed out and exited the complex. "And we're off. I figured we'd drive as far as we can tonight, even straight through if we can make it."

"Don't push yourself."

"We'll play it by ear." He blended onto the highway, and we headed for Texas, headed home.

Beth-

I can't believe your little guy is crawling already. He'll be a busy one!

Great news about Patrick's promotion. Tell him congrats!

Sticks stopped by the other day. He had his baby girl with him. She's beautiful, so tiny. Looks like him a little, too.

Don't bother lecturing. He didn't come to see me, only to pick up Scooter. They went for burgers. It's really hard not to tell Scooter the truth now that he has a sister. Oh, and it was silly to worry that Sticks would forget about showing up. He's made it to almost every one of Scooter's baseball games, they play catch any chance they get. Sticks has made a point of carving out time for Scooter.

For a while, I couldn't figure out why Sticks spent so much time with Scooter, but I think I know. We both know that Sticks isn't a noble soul fulfilling his duty to his son. He doesn't even want people to know they're related. I think Sticks likes the way it makes him feel to have Scooter looking up to him, proud of him.

Just like it was when we were in college. It wasn't about how I felt. It was all about how I made him feel. I just hope he continues to like the way it feels to have Scooter love him for a long, long time, because that kid is really attached. If Sticks ever quits coming around, Scooter will be crushed.

I wonder what he tells his wife about why he leaves. I'm envious of her. I know that sounds like a horrible thing to say, but she has everything I wanted.

-M

September 1984

Beth-

Remember how I said she had everything I wanted? Well "her" husband keeps showing up at my door, long after Scooter has gone to bed. His wife has to know, not that it's me . . . just that he's seeing someone else, spending half his nights away from home. Does she notice that he comes home smelling of perfume? I started wearing it again when he began coming around.

I slept alone only twice last week. That little girl is the only reason he stays with his wife. I just know it. I'm not envious of his wife anymore. I don't know if I could handle being cheated on repeatedly and living like nothing was wrong.

I need to tell him that he's welcome to see Scooter, but I can't continue like this. Sleeping with someone else's husband isn't what I wanted either.

There's a new guy at work. He's nice—the kind of guy you want to take home to Thanksgiving dinner. Why can't I find someone like that?

-M

CHAPTER SIX

January 22, 2016 – 4:12 pm

Alex negotiated traffic, not daring to take his eyes off the road. He couldn't wait to get Kate settled in Texas. He looked forward to showing her around San Antonio and the Hill Country; to strolling the Riverwalk and watching her reaction to the music, color, and food; and to watching movies with her—just being a normal dating couple, not chased by anyone.

"You like movies?"

"Yeah, and popcorn." She laid her phone on the center console. "With butter."

"I got to ask your friends questions. What would you ask DJ and Becca about me?"

"What do you mean 'would I'? I already asked Becca."

Alex raised an eyebrow but didn't have a chance to respond because Kate's phone beeped a text notification.

"LeAnn wants us to stop by Jeff's before we leave. Says it's important."

They hadn't even left the Denver city limits. "Tell me where to go." He didn't have to ask if Kate was concerned; her furrowed brow left little doubt.

She wrung her hands as she directed him to the apartment. She'd texted LeAnn back but hadn't gotten a response. Thirty-five minutes later, when he turned into the complex, Kate gasped. Two police cars and an ambulance blocked the spaces near Jeff's door. Kate started to open the door before Alex had even stopped the truck.

"Let me park before you jump out." He found a place where he could pull out of the way, then jumped out and nearly had to run to keep up with her.

She stopped when a gurney rolled out of the apartment. "LeAnn?" Kate bolted toward the commotion.

Alex stepped up beside her as she reached LeAnn, who waved at the medic and asked for two minutes alone with Kate and Alex. The medic hesitated but walked away holding up two fingers.

LeAnn winced as she shifted. "Oh, Kate."

"What happened?" Kate choked out the question.

"They took Jeff. You can't tell the police, though. They think someone broke in when I was at Jeff's alone. You can't tell them what happened." LeAnn stifled a sob. "Promise?"

"Just tell me, LeAnn."

"Not until you promise."

"Okay. I won't tell them." Kate shot Alex a sideways glance when he nudged her in the side.

"That guy . . . I mean . . . trying to find you. He said it was your fault. He hit Jeff so hard. I finally talked, told him what he wanted to know. If he doesn't find you there, they'll kill him. Please, no police."

"What did he want to know?" Alex leaned over, his fists clenched.

"Where Kate was headed."

The medic walked up, unwilling to waver on the agreed upon two minutes. "Time for her to go."

"I need him." LeAnn wiped at tears as they lifted the stretcher into the ambulance. "I need him safe."

Kate ran back to the truck at a full sprint. She was already buckled in, her face as white as a slice of sandwich bread, when Alex climbed in behind the wheel.

"We *are* calling the police." He slammed his door and reached for his phone. *How can this be happening again?*

"We can't." She grabbed his arm, her eyes pleading with him not to make the call. "They'll kill him. At least wait until we know more."

He started the engine and drove out of the lot, fuming.

Deep breath. Calm down.

A mile down the road, he finally gave voice to his fears. "Did you miss the part where she said, 'If he doesn't find you'?" It took all the willpower he could muster not to raise his voice. "Someone willing to kidnap and kill is after you."

At those words, she erupted into tears.

Watching her cry like that was a special kind of torture. He spied a lot where he could park the truck and trailer. Once he stopped, he reached over the console and stroked her hair. "Kate, I'm sorry. I didn't mean to make you cry." After unbuckling, he leaned over, wishing he had a bench seat so he could pull her into his arms. "I just want to keep you safe. If Jeff's life wasn't on the line, I'd be driving the opposite direction and keeping you out of Texas until I knew the coast was clear."

She didn't answer. Her shoulders shook, her face still buried in her hands.

"I hate seeing you this upset." He pulled out tissues and handed them to her. Helpless to fix the situation, he gripped the steering wheel until his knuckles turned white. "I should start driving."

She grabbed his arm. "Can we give it until we get back to Texas? Right now, I'm not even sure what to report."

"But when we get back—"

"We'll involve the police." She blew her nose, then chuckled, but there wasn't a hint of happiness in it. "Apparently, I attract trouble. It would've been easier for you if you hadn't answered when I knocked."

"Kate, don't." He wiped a tear off her cheek with his thumb and kissed her hand. "All I care about is keeping you safe."

Exhaustion evident on her face, she leaned back against the headrest. Already tired, the stress had drained her of what little energy she had left.

He reached into the backseat and grabbed a pillow. "Try and sleep."

She gathered the pillow into her arms. "Alex—" Her voice cracked, and she shook her head before dropping it onto the pillow and squeezing her eyes closed.

They were well out of Denver before she relaxed enough to sleep, and her breathing fell into a restful rhythm.

South of Colorado Springs, traffic lightened. He rested a hand on Kate's head, stroking her curls. Dealing with the threat had been much easier for the walled-off Alex. Danger was a short brunette, and he could no longer imagine life without her. He didn't want to.

He shifted in his seat, ready for a break to stretch his legs. Kate stirred. The radio turned down low, he'd tried to let her rest without interruption, but a stop was necessary. He glanced in the rearview mirror for about the one-hundredth time. No one followed behind them, hanging back or keeping pace. He exited the highway, and, as he slowed down, Kate's head popped up off the pillow.

"We stopping?" She rubbed her eyes.

"Need fuel and a bathroom."

"It's dark. I slept hard."

"You needed it."

When he pulled up to the pump, Kate reached for the door handle, and his heart raced. *You haven't seen anyone following you. Surely it's safe.*

"Want me to grab you anything?" She slung her purse over her shoulder.

"Please be careful." He slid out of the truck and swiped his card at the pump. "I'll be in as soon as I finish."

She surveyed the parking lot but didn't take a step. "Never mind." She shook her head and walked around the truck. Coming up behind him, she wrapped her arms around his waist and laid her head on his back. "I'll just wait for you."

He twisted around until she was in his arms, facing him. Leaning down, he dropped a gentle kiss on the top of her head. *She can read your mind.*

Inside, Alex stood near a shelf, not far from the ladies' room door, trying not to look like a creepy stalker. Once he laid eyes on her again, his heartbeat would resume.

She flashed a weary smile as she stepped out. "Watching out for me?"

"That's what bodyguards do."

In the store, she stayed close, watching anyone who wandered within a few feet of her. Glad for her naturally cautious tendencies, he managed to breathe a little easier but still kept a watchful eye.

Fifteen minutes later, they were back on the road with drinks and sandwiches from the hot food counter. No headlights followed them out of the lot.

"Did you learn anything about Emma's family when you searched?"

"A little. I found parents' names."

"Confirm the siblings?"

"Randall, Elizabeth, and . . . Justin."

"So you do have an uncle Justin. We still don't know for sure the guy that called was him, though. Figure out anything else?"

"My search got . . . I haven't finished researching."

"Did you talk to Travis today?"

"Earlier. I missed a call, too. Justin Carson left a message asking me to call him back."

"More of the so excited that you're back?"

"Pretty much. I texted Travis after Justin called the other day. Travis messaged back and asked me to wait until after I got settled in Texas to call or message Justin. There's a story I need to hear, apparently." She sighed. "Again."

Hours later, the moon far above the horizon, two state lines lay between them and Denver.

Kate yawned. "How are you? Tired?"

"We're about an hour out of Amarillo. I'll see how I feel when we get there. It's getting pretty late, and we jumped ahead an hour crossing back into Central time."

"Tell me about your siblings. Where do they live?"

He didn't even flinch at the random change of topic. Her efforts to keep him awake and talking were welcome. "My brothers are in the Virginia area, not far from DC. One sister is in California, the other in Austin."

"How often do you see them?"

"Not often. I haven't seen the three of them since the funeral. I see Marisa more often. We try to get together before the holidays and make tamales."

"Tamales?"

"Ever had them?" Alex stifled a yawn.

"Yes. Love them."

"It was a family affair before Mom and Dad died."

"I want to learn how to make them." Kate reached into the backseat and shuffled through the snack bag.

His heart danced a little. Her interest in his family traditions added more plusses in her perfect-for-him column. "Music to my ears."

She opened a bag of bacon jerky and set it where Alex could reach. "Are any of them married?"

"No. Not last I heard. One brother is engaged."

"Were you close growing up?"

"We were. And after my parents died, I worked at keeping it that way, but then . . ."

"I'd like to meet them."

Alex took his eyes off the road for a moment. "Tell me more about you and Meg."

"What haven't I told you? Meg was easy to get along with as long as I followed her advice."

"But you weren't close."

"We drew closer after Dad died. When he died, it felt like the ship sank, and we just clung to each other to stay afloat."

"She was already in Texas when it happened?"

"Yeah. I'm not sure how this will all work out. Our conversation didn't end well."

Before he hit the outskirts of Amarillo, he knew he needed to stop for the night. All the stress and chaos finally caught up with him, leaving him wiped out.

Kate didn't miss the cues. "Can we please stop soon? I'm exhausted, and you must be, too."

He nodded and yawned. "Yeah." Two miles down the highway, he exited and pulled into the nearest hotel. "Kate, when we stopped before . . ." He cleared his throat. "Will you please share a room with me? I'm not asking you to sleep with me."

She stared out the window, her cheeks a shade darker than before. He guessed her hesitation was prompted by the intimacy and heat generated when they were close. And the memory of the shower surely deepened her tint.

"Please. I'll sleep on a chair, or even on the floor." He opened his hand, hoping she'd take it.

She tangled her fingers with his but didn't look at him. "All right."

He grabbed the luggage, and they stepped into the quiet lobby. A minute later, a clerk appeared at the front desk.

"Hi. How can I help you?" He looked much too well-dressed for the late hour.

"We need a room." Alex clutched Kate's hand hoping they had at least one room available. He'd pushed himself, and driving farther wasn't a safe option.

"Just for tonight?"

"Yes."

The clerk tapped the keyboard. "We have one room left. A double queen."

"We'll take it." Alex pulled out his wallet.

Kate laid a credit card on the counter. "Let me."

"No." Alex picked up the card and handed it back to her. "I want to."

"I'm costing you too much."

Alex passed his card to the clerk. "Please let me pay, Kate."

"Thank you." She slipped her card back into her purse.

Beth-

I've been struggling with breaking it off with Sticks. I want to, but when he's with me, my nerve withers. Suffice it to say, he's been on my mind a lot.

Please don't lecture me when I tell you what I did.

I dropped Scooter off to spend the night with Dad. Curiosity got the best of me. Instead of leaving via Flat Rock Road like I always do, I drove into town and passed by Sticks' house. I saw his wife.

Never thought I'd be the other woman. I knew he was married this whole time, but now that I've seen her, I feel awful. There she was, swaying on the porch holding the baby. Her face is branded in my brain. What frustrates me is that she looks familiar. I think I know her from somewhere. I haven't been able to place her, but it'll come to me.

-M

Chapter Seven

January 23, 2016 – 4:30 am

I'd woken several times in the night, a common occurrence when I slept in hotels. Just as I lulled back to sleep, Alex startled me.

"Kate! Rainy!"

I bolted upright.

He thrashed in the sheets, reaching toward the ceiling. "Where are you?" Panic reverberated his words.

The expression on his face, the worry in his voice begged to be settled.

I slipped out of bed and shivered as the cold air nipped at me. Clutching his hands, I put them to my face. "Shhh. I'm okay."

A relieved smile spread across his face. He grabbed me and hugged me to his chest. "You're okay."

He's not even awake.

"I'm fine." I extricated myself from his sleepy embrace. Sleeping in his arms would be warmer and more soothing, but I climbed back into my bed. After tossing and turning, I finally drifted back to sleep.

When I opened my eyes hours later, the sun poured light on the world outside. The running water in the bathroom clued me in to where Alex was. I checked my phone hoping for news about LeAnn, then pulled out clean clothes. When he walked out of the bathroom, I was sitting on the bed texting with Becca.

"Morning." He strolled across the room and leaned toward me. His eyes glinted as he kissed me. "How'd you sleep?"

"I never sleep well in hotel rooms."

"Hope my snoring didn't keep you up."

"You're really worried about me. Aren't you?" I hadn't intended to sound so direct.

He sat down on his bed and stared at me. "What did I say in my sleep?"

I walked over and stood between his knees. My hands on his clean-shaven cheeks, I kissed him. "You called my name. From the way you sounded, it was quite a nightmare."

"To say I'm not concerned would be a lie." He put his hands on my waist, his green eyes burning with intensity. "I'm worried we're doing this all wrong. If anything happened to you . . ."

The intimacy hovering between us overwhelmed me as did the fear of something happening. I gave him a quick peck. "My turn in the shower. Be out in a bit."

Two hours closer to home, I pulled munchies out of the back seat and grabbed water bottles out of the cooler. "Travis said he'll meet us at The Castle."

"You were texting Becca this morning?"

"She wanted to know how things were going."

"Did you tell her anything about what's going on?"

"No. She'd just tell DJ."

"We *are* calling the police."

"I said I would." Frustration added an edge to my voice, but he hadn't caused it. I hated that trouble had intruded on my life again. I trailed my fingers down his arm, wishing for half a second that he wasn't behind the wheel. "I'm worried about Jeff, and I haven't heard anything from LeAnn, even though I've texted her a few times."

The closer to home we got, the more pensive Alex became. He

hadn't spoken a word for the last forty miles, which even for him was unusual.

"We going to stop at the cabin first? I wanted to let Travis know we're getting close."

"I'm not taking you anywhere *near* the cabin."

"Okay." Confused and irritated by his answer, I texted Travis and shrugged off the inferred slight. Instead, I gave way to the excitement that bubbled through my blanket of worry. *The Castle. My house.* I couldn't wait to be inside, to see it with my own eyes. I stared out the window, the terrain looking more familiar by the minute.

Alex touched my hand. His tone much softer, he said, "We left my address with the office when you dropped off your apartment keys."

It never occurred to me to worry about that. "Then you shouldn't go to the cabin either."

"I won't. For now, I plan to stay with you, if that's okay."

"Yes, of course."

"Have you heard from LeAnn?"

"Mona texted me. LeAnn's okay, just a bit bruised."

It was mid-afternoon when we pulled up next to the Arts and Crafts-style bungalow. A white picket fence marked the property line, and a stone walkway curved around the house from the drive-way to the front where three steps led to a large porch.

Alex parked next to Travis's red Porsche in the driveway. Travis stood just off the back porch of The Castle. His smile and relaxed demeanor left no doubt that Alex hadn't told him about anything going on.

I jumped out of the passenger seat, and as soon as I neared the back door, Travis handed me a key. I took a deep breath and held back tears, not easy given all that'd happened.

Alex came up beside me. "Need a few minutes alone?"

"No. I want you with me. And you too, Travis."

Travis hugged me and shook Alex's hand. "I wasn't sure if y'all had eaten. I picked up pizza rolls on my way out here."

"Pizza rolls?" Alex grinned.

"Let's eat, and then you can give me a tour." I pushed open the door and gasped. "This place is amazing! Even better than the pictures."

"Emma and I remodeled just before she got sick. We redid the floors, knocked out some walls, and added a second-floor bonus room.

Alex tucked the pizza rolls in the oven and set it on low. "Let's have the tour first, then we'll eat."

Travis pointed to the back door. "Indulge me, if you will. Let's go around and come in the front door."

"Sure." The first one out the back door, I outpaced them around the house. As they came up the front steps, I walked the porch, running my hands along the rails, touching everything in sight, admiring the colorful exterior, and imagining a porch swing at one end. "I love the red door."

Travis's smile lit his whole face. "Emma insisted. When we repainted the exterior, she said I could pick any color I wanted as long as the house had a red door." He nodded to the knob. "Use your key."

I fumbled with the lock, then pushed the door open. Wooden beams and columns accented the great room. Off to the right, a farmhouse table with eight padded upright chairs caught my attention.

"It's gorgeous. The table is amazing."

"Emma picked that out. She fell in love with it and thought it would be perfect here." Travis watched as I ran my fingers along the wood grain.

"It is."

The rest of the great room sat empty. A space to the left of the front door would become a sitting area or living room. A counter-height bar separated the dining area from the kitchen.

"There's very little furniture here, the dining room table and a bed in the master. I had almost everything else emptied after Emma died." Travis studied me. "I had a cleaning crew out while you were in Denver to scrub and dust."

"Thank you. I love this house."

"I want you to make this place yours. Decorate it however you want, buy new furniture." He pointed toward the back of the house. "Follow me back to the den. This was added years after the house was built."

Beyond the kitchen, a room sprawled across the back of the house. Windows filled two walls.

"This room needs new carpet and fresh paint. I want to cover any remodeling expenses."

"You don't have to do that." I cringed as I realized I'd responded too quickly.

"Kate, please let me do these things. I've waited many, many years to have you in my life. Let me spoil you a little, please." He handed me a sealed envelope.

I leaned back against the wall and tore open the envelope. Aware of Travis and Alex's eyes on me, I braced to hold back a flood of emotions. When the prepaid credit card slipped out and I read the words in the card, I lost that battle.

Kate,

There are no words for the joy of having you home. Your choice to live in The Castle means so much. Make it your home; decorate it any way you like. I have decades to make up for—decades of birthdays, Christmases, smiles, and tears. Thank you for letting me be a part of your life. I've waited years to spoil my little girl.

Though we've only just met, I love you, Kate, because, in my heart, you are my little Claire.

Love Always,

Travis

Travis studied my reaction as I read the card. "If you need more than that, please tell me."

I wrapped my arms around his neck. "Thank you. It's more than generous." I couldn't tell him I loved him, not yet. "The light in this room is wonderful. What color should I paint these walls?"

"What do you think, Alex?" Travis motioned for him to join the conversation.

"Anything but white." Alex leaned against the doorframe. "This place is beautiful, Mr. Bentley."

I didn't understand the dynamic between them or why Alex called Travis Mr. Bentley. They each went out of their way to include the other, almost to the point of awkward.

"Take a peek at the bedrooms." Travis led us down the hall and pointed into the first room on the left. "This is the one we called the guest room."

Blue toile curtains framed a sunny window. A large dark blue area rug filled the center of the room. White beadboard covered the bottom half of the walls. Pale coral paint added a punch of color.

"Is this the room she decorated for me?"

The tears in Travis's eyes answered my question. He nodded. "She worried about what to choose because she didn't know what you liked."

"It's perfect just like this. I love blue."

Alex rested his hands on my shoulders.

Travis smiled. "She did, too. Across the hall is the guest bath, decorated in blue. And down here is the extra room."

Plain white walls and bare wood floors gave the room a blank canvas feel. A large pile of boxes filled the room.

"I apologize for all these boxes. This is from our big clean out after my mom died. They were all over the house, but after Scott left, we moved them in here. There is another large closet filled with boxes in the den. I'll send someone to get them out of your way."

"Would you mind leaving the boxes? I would love to go through them." I leaned against Alex. "If that's okay?"

"I'm happy to, if that's what you want."

Travis walked back into the hall and for a moment disappeared as he turned a corner. Alex and I followed and found him just inside the last bedroom.

Travis spread his arms. "The master."

I walked into the bedroom. "Look at this bed!" A king size sleigh bed anchored the room. Crisp floral sheets covered the mattress. A quilt lay draped near the footboard.

"Emma bought that about the same time as the table."

Alex squeezed my hand and stepped aside.

"I had the cleaning crew pull out the linens that had been boxed up and wash everything. They put clean sheets on the bed." Travis walked up behind me and rested his hands on my shoulders. "This feels like a dream come true."

"I'm excited to make this my home."

While we ate, I chatted with Alex and Travis about paint colors and carpet, the perfect distraction from the fear of who might be in pursuit. The guys ate pizza rolls, interspersing comments, letting me know they were listening.

When everyone had their fill, I stuck the leftovers in the refrigerator. Alex carried in our bags and the cooler. As I emptied it, Alex and Travis talked quietly about small towns and college sports.

Alex wanted to tell him what had happened, I could tell.

Travis stood up. "I should probably head out."

I hugged him. "Thank you or everything."

"Please call if you need anything. I haven't forgotten about Justin, but we'll talk more about it later." He shook hands with Alex. "Could I speak with you outside a minute?"

Alex reached for the doorknob. "Of course, sir."

I listened at the door trying to make out the conversation outside, to no avail. *Did Travis just play the dad card?* That was odd. He'd sounded nothing but fond of Alex.

I wiped off the counters near the door, straining to hear. A flurry of curses—from Travis—rang out. Alex must have told him about what happened in Denver.

When the knob turned, I retreated closer to the table. "You told him?"

Alex nodded.

"What did he want to talk to you about?"

Alex kicked at a crumb on the floor. After several seconds, his pinched brow relaxed. "He wants to know his little girl is being taken care of."

Dang it. I really wish I'd heard that conversation. "What did you say?"

"What do you think I said?" He wrapped his arms around me.

"He saw you bring your bags in, didn't he?"

"Until those guys are caught, I'm a permanent fixture." He kissed my cheek. "It's time to call DJ."

"I know." I walked through the house again, arranging furniture in my head, anything to keep my mind off Jeff and my unknown hunter.

Alex called DJ. Standing in the large upstairs bonus room, I heard when Alex ended the call and hurried down.

He met me at the bottom of the stairs and tucked the phone in his pocket. "Becca's coming with him."

"Did you tell him what it was about?"

"Said we wanted them to see the place and also needed to talk to him about a police matter."

"What have I gotten us into? You can't even go home." I leaned on his chest.

He tangled his fingers in my hair, kissing the top of my head.

"I've robbed you of all your time alone."

"I'm not leaving you alone. I am concerned that everything happening—all this time together, being chased—isn't good for *us*." He rested his cheek on the top of my head and held me tight.

What is that supposed to mean? I had another worry to add to my list. Being with him non-stop did make the relationship feel more like a race rather than a stroll on the beach.

"I'm trying to slow it down." He rubbed his thumb on my neck.

Did a thought bubble appear above my head? It unnerved me how often he knew my thoughts. I wriggled out of his arms and tried not to add unsaid intentions to his words. The hurt look on his face as I backed away prompted tears I couldn't hold back.

When he reached for me, I shook my head. "I'm sorry."

"I didn't mean . . ."

Whatever else he said, I didn't hear. I ran down the hall, swung my bedroom door closed, and threw myself on the bed—not my most adult moment. Stretched out on the bed, I let my tears fall. My face buried in the sheets, I contemplated the thread count and ways to pull back so Alex wouldn't feel dragged into a relationship, though at no point had he said such a thing.

Ten minutes later, car doors sounded outside. I jumped up and wiped my face. It wouldn't do to have Becca see me upset, prompting questions I didn't want to answer. I opened the bedroom door and stopped. Alex sat on the floor in the hall, knees up, his face buried in his crossed arms. When he looked up, instead of tears, a drawn and worn expression met me.

"I made you cry." The tenderness in his voice nearly prompted my ever-ready flow of tears. "I'm trying to do things the *right* way."

I dropped onto the floor next to him and rested my head on his arm. "They're going to knock any minute."

"You know I didn't mean I don't like spending time with you, right?"

I nodded against his shoulder. Words couldn't be wrestled into sentences that explained how I felt. Nor did I want to try and explain how logically, I knew what he meant, and it made sense, but emotionally, his words stung. I didn't understand it myself.

The expected knock echoed down the hall.

Alex stood up and held out his hand. "We get interrupted a lot."

I took his hand and let him pull me up. "I've noticed that."

When I opened the front door, Becca beamed as she stepped inside. "This is amazing!"

"Isn't it?" I hugged her.

DJ sauntered in behind her, his arm no longer in a sling. "Nice place." After being shot trying to capture my kidnapper, he'd healed, though he still favored his arm just enough to be noticeable.

Alex and DJ followed behind while I gave Becca the grand tour, explaining bits from my mom's letters, like why I called the house The Castle.

Once we'd wandered the house twice, discussing my new family, paint colors, and furniture arrangement, we all settled in the kitchen. Alex sobered as soon as he dropped into a chair.

It was time.

Ignoring the police matter didn't solve anything, but talking about what happened made it feel more real.

DJ barely waited until we were all seated. "What police matter?"

Alex shot me a sideways glance, and I slipped my hand in his. "The night before we left town, someone tried to break into Kate's apartment." He cleared his throat, trying to stay calm.

I stared at the table. If I looked at anyone, I wouldn't be able to hold it together.

"Yesterday, when we were headed out of town, her friend, LeAnn, asked her to stop by. Police and an ambulance were there when we arrived. She'd been smacked around." He tightened his grip on my hand, and I made the mistake of looking at him. Tears brimmed in his eyes.

I breathed in deep and picked up where he left off. "She didn't tell the police what really happened. Apparently, there's a man that blames me for something. To get him to stop hitting her boyfriend, Jeff, she told the man I was moving to Texas, near San Antonio. He left and took Jeff with them. She asked us not to tell the police that Jeff had been kidnapped."

"But you did, right?" DJ leaned on the table, focused on Alex.

"That's why we called you." Alex's voice was measured.

"You waited until *now* to report it?" DJ jumped up and ran his fingers through his hair.

Alex's tense shoulders heaped guilt on me.

The flaw in my thinking seemed so obvious. I rubbed my temples. "He waited because I asked him to. They threatened to kill Jeff if anyone told the police."

Becca dug through her purse and pulled out tissues.

"They're coming after her." Alex's intensity could've bored holes through the walls. "We don't know who he is, why he blames Kate, . . . nothing."

DJ paced. "Have you talked to LeAnn since then?"

"My friend, Mona, said she was okay, but I haven't spoken with LeAnn."

"Start from the beginning and tell me everything you remember." He dropped back into his chair.

For the next half hour, Alex and I recounted the events again and again. When we finished, DJ stepped into the den. The rest of us waited while he called it in. With so little information and over a day's delay—not to mention the jurisdiction issues—we weren't even sure it would be treated with any seriousness.

Before he cleared the doorway, he started talking, the phone already in his pocket. "Becca, I'm gonna help Alex bring in the bags."

His premise for going outside didn't hold water. The bags were piled in the kitchen.

DJ walked out the back door, and Alex followed.

"They are going to talk about this where I can't hear, aren't they?" I didn't even look at Becca as I asked the question.

"That'd be my guess."

I gently pounded my head on the table. "It's as if someone switched the polarity on my trouble magnet."

"How are things between you and Alex?"

"He's great." I studied the lines in the table.

"Kate, be careful with him."

I shot Becca a puzzled look. Her hint of accusation rang out loud and clear. "You were thrilled days ago. What changed?"

"He loves you. I don't want to see him hurt. Just know what you want before . . ."

"Before what?" I worried enough that I'd put him in danger, but the implication that I'd be reckless with his feelings infuriated me.

"You know what I mean. Before you sleep with him."

"We're not sleeping together." I slammed my hands down on the table top and glared at Becca. "Why the hell does everyone assume we are sleeping together?"

The shock on Becca's face calmed me down.

"I'm sorry." My voice dropped. "He hasn't even used the word love, not once." Words poured out before I gathered my thoughts. She had no right to know what I'd just told her. Becca and I had become fast friends, but her interference and too-personal questions weren't welcome. "Anyway, that's between Alex and me."

"I'm telling you what I see. Please don't hurt him." Her words stung.

Indignation chased away any tears. "Becca, I know you mean well, but don't."

"Don't what?"

"Meddle."

The back door opened, and our conversation ended.

Beth-

I remembered. Woke up in the middle of the night and remembered where I'd seen her. I'm beyond embarrassed. Why didn't you say anything?

You must think I'm horrible. I won't ask you not to say anything. I mean, obviously, I don't want you to tell her, but it seems wrong to ask that of you.

Having you as a friend means the world to me, but if you'd rather I quit writing to you, I understand. All of this has put you in an awkward spot. I apologize.

-M

Beth-

Thank you for your last letter. Without a place to pour it all out, I might go crazy. Some men should come with warning labels.

I hope you burn these letters after reading them. If anyone ever got a hold of them, they'd think me an awful person.

After my big discovery, saying "no" got a little easier—actually, a lot easier. Seeing her, knowing who she is, changes things. Hopefully, they can work things out in their marriage.

And I understand about complicated. I won't breathe a word. Your secret's safe with me. I'm sorry, though. That must be hard. For what it's worth, my parents said the same thing. Don't really talk about them like that anymore, but when I was younger, I rarely heard their family mentioned without "bad stock" added, not that I paid much attention, clearly.

In other news . . . remember that new guy at work, the new manager I mentioned? The nice, settling down type. He asked me out. Cross your fingers for me. I really want this to work.

-M

❧ ～ ❧

Beth-

How was your Christmas? How are you? I bet Christmas was a blast now that your little guy is walking.

Remember I told you about my new someone. We've been dating. He's a gentleman, treats me well. He's an all-around great guy. And he proposed on Christmas Eve!

I am elated. Brad is everything I want.

The only problem is—Scooter doesn't like him. My little boy compares every man to Sticks. No one is as fun as Sticks. Mr. Brad doesn't throw the baseball like Sticks. Sticks has a cool truck. How can anyone else compete? Sticks charms everyone.

I need to find the antidote to that charm or my happily-ever-after is going to pick up and leave. The night before Christmas Eve, Sticks stopped by, really late, after eleven. Scooter was at Dad's house, and I was alone. Arms loaded with gifts, Sticks flashed that winning grin. I let him in. And, yes, I did what I promised myself I wouldn't. Hopefully, Brad never finds out.

The wedding is next month, something small at the courthouse. Will you come?

-M

CHAPTER EIGHT

January 23, 2016 – 5:18 pm

Alex waved to DJ and Becca, then bolted the door. Kate trudged to the master bedroom, sullen. *What did she and Becca talk about?* He knocked at her bedroom door.

"Come in." She sat on the edge of the bed, wiping her eyes.

He leaned on the door frame. "What's wrong?"

"I don't want to talk about it right now."

He laid down on the bed. With so little furniture, it was either the bed or the floor, and he hoped she knew he'd respect her wishes no matter where they were.

Without waiting for an invitation, she snuggled alongside him and used his shoulder as a pillow. "It's just . . ."

"Shhh. Not right now." He couldn't imagine what Becca could've said to upset Kate, but one thing he was sure of—it had something to do with him. "What do you say we go to the home improvement store and look at carpet and paint swatches?"

"I like that idea. And we can get some food while we're out."

"And a sleeping bag."

"Or an air mattress." She picked her head up and gazed at him. Whatever she and Becca had talked about visibly weighed on her mind.

Alex and Kate walked into the home improvement store, and he squeezed her hand. He'd done this before, experienced the excitement of setting up a new house, but this was different, which helped. It was her house. He didn't live there. *Yet.* He glanced down, hoping she hadn't overheard his thought. *Where did that thought come from?*

Her eyes danced as she read the signs hanging from the ceiling. "Flooring or paint?"

"Painting before you change the carpet is probably a good idea." He kept pace with her as she hurried away to the walls cluttered with colorful sample cards.

"I want a blue for the master bedroom. What color do you think would be good in the den?"

Alex held up a mushroom color. "Something like this?"

"Ooh. I like that. Write den on the back."

"Dark blue or light blue?"

"I was thinking a denim color." She picked up several sample cards.

"What about the extra room?"

"Don't know."

He didn't even ask about paint for the guest room. She'd told Travis it was perfect as it was, which meant she wanted that room to stay just the way her mother had decorated it.

Twenty minutes later, she'd settled on paint colors for the den and master bedroom. She waited to choose a color for the extra room until inspiration hit. Alex grabbed a cart, and they loaded up the paint supplies. While the paint tech mixed the cans of color, Alex and Kate wandered over to the flooring section to scout out carpet.

Alex chuckled at her wide-eyed expression. "I grabbed an extra paint chip of the den color to help choose carpet."

She stopped and gasped, awareness dawning in her brown eyes. "You've done this before. With Ellie."

He'd never tell her how hearing her say Ellie's name pulled his heart in multiple directions. "I'm enjoying watching you."

"We can stop, and I can come back later."

Taking her my hand, he whispered, "I'm okay." He pointed to a pale turquoise carpet sample. "What if you paint the walls that color and then get a mushroom color for the carpet?"

"I want a red sectional in that room, so the turquoise would be perfect. Think it's too much?"

"Nah."

"But he's already mixing the paint."

"Use the mushroom color in the extra room."

"That would work. I could use denim accents and bandana pillows."

"Sounds *perfect.*" Alex grinned as he scratched out the word den and wrote *guest room.*

After picking out a carpet color, they asked the paint clerk to mix a can of Colorful Dream. That was the name listed on the sample card, but it was a pale turquoise.

The truck loaded with their purchases, they headed to the local big box store. While she grabbed a few staples, he went in search of an air mattress or sleeping bag and a set of sheets. After a brief hunt, he found what he needed. He caught up with her in the baking aisle.

"Whatcha getting?" He dropped items into the cart.

"I want to make a cobbler."

He walked the aisle, picking up boxes and bags, and returned to the cart with a wide grin on his face, his arms loaded with flour, sugar, brown sugar, chocolate chips, and vanilla extract. "Not sure I got all the right stuff. I thought you might want to make cookies."

"You're encouraging my habit?"

"I want to keep your stress level down, and I like cookies."

"I'm not sure how I feel about it. Should I be feeding you all those cookies?"

"You know where they go?"

She poked him in the stomach. "Here?"

He pressed his hand to his heart. "They fill me up, right here."

She laughed and tossed in other supplies rounding out what she needed to make a berry cobbler and, hopefully, cookies.

He pointed at the disposable bakeware. "Need that?"

"Yes. Good thinking."

He needed to set up her internet. Wi-Fi was a necessity for her genealogy research and his work, if he got a chance to get anything done. Silently ticking off a list of what he'd need, he figured he'd find most, if not all, the items in the electronics department. But he could order it online if it wasn't going to be connected for a few days.

"What about internet?" He switched from thoughts to words in the middle of the conversation in his head.

"Huh?" Kate stared at him, confused.

"When will you have internet connected?"

"It already is. Why?"

"I'm going to grab what I need to set up your Wi-Fi."

"I hadn't even thought of Wi-Fi. But I'd have missed it the first time I tried to research." She followed him to the electronics section and looked at televisions while he gathered the items he needed.

"I think I got everything." He pressed his hand into the small of her back, and they made their way to a checkout aisle. While Alex checked out, Kate texted. Whatever the response, it wasn't good. Her smile faded; her shoulders sank closer to the floor.

In the truck, she swiped at tears as he loaded groceries. She sat silently almost all the way home.

When they neared her house, he couldn't keep quiet any longer. "Please talk to me, Kate."

"I told Meg I was back in town and invited them over for cobbler."

"And?"

"She only replied that she's not my sister."

"You can remind her that you are still cousins."

"That's not exactly the same thing, Alex." The edge in her voice served as a warning that her hurt threatened to explode at any moment.

"You have to choose to build a relationship with what you have, not be derailed by what you don't have." He wanted to laugh at the irony of his own words.

"She blames me. As if I chose to be kidnapped."

He shook his head at the ridiculous accusations. "Which time?"

Fire flashed in her eyes, and Kate set her jaw. The nasty look she shot him wasn't needed for clarification. She turned toward the window, silent again.

"I'm sorry, Kate. I was trying to inject some humor. It's nonsense for her to blame you."

"It wasn't funny." Her tone was sharp, but her sniffles betrayed her battle with tears.

When he stopped in the driveway, he reached for her hand. "Look at me, please."

"I can't joke about it. She's right. She's not my sister, but saying it feels like I'm ignoring all the years of growing up together."

"Tell her that. She's your sister not because you shared a parent's DNA, but because you shared a life together."

"I invited her for cobbler."

"It's not exactly the same thing, but it's close." He climbed out and opened the passenger side door. "I feel like a heel. I'm always making you cry."

She shook her head and kissed the cleft in his chin.

"I want to make things better."

"Alex, you can't fix this." She brushed the steady stream of salty droplets off her cheeks.

"I feel useless when I can't fix it." He needed her to understand how much he cared.

A laugh bubbled out of her.

He raised an eyebrow. "I wasn't trying to be funny."

"I didn't mean to laugh, but I thought about the neighbors. They probably think we're nuts, with me sitting here crying in your truck for all the world to see."

"I could carry you by Gram's window, and you could wave."

She snickered. "Only if you take off your shirt."

He winked and shook his head as he walked to the tailgate. After dropping it open, he picked up as many bags as he could hold. He carried them in, set them on the kitchen counter, and then went back out for the second load.

Kate started emptying the plastic bags and putting groceries away. Alex pulled out the electronics and his temporary bed before heading to the extra room. After shuffling the boxes out of the center of the room to make space for sleeping, multi-tasking, he set up the router and inflated the mattress.

In the kitchen, Kate mixed flour, fruit, and whatever magic necessary to make her berry cobbler.

Once he finished, he wandered back toward the kitchen but stopped at the end of the hall. Kate bounced around the kitchen putting away the non-perishables, seemingly ignoring whatever danger lurked outside. He enjoyed watching her organize the pantry as she tucked items away. She whipped around when his knee popped.

She handed him oven mitts. "Instead of gawking, you can pull the cobbler out in three-two-one-now."

He opened the oven and inhaled before grabbing the foil pan with both hands. "Bed's all set up."

"Which room?"

"The one closest to the master. Is that the extra room?"

"Yep. Did it fit with all that other stuff?"

"I made it work." He tossed the mitts on the counter and dropped into a chair. "Are we okay?"

"I don't know what okay looks like." She walked up next to him and sat her phone on the table. "I'm thirty-one and single. Long-term relationships aren't my specialty."

He slipped his arms around her waist and pulled her into his lap. "How many relationships are we talking about?"

She glanced down as her phone sounded a text notification and grimaced.

"Your sister?"

"Nope. Jerry." She showed Alex the text.

Glad you're finally in Texas. Dinner soon?

"What are you going to tell him?" He allowed himself a smug grin.

"I can thank Meg for this." She teasingly handed him the phone. "I don't know. You want to respond?"

He took the phone and clicked out a response but didn't hit send. "How's this?"

My boyfriend wouldn't like it.

"I can't send that. I need to be nice. It's Tom's brother."

Alex cleared the message and typed out something else. "This any better?"

I met someone.

She squeaked a happy little sound and kissed him, then wriggled the phone out of his hand. "I'm not sure. What about . . .?" She tapped out a text: *Just arrived yesterday. Alex is here helping me get settled.*

Alex read it before she hit send. "He's only going to text you again. You didn't answer his question, and he'll want to know who Alex is."

"Really? I thought that was clear. I avoided the question which implied a no, and I let it drop that there was someone else."

He laughed when her phone beeped again.

Jerry texted back: *Dinner? Meg didn't mention a roommate.*

"You were right."

"What was that?"

She poked him in the shoulder. "Don't push it."

"Be straight with him, Kate. He'll appreciate it."

She texted back: *I'll pass on dinner. Alex is my boyfriend.*

Jerry responded: *Sorry. Your sister didn't mention that.*

Kate answered, trying not to overthink the reply: *No hard feelings.* She laid down the phone. "Better?"

"Yes. Please don't expect me to read between the lines."

"I'll try to remember that." She started to stand up.

"Wait. You never answered my question."

"Sorry. Remind me of the question." Her cheeks colored a soft pink. She hadn't forgotten.

"Relationships?" He'd asked almost in jest, wanting to hear more about her life, but the look that crossed her face when he brought up the question the second time made him regret asking it. "You don't have to tell me anything."

"I'll ignore questions I don't want to answer." She cocked her head. "What do you consider a relationship?"

"More than 3 dates? I don't know."

"So, we wouldn't qualify?"

"Now you're stalling." He waited for her to elaborate.

She drew invisible circles on the table. "I dated a guy in college, but he was also dating someone else at the time. When I found out, it ended the relationship."

"Ouch." He rubbed her back when she tensed.

"After college. Meg set me up on a blind date. We dated for a few months." She blinked back tears.

Alex pulled her closer, sorry that the question had stirred up unpleasant memories. But he wasn't sure what to say.

"He quit calling. I'm not exactly a dateable kind of girl."

"Is that so?"

"What about you?" She patted his chest, ready to get the attention off her past.

"*Besides you,* three. One in high school. We were pretty serious—dated all through our junior and senior year—but she went off to college somewhere in the Northeast. I stayed in Texas. She quit writing to me, and life went on."

"And?" The wheels turned behind her brown eyes, probably wondering how she compared.

"I dated a girl in college for two years. I don't know what happened. One night we broke up, and that was that."

"And then . . ." She let the empty air finish the thought without saying Ellie's name.

He nodded. "I met her at a party. We dated for over a year before I proposed. I wasn't even sure she'd say yes. But she did, and nine months later, we got married." Talking to Kate came as easy as breathing. He hadn't spilled so much personal information to anyone in the last three years. DJ didn't even know how Alex had met his late wife.

"It's ready whenever you want some cobbler." She kissed his cheek, and he responded by dotting kisses on her neck. How she'd stayed single so long confounded him.

Feelings that should have taken months to develop pounded in his chest begging to be said. "Kisses, cobbler . . . my life keeps getting better and better." He gave her one more kiss before she hopped up.

After a delightful dinner of berry cobbler with vanilla ice cream,

Alex locked up the house, checking every window twice, while Kate showered. He checked his phone when it jingled.

DJ texted: *No leads yet, but I'm trying. Let me know if she hears from LeAnn.*

Alex tapped out a quick reply: *Thanks.*

Before he stuck it back in his pocket, the phone sounded. DJ had messaged again: *Becca wants to know if we can bring breakfast tomorrow. She needs to talk to Kate.*

Alex replied: *Sounds good.* Then he clicked off the sound and shoved the phone in his pocket. Staring out the bare windows of the den, he pondered the situation. More than anything, he wanted Kate to be safe, and he was willing to do whatever it took to keep her that way. Somewhere outside two men lurked, hunting Kate.

"There you are." She toweled off her dark, wet curls.

Beautiful.

"You found me. Now it's your turn to hide." He wanted to hear her laugh, see her smile.

She rewarded his feeble attempt at humor. "You're in a strange mood."

"Becca and DJ are bringing breakfast in the morning." He opened his arms as she walked toward him.

"Oh." A little line dimpled between her eyebrows momentarily. She bit her lip, then forced a small smile. "Good."

He focused his gaze on her. "Kate, if you hadn't noticed, I can read your tells pretty well. What's up with you and Becca?"

"Nothing." Did she think that answer would appease him? She hadn't even glanced up from the floor, not a convincing act.

He raised his eyebrows and stared at her.

She finally looked at him from under those dark lashes. "Becca got a bit too personal."

"About?"

"Us."

Becca needs to mind her own business. Careful not to let his irritation show, he asked, "What did she say?"

Kate focused on her fingernails, another tell. Whatever Becca told Kate irritated her like a splinter under a fingernail. "She's afraid I'll break your heart."

He bit back a laugh. Of all the comments he'd braced to hear, that wasn't on the list. "I didn't see that one coming." He tucked a curl behind Kate's ear. "Like someone who has taken in a wounded animal, Becca's a bit protective of me."

Kate didn't meet his gaze.

"There's more you aren't telling me."

She nodded.

"Kate?"

Dark eyes, full of uncertainty and tinged with fear, focused on his face.

"It's my heart to risk." He wouldn't allow himself any more words. Promises weren't his to give yet, because he couldn't give away what he was still trying to mend.

His heart thumped wildly as she slipped her arms around him and buried her face in the curve of his neck. As much as he liked to think himself her protector, there was a certain safety in her touch. But he couldn't get caught in the rapid swell of emotion that overtook him in moments when he opened up. He needed to know he'd feel the same way if he wasn't with her, couldn't feel her, touch her, or kiss her. Circumstances didn't allow that.

Her tears wet his tee shirt. Saying the wrong thing made her cry; saying the right thing made her cry. If there was one thing he could do well, it was make her cry. He closed his eyes and imbibed the scents of lavender and chamomile. If the rest of the world disappeared, he'd be content, even if she were crying. These were happy tears.

When she lifted her head, he wiped tears from her cheeks and kissed her forehead. "Don't let whatever she said bother you."

"Did you lock up everything?" She stepped back and looked around the room.

"I double-checked all the windows."

"It's been a long day. You've got to be exhausted."

"It has been. I should let you get some rest." He resisted the urge to pull her close again. "You know where I am if you need me."

She tightened her grip on his shirt and opened her mouth. After a quick shake of her head, she let go and smoothed out the wrinkles.

"Goodnight, Kate."

She planted a kiss, quick and soft, on his cheek. "See you in the morning."

He followed her down the hall and watched her walk into the master bedroom before making his way to the air mattress. Tucked under the covers, he listened to her tossing and turning in the other room. She reminded him of Bureau, taking forever to find the perfect position. He battled the urge to join her. Nestled against him, she'd sleep peacefully. But her reaction, the fear in her eyes, the recoil, played in his head. Remembering that fear kept him in his own bed.

After several more minutes of shuffling, Alex stood up and pulled on his shirt. Did she want the safety of his embrace? Would it trigger whatever memory haunted her? He waited in the hall, listening. The movement stopped. She'd settled in. He dropped back into bed and closed his eyes. Sleep pulled him under almost immediately.

Voices in the kitchen woke him up. He bolted upright to discover the morning sun streaming in the windows. He'd slept. Hard. After a quick stop in the bathroom to make himself presentable, he padded down the hallway. Gram sat at the dining room table with Kate, coffee mugs in front of each of them.

"Good morning." Gram pointed at a third mug. "Coffee?"

"Yes, please." He kissed Kate as he walked to a chair.

Gram poured him a cup from a white carafe. "I've been talking Kate's ear off, and I almost forgot." Gram laid a photo album on the table and handed Kate a card. "Someone asked me to give this to you."

Kate tore open the letter. After a minute, teary-eyed, she handed it to Alex.

Dear Kate,

I'm beyond happy that you've been found. Some secrets, long kept, are hard to shine a light on even when you want to, but you shouldn't have to wait on me to learn about your mom.

Here's a photo album from our growing up years. Soon I will

*show up at your door, as soon as I've worked up the nerve to
unbury the past.*

Kate hugged Gram. "Thank you. For the coffee, the conversation, and this."

"I need to be going. I'll get the mugs and carafe later." Gram pulled her close one more time. "She'll come talk when she's ready."

"Is it from Beth?"

Gram tapped her lips.

"Why the wait?"

"Guilt is an awful thing. Like chains, it holds people back from what they should, and sometimes even want to do." Gram patted Alex on the shoulder as she shuffled to the door. "Take care of our girl."

Beth-

Scooter is asking to move in with his grandpa. I finally find someone that loves me, and my kid can't stand him.

I hate this. There isn't any question what choice I'll make, but I deserve to shed a few selfish tears about it. I just have to figure out how to tell my husband he has to move out because my son doesn't like the car he drives or the way he throws a baseball.

-M

July 1985

Beth-

Why is life so complicated? I'm pregnant. I can't ask Brad to leave.

I sat Scooter down and held up his two favorite stuffed animals. I asked him which one he wanted to throw away. He got upset, saying he wanted to keep both of them—just as I expected.

That gave me a way to explain that I loved him, but I loved Brad, too. He understood, I think.

I also asked Sticks to talk to him about it. I think he must have, because Scooter's been more agreeable. I'm hoping it will all work out.

-M

CHAPTER NINE

January 24, 2016 – 9:15 am

I set the mugs in the sink. "Travis texted. I told him to come on over." Wiping off the table, I filled Alex in while he rinsed and loaded the few dishes. "Maybe he'll tell me about Justin. And who the album is from. I'm guessing from the Aunt Beth person he mentioned."

"How long had Gram been here?" He flung a dishtowel over his shoulder.

"Forty-five minutes, maybe."

"I can't believe I slept so long."

"I'm glad you did. You needed it." I picked up the card and the album. My phone sounded a text alert, and I grimaced when I read it. "Meg wants to come see my new place."

"That's a drastic change."

"It's her idea today. She wants to be in control—won't come when I ask but invites herself over when she feels like it."

"Even so, you should let her come."

"I'm not sure I'm ready to face her. I was last night, but now . . . I don't know."

"Want me to text Travis and ask him to bring the DNA results when he comes?"

"Yes, please. And the family photo he showed me." I texted Meg my address.

Alex texted Travis, and I flipped through the album. Page after page of family pictures spread out in front of me.

"What's wrong?" Alex squatted beside me.

"I'm okay."

"You look like you're about to cry. Tears are usually my job."

I pointed at a photo labeled *Emma*. "That's my mom."

"Hopefully, whoever sent this will come talk with you soon. I know you'd love to meet your extended family."

"It's all so surreal." I leaned my head on his shoulder. "And you don't *always* make me cry."

He grinned. "I'm going to take a quick shower before everyone gets here. Unit arrives today?"

"Yep. Not sure what time." I tucked the album and card out of the way. "Don't use all the hot water."

He chuckled as he sauntered down the hall. "You going to bring me a towel again?" Laughter echoed off the walls of the bathroom as he closed the door.

As soon as the shower stopped, I hurried back to the master bathroom to take my turn in the shower before people arrived.

When I stepped out of the shower, on the counter, next to my towel, was a cup of coffee. *Someone bought coffee. Who put it on my bathroom counter?* After toweling off my hair and throwing on something presentable. I made my way out to the great room.

As soon as Becca saw me, she beelined straight to me. "Forgive me?"

I hugged her. "Of course."

Alex pointed to the dining table. "Donuts are here. And Travis brought coffee."

"I found my cup. Thank you." I bumped against his shoulder.

He winked and leaned in close. "You already had a towel."

Travis walked up next to me.

"Thanks for the coffee." I needed a new subject before my face turned red.

Alex's shoulders tightened a hint, and the teasing disappeared.

Travis wrapped me in a hug. "Good morning, sweetheart."

I hadn't figured out the dynamic between Alex and Travis. He texted Alex more than me, but Alex tensed a little anytime Travis was close by. Given the crazy circumstances, I couldn't worry about it until later, but it patiently waited at the bottom of my things-to-worry-about list.

Becca dropped into a chair. "Y'all need to start eating before DJ eats them all."

DJ chuckled as he licked glaze off his fingers. "I've only had two. So far."

Travis set the papers and photograph on the table, then sat down next to me. "Alex said you might need these this morning."

"My sister should be here any minute."

"Then it's good I brought her a cup too."

As if on cue, a knock sounded. I hurried to answer but took a deep breath before opening the door.

Meg forced a smile and smoothed her sweater, not a blonde hair out of place on her head.

"Hi, Meg."

She scrunched up her nose, and the complaining began before she set foot inside. "Kate, this is in the middle of nowhere. Why do you want to live here?"

I tamped down the irritation gurgling in my gut. "I like it."

"How did you even find this place?" She surveyed the house, disdain apparent in her expression.

"Come on in. Do you want to see the rest of the house?" I acted as if I couldn't tell she disapproved.

The manila envelope and the pictures remained at the table, but the others had vacated the space, leaving the donuts.

Meg fingered the beautiful long table and tossed her purse into a chair. "Not really. I'm not sure why I drove *all* the way out here."

I pushed a coffee cup toward her. "Travis got this for you. Help yourself to a donut."

She perched on the edge of a chair as if it would swallow her whole if she let her guard down. Awkward silence clanged in my ears. I hesitated, trying to decide how to start the conversation.

I'd just opened my mouth, still unsure what to say, when I heard a large truck outside. Just then, Travis walked into the kitchen.

He nodded at Meg. "Sorry to interrupt. The storage container just arrived. I'm headed back out there." He hurried to the door, and I guessed that the others had gathered out back, watching the unit get unloaded.

Meg gripped my hand in surprise. "He looks like Dad. Who is he?"

"That's Travis. We talked about this on the phone." I shook my head at Meg's obvious denial. *She watched the news story.*

"I'd hoped it was all a product of bad Chinese food." Meg poked through the box of donuts, finally choosing one with strawberry icing and sprinkles.

"He's Dad's brother."

"Dad never mentioned any family."

"Because he was hiding from them." I braced for her reaction.

"Very funny, Kate." She leveled a glare at Alex as he whistled his way through the kitchen into the den.

I tried to hide my smile, knowing he'd wandered into an empty den just to eavesdrop on the conversation. *He wants to make sure I'm okay.* "Dad's name was really Scott Bentley, and he kidnapped me when I was two."

"Not true." She might as well have put her hands over her ears and sung "la la la."

"In 1981, Scott married Emma."

"First of all, Dad's name was Gavin. Second, I think Dad would've mentioned if he was married before." She pinched off a piece of the donut.

If I kept talking, maybe the truth would penetrate her denial. "After they'd been married for two years, Scott left early one morning. The only explanation Emma got was a note on the pillow that said he'd be gone for a while."

"Is this leading somewhere?"

"There is more to the story, but one night Emma and Travis slept together."

"And that's who you are choosing?" Her biting disdain oozed out of every word.

I dug my nails into my palms, struggling to contain my anger. "Choosing parents? That's not how it works. Would you have *chosen* Dad?" I hadn't meant to throw daggers, but he was far from the perfect dad. Even though I had good memories, in hindsight, I saw the problems. "When Scott found out that Travis was my dad, he took me and left. He changed our names and started a new life."

"This is all crazy talk. What proof do you have?"

I slid the family picture across the table. "Travis showed me this picture when we met for brunch."

She blinked back tears and set her jaw. "I refuse to believe it. Photos can be faked."

"Do you see Cuddle Bunny in that photo? Monogrammed? Besides, we had a DNA test run." I pulled the results page out of the envelope.

She waved it off. "I can't believe it's true. And how could you? You are calling Dad a kidnapper and saying that Mom lied to you."

I was so furious my tears evaporated before leaving my lashes. "He was, and she did."

Meg crossed her arms.

I held the graduation photo up in front of her face. "Mom mailed them this!"

She gasped. "How you can so easily turn on our parents after looking at one piece of paper breaks my heart." She sprang up, sending her chair skidding, then stomped off, her half-eaten donut left on the table.

The walls rattled as the front door slammed. I stood up, and Alex pulled me into his arms. Keenly aware of our company, I buried tears by sheer will, an ability slowing returning.

He stroked my hair, fully expecting sobs. "I'm so sorry. I don't know what to say."

"Me neither." I wrestled with anger toward my parents, or rather the people who'd called themselves that.

Travis, DJ, and Becca hovered just outside the back door. Alex motioned for them to come into the kitchen.

"I'm sorry, sweetheart." Travis's jaw was set, his blue eyes dark with anger.

"The nerve of her. I know she's your sister, but ugh." Becca fumed, and DJ rubbed her back.

"I'm okay. I knew this would be hard for her. I just didn't quite expect that reaction. She needs time. It took me a few days to let myself believe it."

Alex relaxed a little but didn't let go of me.

"Container's here. Are we going to unload it, or what?" Becca rubbed her hands together.

I shook my head. "Not today."

"We'll call when she's ready to unload." Alex nodded toward DJ. "He can hold the door open."

"I'm glad to help." DJ laughed, gripping his arm, his recent injury getting him out of the heavy lifting.

Alex turned to Travis. "What you can help me with, Mr. Bentley, if you have a few minutes, is moving boxes from the extra room."

"Sure." He started down the hall, DJ and Alex right on his heels.

Becca and I sat down on the floor in the den. She put her hand in the air as if she were going to swear an oath. "I'll stop meddling."

"I already said I forgive you."

"Why are they moving boxes around?"

"Moving them from the extra room to the guest room."

"Why?"

I lowered my chin and eyed her, waiting, watching her squirm with curiosity. "No meddling, huh? Alex is using the extra room, and the boxes are in the way."

Becca raised her eyebrows and ran a finger along her sealed lips.

While I didn't want to share details of my relationship with Alex, Becca had become a friend, and she'd known him for years. I didn't want to shut down all communication on the topic. "I still feel like I need someone to pinch me."

"It is like a fairy tale."

"Ugh. Don't say that." I groaned as I laughed.

"Well, you both look really happy."

I glanced toward the door. "What if . . .?" I wrestled with whether to ask my question. "What if it's not *me*? I mean, maybe I'm just the first girl he's been around since, you know."

Becca shook her head. "No. He . . ." Her sentence dissolved into giggles, then built into a full belly laugh. "I . . . He . . ." Each time she started again, her words disappeared in a new wave of laughter.

"What's so funny?" Alex stepped into the den and dropped onto the floor next to me. DJ and Travis followed.

Horrified, I stared at Becca, telepathically willing her not to repeat what I'd asked.

"Tell Kate about when I tried to set you up." Becca wiped tears and stifled a final giggle.

"Which time? As I recall, you did it more than once." Alex turned toward me, a relaxed grin on his face. "Becca thought it wasn't good for me to be *all alone out in the woods.*" He said the last few words in the highest pitch he could manage, trying to imitate Becca. "Shows what she knows."

She turned a deep shade of red, and we all laughed.

"How is Evan, anyway?" Alex brushed his fingertips along the side of my hand.

"You set him up with a guy?" I let my mouth hang open for added effect.

Everyone roared with laughter.

Alex gripped his sides and caught his breath. "Evan is the neighbor who always ended up with my dates. DJ texted him after Becca ambushed me, all three times."

"Evan's doing great, by the way. He and Kelli are expecting a little one any day now." DJ poked Becca. "That last set-up was a winner."

"You set him up with a Kelli?" I couldn't believe Becca had made such a faux pas. "That's just mean."

Alex pointed at Becca. "See?"

"Her name was K-k-k-Kelli. With a K." Becca waved her hand. "It's all in the past."

Alex nudged me with his shoulder. "Now you see why I was so irritated with her when she said you went home." He stood up and reached down to help me up.

Travis checked his watch. "I have a meeting, so I really need to go. I'm sorry to run out."

"Thank you for coming. When you come next time, maybe you can tell me about Justin." I hugged him. As much as I wanted to call him dad, I wasn't ready yet. I needed more time, but the genuine care in his eyes filled up places in my heart.

"Yes. Sorry we didn't get to that today." Travis pulled me back for another quick hug. "Remember if you need more . . ."

Alex shook his hand. "Thank you, sir."

"Please, Alex, call me Travis."

"I can do that."

Becca and DJ pushed up off the floor. "We need to be going."

"Thanks for everything."

"Call me when you want help." Becca hugged me. "I mean it."

"I will. I promise. How are you with paint?"

"An expert." DJ laughed. "She's repainted every room in our house at least twice." He caught Becca's hand.

"I'd love to help you paint." Becca hugged me again with her free arm before they strolled out to their car.

Alex closed the front door. "I need real food, something not covered in glaze or powdered sugar. Want to walk to The Drugstore?" He crossed the room and wrapped his arms around me.

"Sure. I wonder if the whole town has heard the news."

"Besides Maggie?" Alex cocked an eyebrow.

One of the two waitresses at the only restaurant in the tiny town, Maggie loved to share the goings-on of everything she heard. Her willingness to share the story of the child kidnapped long ago and the look-a-like returned lately had earned me a spot on the news cycle.

I momentarily reconsidered the idea of going, imagining her rehashing my story. "Point taken."

"Still want to go?" Alex held out his hand.

"Have to go sometime. Why not today?" I locked the door before we headed down the street.

Enjoying the mild January day, we strolled past Gram's to the restaurant. Alex grinned as he pulled open the door. Maggie, the lady who acted as if she'd seen a ghost the last time we stopped in, stood behind the counter.

"Come in and have a seat. My name is Maggie." She wiped her hands on her apron before shaking my hand.

I sat on a barstool. "Nice to meet you. I'm—"

She held up her hand. "Everyone around here knows who you are. We just aren't sure whether to call you Kate or Claire."

Alex bumped me with his leg. "Maggie, I'm Alex."

A wide smile cut through the wrinkles on her face. "And people are talking about you, too. Y'all are a lot of excitement for this little town."

Alex chuckled and flashed a wary grin.

"I'm sorry for my behavior on your last visit, but you near gave me a heart attack. You do look like Emma. I hurried out of here to call Travis, thought you might be his daughter. Looks like I was right." She laid menus on the counter. "What drinks can I get started for ya?"

"I'll have a vanilla peppermint cream soda."

"I'll have the same." Alex closed his menu.

"Coming right up." She pulled glasses off the shelves and syrup bottles off the wall.

"Not having your usual?" I flipped open my menu.

"Nope."

"Know what you're going to eat?" I spent more time looking at him than at the menu.

"Today's special." Alex pointed at the chalkboard.

"Yum. Chicken fried steak."

Maggie slid our glasses across the counter and asked for our order.

"The special for me." I pushed the menus across the counter.

"Same for me." Alex sipped his soda.

"I'll have those out in a few." Maggie walked through the swinging doors back to the kitchen.

"You like?" I tapped the side of his glass.

"Yeah." Alex held my hand and ran his finger along my knuckles.

"So, Becca set you up on blind dates?"

"I wasn't a good sport about it." While we waited for food, he recounted the episodes of Becca's misguided interference.

Maggie pushed through the swinging door with two plates on

her arm. "Two specials." She set the food in front of us. "Can I get you anything else?"

"No, this looks wonderful." I cut into my chicken fried steak.

Maggie pulled up a stool behind the counter. "This whole town is buzzing about you. Travis has been waiting a long time for you to come home."

"I'd have come sooner if I knew. Did you know my parents well?"

"As well as most in town. I went to school with Travis. Your mom was a few years younger. Even younger than Scott, I think." Maggie almost choked on his name. "Sorry. No one really mentions his name much anymore."

I didn't want to talk about Scott, but it was easier to just let her say what she wanted to say. "Please, continue."

"The whole town was surprised when Scott and Emma married. It seemed everyone except Scott knew that Travis was heartsick for her. I don't know what happened. Don't know if Travis just waited too long, if Emma got tired of waiting."

My mouth full of food, I nodded, silently wishing I hadn't asked.

"Every girl liked Travis. So, when the one that he liked married someone else, a collective gasp went up from every girl around. Even with all that history, when we heard about what happened and the . . ." Maggie dropped her voice to a whisper even though there was no one else in the restaurant. ". . . *the affair,* we were shocked."

Alex, sensing my discomfort with the direction of the conversation, rubbed my back. "Kate would really like to know more about Emma. What was she like?"

"Emma was a doll. Short, a lot like you, Kate. Before you left, she always wore a smile. After, she was more subdued but always nice. Honestly, though, I didn't know her well."

"Is there anyone in town she was close to?" I dragged a bite of steak through the gravy.

"Not so much that I know of." She drummed fingers on the counter. "Nope, no one stands out, except Gram. That's Mrs. Crawford. Gram is what everyone calls her, she's lived here a long time. She's got plenty of stories to tell."

Alex finished off his drink. "We met her. She's a fascinating lady."

"Let me grab you a box so you can take home the leftovers."

"Thanks." Alex signed the check and tossed a tip on the counter.

As soon as the remaining food was packed up, I made my way to the door. "Nice to see you again."

Alex carried the boxes of leftovers while we walked home hand in hand. "Now you know where to go to uncover secrets."

"No kidding. Probably best that I didn't hear her story before meeting Travis and reading the letters."

"I'd say so." He kissed my hand.

"I didn't mean to make you star of the rumor mill."

"We haven't given them much to whisper about . . . yet." He winked as I pushed open the front door.

After tossing the leftovers in the refrigerator, I laid on the den floor envisioning new carpet, turquoise walls, and a red sectional dividing the room.

Alex walked in from the kitchen. "If you put the television there and the sectional in the middle, there would be room for a table or desk in that corner." He stretched out next to me.

"Good idea."

"You'll get a coffee table, right? I need somewhere to put my feet."

I loved that he included himself in my future, acting as if it was a given that he'd be over, needing a place to kick up his feet. He lay on his back, staring up at the ceiling. I stared at him, acknowledging that what I felt had moved past infatuation.

"It feels like a dream." The words tumbled out, and I scrambled to recover, not wanting to explain that I meant him. He was my dream come true. "I moved out of a one bedroom apartment into a three-bedroom house. I even have money to decorate it any way I want. This is what fairy tales are made of." I cringed as the words left my lips. Fairy tales were for the pages of a book, not real life.

"That makes you the princess?"

"Very funny."

"I'd save you from an ivory tower."

The words bounced around in my head like a rubber ball in a cement room. He'd struck on a truth I never cared to discuss. A little separation made for less vulnerability, and I was all about that. He'd plowed up the stone staircase and made me forget that I didn't want people close. I sat up and stared at him. My reaction alarmed him at first.

"Did I say something wrong?" He studied me, concerned with the tears pooled in my eyes.

I shook my head and laid back down letting tears run past my temples. And, as always, my thoughts flashed like a neon sign on my forehead.

He rolled onto his side and raised up on his elbow. His other hand drew figure eights on my shirt above my stomach. "Meeting your friends in Denver was intriguing. They—well, not LeAnn—described a sweet, unadventurous, stoic Kate. Not just Mona, either, even some of the things that Sarah, Lindsey, and . . ."

"Ashley."

"Yeah, Ashley. I think maybe . . . around them . . . you were keeping Kate in here." He ran his thumb and index finger up and down, parallel to each other, where my six pack abs would be in some alternate universe. "Behind walls. LeAnn was right when she said you only let a few people in."

I'm my own ivory tower. I kept still, not wanting him to withdraw his hand or stop talking.

"And as it happens, I know a thing or two about walls."

My laughed bubbled out unexpectedly, and crinkled lines near his eyes conveyed his delight.

"The woman that fell into my arms that night had escaped kidnappers and ventured through the dark in an unknown terrain until she found safety."

"Until I found you."

"And we both know you hold tears always at the ready. There were no walls."

"I was too scared to think about my walls."

"But they stayed down for a few days. I think when you forgot who you were, you forgot you had walls."

I swiped at my eyes, unable to stop the flow of tears as vivid recollections of my memory returning came flooding back.

"What I don't understand is . . . why the walls? I'm not asking you to tell me." He laid his head in the crook of his arm so that our faces were inches apart. "Kate, you're adventurous, intelligent, passionate, and beautiful. Why hide that?" He flopped onto his back and held out his arm.

I slid up beside him and rested my head on his chest. I breathed him in as his arms encircled me. "I'm not a princess."

"But you live in The Castle."

My charming prince and I laid there in the empty den for a half hour in silence. I shifted when I noticed Alex pumping his fist trying to wake up his numb arm. "I love this place. I can't wait until—"

"This place!" He bolted upright. "Did you tell anyone about this house?"

The meaning of his question, instantly clear, sounded like bricks collapsing around me. "I told LeAnn."

"Let's go."

"But my house."

"We can find a hotel until things are safe."

"I didn't tell her the address."

"Did you tell her the name of the town?"

"Well, yes, but . . ."

"All they have to do is ask anyone around here. The whole town knows about you."

My disappointment mounted as I looked around the empty room. This was supposed to be mine. No sooner had I gotten here, he was asking me to leave.

"Kate, please. We need to go." He tangled his fingers with mine. "I cannot risk losing you. I won't." That dogged stubbornness that reared its head a few times the last two weeks dared me to disagree. My safety served as a shield from his past pain.

"I haven't even unpacked."

"Good, I'll grab our bags."

I quietly slipped out the back door, my disappointment morphing into anger.

Beth-

I don't know what kind of magic dust Sticks carries in his pocket—the stuff he uses to get people to do what he wants—but Scooter is like a different kid.

The two of them still hang out at least once a week, but at home, Scooter talks to Brad, does chores without complaining. Last night Scooter even asked Brad for help on homework. Maybe my dream of happily ever after isn't dead yet.

-M

Chapter Ten

January 24, 2016 – 4:15 pm

Alex dropped their bags on the floor just inside the door. "At least we have luggage."

"You could've asked first before getting *one* room." Angry at the trouble that ran her from her castle, she had only one person to take it out on.

"I'm trying to protect you." Alex let irritation show in his tone.

"I would've said yes. It's just . . ." She shook her head and dropped onto one of the beds, giving him her back and scrolling through social media posts.

He closed his eyes and rubbed his temples. In the three years of being alone, he'd forgotten how complicated women could be. The purely rational side of his brain argued that if she would've said yes anyway, frustration over not being asked was silly. *Don't say that out loud.*

But the other part of him understood. She liked to be protected, but she didn't like being told what to do. He threw himself onto the bed next to her with enough force to bounce her a little.

She didn't even crack a smile.

"I should've asked. I'm sorry." He eyed her, waiting for a reaction.

She cast him a side look. "Before all this, I . . ." Her focus moved to her nails as she pushed back her cuticles. "I mean, I want your help. *I do.*"

He leaned down, making eye contact. Staring into her dark eyes was becoming a favorite pastime. "Forgive me?"

Those were the magic words.

Her answer came in a swift and passionate kiss. He fell backward onto the pillows, and she moved with him, never breaking away. After several delightful minutes, she pulled back, a hint of a smile peeking out the edges of her mouth.

"You could've asked. I'd have said yes." He winked.

She swatted him on the arm and jumped off the bed.

Alex laughed as he dialed DJ's number. He dodged a throw pillow just as DJ answered. "Hey, Kate remembered that she'd told LeAnn about Schatzenburg so, just in case, we vacated the premises."

"I was just about to call you. Had a car roll by your cabin to check on it." DJ left the thought hanging which made Alex tense.

"And?"

"You need a new door again. It'd help if you could come out here."

Alex choked back profanities, not wanting Kate to know how upset he was. "I'll get over there as soon as I can. I just need to . . ." He glanced over his shoulder and dropped his voice. "I'm not leaving her alone. I'll text you." He tucked the phone in his pocket and rolled his shoulders, trying to relax.

"They broke into your place?" She fell back onto the pillows.

"Yeah."

"You can go meet with DJ to do a walkthrough and file a report. I'll be fine."

"Please, let me call someone. *Please.*"

"I don't want you to call Becca. I'm not getting her mixed up in this. DJ's at your place. And if they know who I am, they could be following Travis. You need to warn him."

Alex ran his fingers through his hair. "I hadn't thought of that.

What if . . ." Without many options, only one name came to mind, but part of him hesitated. "If you don't mind, I could ask if Detective Torres would be willing . . ."

She shrugged. "Whatever."

He fished a business card out of his wallet and dialed. Tapping his foot, he waited through the first, second, and third ring. He started to pull the phone away from his ear when the detective answered. "Torres."

"Detective Torres, this is Alex Ramirez."

"Kate's . . ." the line was quiet for a full second. ". . . friend?"

"Yep. Listen, I have a situation and could use your help."

"Situation?" Commotion in the background made it hard to hear his question. "What's going on?"

"There are some guys after Kate."

"Again?" Voices faded, and a door closed. "Sorry, I thought you said guys were after her."

"Yes, *again*. Anyway, they broke into my cabin. I need to go over there, but I'd feel better if Kate wasn't by herself. I don't want to take her to the cabin either just in case they return."

"I get it. And yeah, I can head that way. I'm just wrapping things up here at the office. Dinner okay? Or would you rather me stay with her at—where are y'all?"

"A hotel, not far from the mall." He muted the call. "He says he'll pick you up and take you to dinner. That okay?"

She flashed an almost wicked smile. "Sure. I'll put on something nice."

Alex shook his head and unmuted the phone. "Dinner works." He told Torres the name of the hotel before ending the call. "You aren't making this easy on me."

"If I didn't know any better, I'd say your eyes are greener than usual right now." She hopped off the bed and reached for her suitcase.

"I don't want to leave you alone, Kate."

She slid her arms around his neck and stretched up on her tiptoes. "You really *are* jealous."

The burn in his cheeks betrayed the truth. Not staying closed off meant his feelings showed, even when inconvenient.

"Why did you call Torres?"

"Because I had his number, I trust him, and he carries a gun. Would you prefer I ask if his partner, Miller, is free?"

"Don't even. And I'm not the least bit interested in Torres. You know that. I mean, he's nice and all, but . . ."

"Which is why I suggested it."

"Then why?" Her eyes went wide as she caught on to his train of thought. "*You* think—"

"No. I don't. Probably not. I don't know. I don't want to talk about it." He remembered the day in Travis's kitchen watching Torres pat Kate's shoulder. "As soon as he gets here, I'll leave and be back as soon as I can."

Thirty minutes later, Kate winked as Alex made his way to the door. He pulled it open to find a smiling detective in the hall. *At least he didn't bring flowers.* "Come on in."

She laid her hand on Alex's back. "I'm ready to go. Why don't we head on downstairs?"

Torres, still dressed in slacks and a dress shirt but without his tie, stuck out his hand to Kate. "Good to see you again."

"Thanks for doing this." Alex shook Ben's hand then checked the door to make sure it had locked.

"It'll be fun." Turning to Kate, Torres asked, "You aren't a vegetarian, are you?"

Alex laughed.

"Not even remotely." She grabbed Alex's hand as they made their way to the elevator.

Outside the lobby, Torres pointed to his car, a beige Jetta. "Ladies first."

Alex forced a smile as her hand slipped from his and prayed he wasn't making a mistake.

She took one step before turning back and hugging him. "Hurry back." She planted a quick kiss on his neck.

The feel of her lips lingered on his skin as she walked away. At least he didn't have to worry about her while he dealt with the mess at the cabin. He had to believe that Torres, a police detective, could keep her safe; otherwise, Alex would never be able to leave her.

When he reached the cabin, Alex parked next to the two patrol cars in front. Before his feet hit the ground, DJ strolled up to the truck, frowning.

"It's a good thing Bureau is still with y'all." Alex forked his fingers through his hair.

"It looks like someone just wanted to make a mess, almost as if someone was out for revenge."

"I have no idea who, but it's got to be the guys after Kate." Alex stepped through the broken door frame and froze. Mess didn't even begin to describe the disaster before him. "What the hell?"

The recliner lay on its side. Every drawer hung open, the contents scattered on the ground. The rug, rolled up haphazardly, lay in front of the hearth. In the kitchen, containers from the pantry were strewn on the table, the food from inside scattered across the floor.

"Like I said, they made a mess."

Alex pointed to the office. "How bad is it?"

"I couldn't tell if anything was missing or broken." DJ stepped around books scattered on the floor near the empty shelves.

Alex braced himself. His livelihood depended on the computer equipment in his office. After a brief scan of the room, his muscles relaxed. The equipment sat right where he'd left it days ago. Papers covered the floor. Filing cabinet drawers hung open. But untouched, in the middle of the desk, lay his magnifying glass, half-covered by the photo of Emma and Claire.

"She has no idea why they're after her?" DJ leaned back against the wall.

"Only that the guy blames her for something."

After determining that nothing of significant value was missing, Alex answered questions for DJ's report.

DJ motioned for Alex to leave as soon as the report was complete. "Hurry back to Kate. You told Travis what's going on?"

"Yeah. Called him on the way out here." Alex shot off a quick text to Kate as he walked to the truck, letting her know he was on his way. He started the engine, waiting for a reply. At the end of the driveway, he stopped when a notification sounded. He smiled at her reply: *Don't speed.* After a second beep, a kissing emoji popped up on the screen.

Without any clue about what the men who broke into his house wanted, the police had little chance of making progress in the case. While driving, Alex ran through the events since setting off on the road trip. *How had they found her in Denver?* The attempted break-in couldn't have been coincidental. Had someone seen the news segments and somehow tracked her that way?

When he pulled into the hotel lot, he spotted the detective's Volkswagen. *They're back.* Alex beelined for the elevators, pushed the up arrow, and waited. Tapping his foot, he grew impatient as the numbers lit up when the elevator stopped at each floor, making its slow descent.

Finally, it dinged, and the doors opened. Arms circled his waist before he even took a step.

"They are slower now because of relative time. You know. Einstein stuff."

He spun around. "Crap, Kate. You startled me."

"You made it back." Torres walked up, carrying a bag of popcorn. "This place is great. They have free drinks and popcorn in the lobby."

Alex followed as Kate dragged him away from the elevators toward the free snacks. "Kate fill you in on what's going on?"

"She did." Torres winked at her. "I may have to nickname her *Trouble.*"

She smirked as she handed Alex a bag of popcorn, and it took everything in him to swallow the comments that ping-ponged in his head.

"I should probably get her upstairs, just to be safe." Alex scanned the windows.

Torres tossed his empty cup in the trash. "Probably not a bad idea." He whispered something to Kate before stepping away. "Have a good night. Call if you need anything else."

Alex pushed the button hoping the wait for the elevator wouldn't be long. "Did it go okay?"

"Yep." She finished the last of her Coke and tossed the cup in the trash.

They stepped onto the elevator, and he tangled his fingers with hers. *Please, not the one-word answers.* She stayed quiet as they walked to the room. He swiped his card key and pushed open the door.

"How bad was it?" Kate waited until they were in the room to ask about the cabin.

"A lot worse than the last time."

"I'm so sorry." She dropped onto the edge of the bed. "It's my fault. Again."

He sat down next to her. "Aww, *Trouble*, don't cry." He smirked, waiting for her reaction.

She sat up straight. The flash in her dark eyes told him what she thought of his humor. "*Do not* call me that."

"Yes, *dear*."

Her tone completely changed. She purred, "*That* is not my nickname." She touched a finger to the cleft in his chin.

He pulled her into his lap. "Rainy." He pictured the destruction in his cabin and shuddered. Whoever did it was hunting Kate.

"This guy is determined to find me, isn't he?"

"Seems that way."

"What are we going to do?" She trailed her finger up and down his arm.

"You sleep in that bed, and I'll sleep over here." He had no other plan to offer.

She rolled her eyes. "I want the bed closer to the bathroom."

"Yes, dear."

He stared at the ceiling waiting for sleep. He'd checked the locks on the door ten times or more before sliding under the covers. It'd been quiet for nearly an hour, yet sleep had been chased far away by worry. He about stopped breathing when Kate spoke.

"Alex?"

"Didn't know you were awake."

"You can't sleep either?"

"I'm sure I will eventually. Just thinking about stuff."

"Forgot to tell you that Mona texted me. LeAnn was released from the hospital."

"Did you talk to LeAnn?"

"No. And she still hasn't answered my texts."

"What did Torres whisper to you?"

"I'm not sure you want to know."

"Where did y'all have dinner?"

"Some Brazilian steakhouse."

Alex bolted upright. "Seriously?"

Soft chuckles bubbled from her side of the room. "No. We went to the Mexican restaurant across the highway. The place with all the funny tee shirts."

Alex didn't respond. In the dark, she couldn't gauge his reaction if met with silence. Perfectly still, he waited.

"Alejandro?" Her voice carried more tease than apology.

He rolled his eyes and bit his tongue. She'd surprised him, but her rolled Rs needed work.

"I'll be good. No more teasing."

"Night, *Rainy.*" He rolled on his side and punched at his pillow. "Go to sleep . . . if you want."

The phone buzzed. He squinted at the screen. *Travis texting at 2 am can't be good.* After rubbing the sleep out of his eyes, he shifted to a sitting position and swiped at the screen.

His stomach tightened as he read the text: *Someone was lurking outside Kate's place. Captain Maddox saw the car pull away but didn't get the plate.* As Alex typed out a reply, another text appeared: *Glad you weren't there. I hired security for my house and Kate's.*

Alex responded: *Did they break in?*

Travis replied quickly: *No. Maddox walked around. Everything's secure.*

Alex tapped out another text: *Thanks.*

Kate stirred. Half-asleep, she asked, "What's going on?"

"Shhh. Go back to sleep." He'd tell her in the morning. No point in her losing sleep over prowlers, whoever they were.

Her bed jostled, and she sighed contentedly. "Okay."

Just as Alex set the phone down, it buzzed when Travis texted again: *Give me the cabin's address so I can send security there, too.*

Alex hesitated before responding: T*hey've already been there.*

Send it anyway.

So he did.

Alex opened his eyes. Outside the door, people whispered as they padded by. He strained to make out what they were saying. *Tourists.* Glancing over to the other bed, he smiled. Kate slept facing him, snuggled on her side, her hands tucked under her cheek. He rolled to his side, gazing at her.

Again, danger kept them together. He'd worried that too much togetherness might strain the budding relationship. The opposite had happened. They flirted and swapped stories. Each day was like an extended date in spite of the lurking danger. The more he learned, the more he wanted to know. Familiarity bred something altogether different than contempt. Lost in his thoughts, he didn't think to stop staring when she opened her eyes. Her sleepy smile lit his insides.

"Good morning." She pulled the covers to her chin and snuggled a little deeper into the bed. "How long have you been awake?"

"A few minutes."

"Been staring at me the whole time?"

"Pretty much."

Her lips curved into a delighted grin, the kind that sparks when a woman believes herself beautiful.

Enough staring. Time to get up. He threw back the covers and stood up.

She grabbed a hair tie off the bedside table as she sat up and pulled her hair back. "What was going on last night?"

"Travis texted. People were snooping around your place, but they didn't break in. A guy that lives in town scared them off."

"You were right."

"Normally, I'd relish hearing those words." He perched next to her on the edge of her bed. "Today, what do you say we just stay here in the room? We can order room service." Sitting around, he'd likely have time to complete at least part of a project. Income was a good thing. Although he had savings stashed away, he didn't want to dip into it much.

She scooted behind him and massaged his shoulders. "Sure. I'll look through the album and spend some time researching Emma's family."

He rocked his neck from side to side as she kneaded her fingers into his muscles. "Have Wi-Fi, will research?"

"Exactly." She moved her hands down his back and rubbed circles with the heels of her palms. "Sorry I gave you such a hard time last night."

He chuckled. "So, that's why you're being so nice to me."

She draped her arms around his neck. "Torres was a complete gentleman, nothing weird. I just felt like I was being babysat."

"And you *hate* that."

"It was like I was the kid sister he was trying to keep out of trouble." She rested her chin on the top of his head. "He wouldn't even let me pay for my own dinner."

Conscious of her body pressed against his back, Alex hesitated a second before tilting his head back. Kate met his lips with a forceful, hungry kiss. He slipped his hands around her waist as she slid around him, into his lap, straddling him. Ever-conscious of her wishes, a non-negotiable boundary, he savored her kisses, willing to call a halt when needed.

Without warning, she pushed off his chest. "I can't."

He loosened his hold but kept his hands on her hips. "Kate, I know what 'no' means. I would never—"

She touched her finger to his lips. "That's not what I meant." She kissed him on the cheek and stood up. "I'm going to go take a shower. A cold one."

As she swung the bathroom door closed, he fell back onto the bed, puzzled and a little frustrated. She didn't trust him. The remembered hurt had her rebuilding walls, keeping him out. The start and stop, worse than traffic on a big game weekend, didn't irritate him. The lack of trust bothered him, like a pebble stuck inside a shoe. Someone had hurt her, and her pulling away so abruptly, lumped Alex with that person. It stung.

Beth-

Congratulations! Another boy. I stopped by the other day when I was in town visiting my dad, but you weren't home. Two boys! That little man of yours must be growing like a weed. Is he excited to be a big brother?

Hopefully, I'll catch you the next time I'm in town.

-M

October 1985

Beth-

I lost the baby.

Just when my white picket fence life started to feel like a reality, a bulldozer smashed it all to hell. Brad is beyond despondent. He hasn't spoken to me in days. He looks at me as if it's somehow my fault. I'm not sure what to do.

What's your secret, Beth? Mr. Faithful adores you. He has from the night he first saw you at the Broken Spoke. That night was life-changing for both of us. You're living the life I always wanted. I mean, not with Patrick, but you know. The house, the kids, the husband—you've got the whole package.

What do I have to do to get the same thing? Or did one lapse in judgment make none of that possible?

I'll write again soon.

-M

CHAPTER ELEVEN

January 25, 2016 – 9:12 am

With the photo album open in my lap, and the computer on the desk, I searched names as I came across them in the album. Excitement chased away any thought of tears, happy or otherwise. A tree spread up from the bottom of the hotel notepad—Emma's parents, three siblings, and grandparents. Absorbed in the hunt, I jumped when Alex kissed me on the top of the head.

"I didn't realize you were even out of the shower." I stroked the stubble on his cheek when he rested his chin on my shoulder. "These are Emma's siblings."

"Which one is Justin?"

I pointed to the younger son. "That one. Recognize him?"

"Not a bit." He picked up his laptop.

"Want to help me search?"

"Sure." He tossed the still-closed computer on the bed and slid the armchair next to the desk

"If you need to work . . .?"

"I'd rather do this with you."

I hopped up out of the swivel chair. "Sit here and search. I want to look through the album some more."

"Whoa. You want *me* to search?"

"Why not? You are a computer guy, aren't you?"

He sat in the chair and hovered his fingers over the keyboard.

"I think I already showed you this picture of Emma. *And* I found her birth certificate."

"How did you know which was the right Emma Carson?"

"Because of this." I pointed to a birthday card, dated. "And this is a picture of Emma with her mom."

"Oh, wow. You look like your grandma."

Such a simple phrase, but it melted my heart. I'd waited years to look like somebody. "That's what I thought, too."

"Think Beth sent the album?"

"From Gram's reaction, I'd say yes."

Alex chuckled. "I like her."

"Yeah, yeah. She likes you, too."

Gram liked him enough that I wondered if Alex reminded her of someone who, at some time before Mr. Crawford, she had loved.

Alex's phone chimed a text notification. He shot me a look as soon as he read the message. The smirk that accompanied it piqued my curiosity.

"Who texted?"

"Ben." Alex texted as he answered me.

"Who?"

Alex shook his head and laughed. "Detective Torres."

I'd spent an evening with the detective and didn't remember his first name. To me, he was still Torres. "And?"

"He just asked if there was any update." After hitting send, Alex tucked the phone in his pocket.

"Why does everyone text you for an update?"

"Because they know I'm always with you? I don't know. What should I search?"

"See what else you can find about Emma's brothers and sister."

He clicked on the oldest brother's profile and searched records.

"This could be him. What was the other site that had the death certificates?"

"Familysearch dot org."

He opened a new tab and entered *Randall Carson* in the search field. While he scanned the list of results, I flipped through pages of the album.

"There are only five people in this family photo. One of the brothers is missing."

"After 1961? It's Randall that missing."

"What did you find?"

"His death certificate." Alex turned the screen so I could see the image.

"How did he die?"

He pointed at the line where the cause of death was recorded in barely legible writing. "Measles."

"When—?"

"They didn't start vaccines for that until '63." He answered before I even finished the question, reading my mind again.

"How sad."

"Let me save this and then hunt down the other brother, the infamous Justin." He turned to look at me. "You don't think . . ."

"I hope not, but I texted Travis asking if Justin could be responsible for any of this."

"What did he say?"

"He doubted Justin would do this stuff but said he would talk to Captain Maddox about it. I'm not sure who Captain Maddox is."

"He must live in Schatzenburg. He's the one who chased off the prowlers." Alex tapped the desk. "Back to searching."

Two hours later, I'd put aside the album and hovered near Alex's shoulder, watching as he searched. We found information about Emma's other brother, Justin—no arrest warrants, thankfully—and were just beginning a hunt for Emma's sister, Elizabeth.

"We know Justin is still alive. And Elizabeth must be Aunt Beth, living presumably. Crazy that they're both still alive."

"Emma's siblings aren't that old."

"You're right. I forget Emma died so young."

He squeezed my knee and kissed the side of my head. "Lunch break?"

"Sure. We going to order in again?" Although I enjoyed spending time alone with Alex, the hotel room walls were creeping in. If there were no reason to stay, leaving wouldn't have been so desirable.

Alex leaned back in his chair and laced his fingers behind his head. "I was thinking pizza."

"Sausage and mushroom okay?"

"Whatever you want." He grinned, daring me to test the limits of his offer.

"Anchovies?"

"If it makes you happy."

"I was kidding." I didn't want to try salty fish on my pizza. "The room, even though I can't complain about the company, is getting boring."

"Sorry, Kate. Maybe I'm being too cautious."

"Just order the pizza."

"You can have the last slice." I pulled my knees up in front of me in the chair, clicked on the television, and flipped through channels. Even though I had plenty I could be doing, feeling trapped in one room left me bored, without motivation. Soap operas and anything-but-reality court shows were my only television options.

Alex stretched out on the bed. "I am sorry."

"Not your fault." Chin resting on my knee, I clicked through the series of channels.

"When this is all behind us, we'll take a day to go downtown. Have you been to the Alamo?"

I shook my head.

"Riverwalk?"

"Nope."

"I'll take you on a tour of all the missions, and we'll wander down the Riverwalk and ride a river taxi."

"That sounds wonderful." I continued my hunt for anything remotely interesting. "Think they'd notice if we smuggled Bureau up here?"

"Unfortunately, yes."

"I talked to Mona again. LeAnn got on the phone for a minute, but she only cried and mumbled about Jeff. I couldn't make heads or tails of what she said."

"I can't even imagine how worried she must be. If you were missing . . ."

"I can't even contemplate being in her shoes." I rubbed my face as the thought of Alex in trouble wormed its way into my brain. "LeAnn will be mad that I involved the police. If anything happens to Jeff, she'll never speak to me again."

"Kate, we didn't have a choice. These aren't matters we can handle ourselves."

"I know."

Alex sat up and patted the bed next to him. Pointing at the laptop, he said, "Let's search some more."

By the time the sun had set, we'd found another two generations back on Emma's maternal side. We weren't as lucky finding information about Emma's sister, Elizabeth. The name was too common to know which records belonged to the right one.

"We've been cooped up in here all day. No one has come knocking. Let me wander downstairs, make sure everything seems okay, and we'll walk next door for dinner."

"I could really use some fresh air and a change of scenery."

"Be back in a few minutes."

I bolted the door behind him and contemplated a different outfit, but comfort trumped any thought of changing. I stayed in my yoga pants and tee shirt. I took a few minutes to brush my teeth and apply eyeliner and lipstick. When I stepped out of the bathroom, my phone beeped: *All clear. I'm headed back up.*

I had just enough time to pull on my shoes before he knocked. A text followed the knock: *It's me.*

I unbolted the door and pulled it open. "All good?"

He brushed past me and dug through his duffle bag. "Yeah. It's a bit chilly." He tossed me one of his Aggie sweatshirts. "You might want that."

"Thanks." I slipped it on over my tee shirt, and a wide grin spread across his face.

We slipped out of the hotel, unbothered, and walked down the sidewalk to the restaurant next door. As we stepped inside, Alex tapped his pockets. "I walked off without my phone."

"We'll only be here a little while, and I have mine."

He nodded, and we followed the hostess to a table.

We ordered food at the same time we ordered drinks. The faster we ate, the sooner we'd be back in the room, but the restaurant was a welcome change of scenery.

Tucked in the same side of a booth, as we waited for dinner, I quietly broached the topic I'd been avoiding. "It's been three days. What if . . .?" The question hung in the air.

Alex clasped my hand. "We have to keep thinking Jeff's still alive. Figuring out why they blame you might help sort out some of this."

"Is it something I did? Something I have?"

"I sure hope it isn't that apron." His green eyes glinted.

I poked him in the side.

The waitress balanced Alex's dinner plate while setting mine in front of me. "Careful, the plate is pretty warm." She put his food on the table. "Anything else I can get for you?"

"I think we're good." He flashed her a smile before she turned and hurried away.

Over dinner, the conversation drifted away from Jeff and the kidnappers to my relationship with LeAnn.

"We met in high school. My freshman and sophomore year, teachers sat my classes in alphabetical order. LeAnn's last name is Vaughn."

"So, Miss Westfall got to sit by LeAnn in every class."

"We share a love of Jane Austen novels, but other than that, we aren't much alike."

"Differences make the world go 'round."

CHAPTER TWELVE

January 25, 2016 – 6:42 pm

Alex slipped his credit card back into his wallet. "Ready?"

"I'm going to stop by the ladies' room."

He didn't want her out of his sight, but he couldn't exactly ask her not to use the bathroom. "I'll meet you up front."

Standing near the entrance, Alex chewed on a toothpick as he waited. Two men stepped into the restaurant. Alex froze. Keith and another man, who Alex didn't recognize, ignored the hostess when she asked how many. Suspicious that Kate's neighbor had traveled to Texas, Alex turned, giving them his back, listening and plotting. *I need to get Kate out of this restaurant unseen.*

"She's in here somewhere. Near the back maybe." Staring at the screen of a phone, they muttered to each other just loud enough for Alex to make out what they said. Reflected in the glass, Keith's companion pointed to the back.

The hairs stood up on the back of Alex's neck.

They're tracking her.

The hostess waved a menu in front of the two of them. "Excuse me, gentleman, would you like a table?"

"Yeah, sorry. Something near the back is good," Keith said, still distracted by the phone.

As soon as the men followed the hostess toward the table, Alex beelined for the bathrooms and met Kate just outside the ladies' room. "Give me your phone." He put a finger to his lips.

She handed him her phone, fear swirling in her eyes.

He turned off her phone, yanked out the battery, and grabbed her hand. "Let's go."

She didn't budge. "What's going on?"

"I'll explain outside." He glanced at where the men reviewed the menu. "Please trust me."

She nearly cut off his circulation squeezing his hand as she followed him out of the restaurant.

Out the door, they ran to the truck, parked in the shared lot with the hotel. Alex whispered a profanity. The rims of two of his wheels rested on the ground, the tires deflated.

"Alex, that's Keith."

He looked up in time to see both men jumping out of their chairs. "Run, Kate. That way. Come on."

Surrounded by roadways and fences, their options were limited. After crossing the parking lot and dodging a fence, they ran for the trees. Between the cedars and oaks, a white path glowed in the moonlight. He grabbed her hand and raced down the walking trail. Without looking back, they ran, knowing they were being chased.

How long can she outpace them?

The concrete path curved, but the wide-open trail made it easy for their pursuers. Alex scanned the trees as he ran. When she slowed the slightest bit, he pulled her off onto a dirt trail that wove through the trees and brush. Once they were out of sight of the main trail, he stopped. "Take a second to catch your breath," he whispered, clutching her to his chest.

Voices carried as the men drew close to where Alex and Kate had ducked off the sidewalk. She tugged at Alex's hand and started moving again. He ducked branches, keeping a tight grip on her. Slowly, quietly, they worked their way down the dirt path. When they'd circled around to the main trail, he stayed hidden in the tree line. With Kate pressed against his side, he watched and listened. From the sound of it, the men had doubled back toward the restaurant. Their voices traveled farther away. Alex stepped onto the paved path. He pointed ahead, and Kate took off running. He stayed right on her heels.

"Hear that? This way." A male voice carried through the air.

They can't be too far behind. Alex prayed for a gap in the trees, anywhere to duck out again.

Kate stopped, chest heaving. He clutched her arm and pulled her further down the trail, scanning for a place to hide. As they rounded a bend in the trail, the footbridge came into view. They raced across. He let go of her arm and grasped her hand, then nodded toward the grass. Leading her off the path, he jogged around a short rail fence and slipped underneath the walkway with her in tow.

The wide, metal footbridge stood out in contrast to the surrounding landscape. Large and sturdy, it provided ample coverage for hiding. Careful of each step, stooping as he moved, Alex shuffled out of sight, sat down, and pulled her into his lap. He tried not to think about what other critters and insects lay hidden under the bridge with them. She looked at the drop-off not far from their perch and curled up against him.

Below, the creek—still high from the recent rains—gurgled and spat, warning them not to misstep. In the darkness, they waited. Kate tensed as footsteps approached, and Alex tightened his embrace. Cheek pressed to the top of her head, he focused on the sounds of the men, their footfalls, what they said.

The pursuers ran closer. With each thump on the bridge, fear rose in Alex's throat. Alex and Kate held their breath.

Just above them, someone stopped. "Dammit. Where'd they go?"

Alex winced. The unmistakable tickle of something crawling on his arm brought visions of spiders and scorpions. Staying still required every ounce of self-control. Whatever was on his arm, Alex hoped it didn't have a stinger.

"They couldn't have gotten far. She could be hiding in the trees. Maybe she got tired, and he ran off without her." Keith sounded nearly frantic.

Alex brushed his fingertips against her cheek. Kate clutched his shirt in her fist. Keith's disdain for Alex wasn't lost on anyone within earshot.

"Don't worry about it. We know where they're staying. We'll wait until they come back for their stuff." The other man left little doubt about who was in charge.

One of the men left the sidewalk, crunching through the leaves and grass. "If I grab a flashlight . . ." Keith's single focus was finding Kate.

"Not worth it. Good thinking letting the air out of his tires."

"I'd have slashed 'em if I'd had a knife."

"Come on. They aren't here."

"Let's go just a bit further down the path." Keith wouldn't give up.

"All right, but not far. I don't want to bump into the park police."

The men jogged away, not toward the hotel. Alex released his long-held breath and scrambled to knock the insect off his arm. Kate looked up at him but remained quiet, the bright moon reflecting in the tears brimmed in her dark eyes. He kissed her forehead and whispered in her ear. "We'll stay here a while. Let them give up and leave, then we'll go further down the trail."

She nodded and rested her head on his chest.

Minutes stretched out, but still they waited for Keith and his companion to cross back over the bridge. Alex listened, straining to hear over the sounds of nature. At the first hint of footsteps, he held Kate tighter, his lips pressed to her forehead. The footfalls continued over the bridge and faded as the men headed back toward the hotel.

Alex relaxed his shoulders and waited until silence settled around them before he risked even a whisper. "I'm sorry I suggested dinner out."

"Keith let the air out of your tires."

"Of course he did."

They stayed huddled under the bridge, Kate in Alex's lap, his arms wrapped around her, neither saying a word. His tee shirt was still clenched in her fist. Alex guessed at the time. It felt as if they'd hidden for hours, but more likely, it had been only forty-five minutes since they found the niche under the bridge. Satisfied that they were truly alone, he cradled her face in his hand and lifted her chin.

Before he could whisper instructions in her ear, she breathed, "Thank you for not leaving me behind."

The waver in her voice overwhelmed him. He sought her mouth and pressed his lips to hers. He'd known Kate less than three weeks, and most of that time had been fraught with danger. Leaving her behind hadn't crossed his mind.

After indulging in a couple minutes of escape, he pulled back, then followed with one more peck. "We should go. I'd hate to get caught by the park police making out under a bridge."

"I'd hate to make the news a second time." She crawled out of his lap, hugging the underside of the bridge.

Keeping hold of her hand, he slipped around her and peeked out. Not a soul could be seen either direction. They hurried back onto the trail and trekked away from the hotel. The near-full moon shed welcome light on the walkway. They hung close to the tree line as much as possible but stayed clear of the barbed-wire fence that ran parallel to the path.

Kate tensed as the trees on the left disappeared, a large construction site just on the other side of a tall fence. The openness made her feel vulnerable, easy to spot.

"We'll be past it pretty quick." He glanced around.

The later it got, the longer the sidewalk seemed. Kate faltered, and Alex caught her arm.

"Need to stop for a minute or two?" A bench came into view as they rounded a curve.

She shook her head, trudging on down the path.

He slipped his hand in hers and slowed their pace. "We'll be near a road soon, I can hear traffic."

The road came into view, and she let go of his hand and hurried downhill, out of sight, under the concrete bridge. Alex paused before following her, orienting himself, deciding which direction to go.

She leaned against a concrete column. "Where do these trails go?"

"All over the city."

"What about *this* trail?" Kate pointed in the direction they were headed.

"If I'm right, it takes us by the university, then onto Bandera Road."

"I'm so turned around. I'll just go where you lead."

He stepped under the bridge and pulled her close. "I think I know a place where we can hole up and wait for someone to come get us." He kissed the top of her head before resuming the walk up the path, clutching her hand.

"And go where?"

"I haven't figured that out yet." He turned when she stopped and read the look on her face. "We can discuss it *together.*"

"Thank you." She squeezed his hand.

He paused where the path branched. "I think we want to head up this way. Should take us near the campus."

She followed him up the sidewalk, her pace slower, her breathing heavier. The stress made what would be a leisurely walk seem long and tiresome.

They walked past an apartment complex, but unless he wanted to scale an eight-foot fence, he wasn't getting in there. When they reached the surface streets, they were near the campus, but every-thing was dark. There was no place to retreat inside.

He matched her gait and kept a tight grip on her hand. "Let's walk down this way. I don't think it's far."

They walked along the side of the road, using sidewalks when they could. The construction along the street made it treacherous in places. When he spotted the gas station, he breathed a sigh of relief.

"It's over there, in that tall building. A coffee place."

She hurried her steps. "It'll take DJ an hour to get here."

"Yeah, I'll probably try Torres first." Alex held out his hand for her to steady herself as she climbed the few stairs.

"Finally, a place to sit down."

He opened the door, and Kate stepped inside the coffee bar. A handful of students sat buried in books, sipping drinks.

Alex pointed to a vacant couch. "Vanilla latte sound good?"

She shrugged as she dropped onto the sofa. "Sure."

Alex stepped up to the counter. "Two vanilla lattes. Any chance I could use your phone? I walked off without mine."

"No problem." The barista handed Alex a cell phone.

He paid for the lattes, then pulled Torres's card out of his wallet to be sure he dialed the right number. "Hi, Detective. It's me again." He walked to the front window, his back to the room, then turned around to keep Kate in view.

"Alex, please call me Ben. What's up?"

"We need a ride. Someone let the air out of my tires, chased us down a walking trail."

"Where?"

"The trails behind that financial place with the sign. You know the one that has political sayings on it all the time."

"The one by the hotel?"

"Yeah." Alex flashed Kate a smile when she glanced at him, hoping to ease her worry.

Ben's keys rattled in the background. "Where are you now?"

"Indy Coffee on UTSA Blvd. In the mid-rise building."

"I know the one. How'd they find you?"

"They were somehow tracking Kate's phone, I think. It's off now."

"Battery out?"

"Yeah. I walked off without my phone, unfortunately. I'm using the barista's."

"I'm five minutes away. Be there soon." Ben ended the call without another word.

Alex handed the phone back to the man behind the counter. "Thanks so much."

"Sure thing. Your drinks are ready."

Alex handed Kate her cup and took a seat next to her. "Torres is on his way."

She leaned close, her eyes scanning the room. "He didn't whisper anything bad."

"What are you talking about?"

"Detective Torres. At the hotel." She rested her head on Alex's shoulder.

He waited, hoping she might say what had been whispered that night without making him ask. He patted her leg and sipped his coffee, curiosity making it hard to stay quiet.

"He said he hadn't seen someone so smitten in a long time. He meant you."

Alex grinned. "Is that so?" Knowing Torres said that made it easy to brush aside jealous thoughts. Alex liked Ben more and more. "And why did you not tell me this last night?"

Tearless, fearful eyes stared at him. "Why is Keith after me? And who is the other guy?"

"Tell me you know Keith's last name, please."

"I'll think of it. Let's talk about something else. It'll come to me." Measured and rational, she was handling it better than he expected.

"I have a suggestion about where we should go, but only if you're willing."

"Good, because I don't think you'll like my idea." She sipped her latte, eyeing him over the rim of her cup.

"Tell me." He draped an arm around her.

"The Castle. They know we aren't there."

"I had the same thought." Alex kissed the side of her head. "Travis hired security to monitor the house. I think it might be the safest place for us right now."

"So, you think it's safe to go back?"

"Yes. We can go to The Castle." He inhaled and exhaled slowly, ready for Ben to arrive.

Torres waved as he stepped inside. Wearing jeans and a Rush tee shirt, he looked like a more relaxed version of the detective they'd met the first day at the mall. He nodded at the barista and walked up to the couch. "Long time no see."

Ben's attempt at humor didn't even draw a smile from Kate, only a sharp look.

"Ouch. Sorry." Ben shook Alex's hand. "Listen, if you need a place to stay, I don't live far from here. I have an extra bedroom and a couch."

Alex appreciated the offer and considered it for a second, but a security guard nearby seemed the safest bet. "Thanks, but we're thinking that her place is the safest. Travis hired security. We know the locals. Those guys will stand out like sore thumbs in that town."

"Can't argue with your logic. Want me to get your stuff?" Ben stuck his hands in his pockets.

"I hadn't even thought that far ahead." Alex ran his fingers through his hair.

"Let me drop y'all off, then I'll drive back in and get it."

"What about your truck?" Kate grabbed Alex's hand. The weariness in her voice caught the detective's attention.

"Don't worry about it, Kate. We'll get his truck." Flustered by how upset Kate was, Torres rubbed the back of his head. "If y'all can get by without it for a bit, might be best to let it stay put overnight."

"Thanks for being so nice." She continued to catch him off-guard.

"Nice?" He laughed. "That's why I'm here. To protect and serve."

She stood and hugged him. "You've gone way beyond. Thank you."

He patted her back before stepping backward and nearly falling over the small coffee table. "Let's go out the back door."

Kate stopped just outside the door. "Perkins. His name is Keith Perkins."

"Maybe that will help track him down." Alex held her hand as they walked into the parking garage. He opened the front passenger side door of the detective's Jetta.

Kate hung near the back of the car. "I'll sit back here."

Alex pulled open the door, and Kate slid in. After dropping into the front seat, he turned to look at her, and she flashed a tired smile. "We'll be home soon."

Torres started the engine. "Schatzenburg, right?"

"That's the place."

He handed his phone to Alex. "You need to call anyone else?"

"Thanks." Alex called DJ while they were on the road and explained what all had happened. Before hanging up, Alex repeated Keith's full name. "Make sure you catch him."

"Jeff wasn't with them." Kate blinked several times. "You think he . . . ?"

"I don't know, Kate." Alex reached back and gripped her hand.

Torres glanced into the rearview mirror. "There could be another accomplice that has him stashed somewhere."

Kate nodded absently. "I hope so."

When they arrived at the house, Torres stopped them before they got out of the car. "Mind if I look around inside, just to be safe?"

"Not a bad idea." Alex raked his fingers through his hair.

Torres accepted the keys Kate held out, then got out and talked to the security guard before going inside.

"Alex." Kate leaned forward and rested her head on Alex's shoulder.

He stroked her hair. "Hmm?"

"How did they know where to find me?"

"Your phone, I think. Not sure how."

A door slammed, and Kate jumped.

Alex rubbed her arm. "It's DJ."

Once they were locked inside, Detective Torres headed back to the hotel to retrieve their things. Kate sat in a chair, her knees pulled close to her chest.

Alex handed DJ her phone. "Maybe you can use that to lure them somewhere."

"That's not a bad—" His phone interrupted him, and he answered as he walked away down the hall.

Kate jumped up and pulled out flour, butter, sugar, and all the other ingredients to make cookies. Alex didn't dissuade her. Warm gooey cookies were exactly what he needed, and baking would give her something to do, calm her.

DJ rushed back up the hall, his eyes wide. "An agent is on his way over."

"Agent?" Alex pulled a soda out of the refrigerator.

DJ nodded. "FBI. Kidnapping. Crossing state lines. That's their jurisdiction."

Beth-

Brad left. He packed his stuff, mumbled something about wanting his own kids, and left. I'm just glad Scooter didn't hear. He was just starting to warm to Brad.

He called a couple days later. Said he just needed some time. We're separated.

Hope y'all have a good Christmas. At least I still have my guy, my little heart and soul. Sticks said he might drop by this weekend. I hope he does for Scooter's sake. Things are pretty glum around here. A visit with Sticks will be good.

Oh, I almost forgot to tell you. Scooter begged me to let him get one of those custom mugs. He had me put *I ♥ Sticks* on it. So, when Sticks comes over, Scooter has the gift all ready for him.

-M

Chapter Thirteen

January 25, 2016 – 10:30 pm

I grabbed a handful of chocolate chips out of the bag and tossed them in my mouth before pulling a pan out of the oven. I swapped out pans, slid in another batch of cookies, and then reset the timer. The freshly baked cookies sat on the hot foil pan until they cooled enough to keep their shape. Once they had, I moved them to a paper plate.

Without my normal supplies like spatulas and cooling racks, I had to make do. "Thank you for grabbing baking supplies and aluminum pans."

Alex rubbed my back and picked up a cookie. "Anything I can do?"

"Keep eating. There's another dozen in the oven." I dropped the last bit of dough onto the cooled cookie sheet, prepping the last dozen for the oven.

DJ paced. He spun around at the sound of a car door closing. "I think Agent Jacobson is here. Stay put." He ran out the front door.

Alex walked to the front window and stared out, his jaw tight. I wiped off my hands and stepped up next to him. Without turning away from the window, he clasped my hand. The clamminess surprised me. When I bumped his shoulder, he offered a weak smile.

As DJ and the agent neared the porch, Alex squeezed my hand tighter and pulled me closer. Rigid, he draped his arm around me as Agent Jacobson stepped into the light of the porch. The vein in Alex's neck throbbed in rhythm with his heartbeat.

DJ pushed open the door.

"Alex?" The agent froze in the doorway. Recovering, he stuck out his hand.

He knows Alex?

I stared at the agent. Tall and lean, he could've been a poster boy for the FBI.

"Rory, hi. It's been a long time." Alex shook his hand.

"Three years." Rory ran his fingers through his straight, light brown hair.

Alex shifted and rested his hands on my shoulders. "Rory, this is Kate."

Rory had a firm handshake. "You have someone after you?"

"Yeah." My voice cracked. "Come on in. We can sit at the table. I don't have much furniture yet."

DJ followed the three of us, questions knitted in his brow. The personal exchange had surprised him, too.

I clicked off the timer, pulled out the tray, and slid in the last batch. Puzzling through the little information there was, I tried to figure out the connection. DJ introduced him as Agent Jacobson. Alex called him Rory, and astonishment registered on DJ's face. Rory said he hadn't seen Alex in three years.

Three years? Ellie connected them somehow, which explained loads about Alex's reaction.

Alex sat silently running his finger along the grain in the wood table.

"Cookies?" I motioned toward the plate.

Rory smiled and cleared his throat. "I never turn down homemade cookies."

"Me either." DJ looked at me with raised eyebrows.

I set a plate of cookies in front of them and pulled Cokes out of the refrigerator. Tension hung in the room like a morning fog.

DJ pointed at the Cokes in my hands. "Got milk?" His attempt at humor fell flat; no one cracked a smile. He stuffed a cookie in his mouth and popped the top on the can I handed him.

A debate played out in my head. Should I ask Rory how he knew Alex or vice versa? It connected to Ellie somehow, but I guessed it wasn't a topic either wanted brought up at the moment.

As if reading my mind, Alex spoke. "Kate, Rory is Ellie's brother." His eyes, usually bright of late, were more like they were when I'd first met him, dark and cloudy.

Rory flashed a half-smile. "Nice to meet you, Kate."

"Nice to meet you, too." After I responded, the silence returne and filled several minutes.

"Alex—" Rory stared at his hands, spinning his wedding ring.

"It's okay, Rory. You don't have to explain. I could've called you too."

"But I should have, and I'm sorry."

"Your parents still email me once a year."

"January 9th?" Rory took a long sip of his Coke.

My head swam as I took in their conversation. Ellie died in December. Alex and I talked about it in Denver. The only thing that made sense was her birthday. I'd landed at Alex's door on Ellie's birthday, and he never said a word about it.

"Yeah." Alex tapped the table.

Rory looked up. "They are trying to stay connected in their own misguided way. They don't blame you."

"Yeah, right." Alex didn't take his eyes off the table.

"It wasn't your fault, Alex. Not in the least."

"Did you hear that they closed the case?"

"No. What? When?" Rory's eyes went wide.

"A week ago. A guy from Kerrville. Long rap sheet. When they searched his place, they found her rings."

"Are they sure?"

"DNA evidence matched," DJ said.

I leaned forward and rubbed Alex's arm. He reached across and patted my hand.

Rory took notice. "I haven't heard anything about it."

"The guy is dead, so there won't be a trial. I'm sorry I didn't call you. I thought you'd hear." Alex's voice was even but not void of emotion.

Rory turned to me. "Kate, he's one of the best. He was very good to my sister." He pushed his plate to the side. "But we have another matter to discuss."

Alex draped an arm around me. "She doesn't know why they're after her."

"The name Keith Perkins didn't turn up anything. We're hoping to use your phone to set him up."

"What about Jeff and LeAnn?" I asked.

"DJ explained the situation. I can send some guys to check in on LeAnn. Is she at home?"

"No. She's at a friend's house." I scribbled an address in his notebook when he slid it across the table to me.

"The main problem is that we don't know what Keith looks like. You do."

Alex jumped out of his chair. "You don't need to know what he looks like."

"Kate, two guys may show up when we turn on your phone. If they don't have Jeff with them, from what you said, you're the person who can get Keith to tell us where he is." Rory laid his hand on mine. "Please."

"No." Alex slammed his fist on the counter. "I don't want her anywhere near them."

"She'd be protected."

I cringed. Going with Rory might be the best chance of saving Jeff, but it guaranteed that Alex would be madder than fire ants in a smashed mound. I slipped out of my chair and stood in front of him.

Green eyes pleaded with me. "Rainy, you can't. Please."

"I don't want to, but Jeff—if there's any chance to get him back safely." I buried my face in his chest, hiding the tears spilling down my face. Inconveniently, my ability to suppress them had taken a vacation.

"I'll have a team ready in the morning. I'll be back then." Rory pushed back from the table and let himself out.

"I didn't know, Alex." DJ swore under his breath. "I'm gonna leave y'all to talk." He followed Rory out the door.

Alex wrapped his arms around me and buried his face in my hair. "I gotta bolt the doors."

As he walked toward the front door, after locking the back one, someone knocked, and I tucked out of sight. Alex peeked out the window before opening it. "It's Torres." He turned the knob and stepped back, letting the door hang open.

"Sorry it took me so long. I made sure I wasn't being followed." Torres dropped our luggage onto the floor and handed Alex his phone. "I'll get your truck in the morning. Tonight, I stayed clear of it. Didn't want to arouse suspicion."

Alex nodded and walked toward the kitchen.

I hugged Torres again, grateful for all his help. "Thank you."

He didn't miss the tears streaked down my face. "What's wrong? Alex?"

Alex clenched his jaw and, after a slow inhale and exhale, explained what the FBI had asked me to do.

"She doesn't have to. They can't force her, you know." Torres dropped into a chair.

I slid a plate of cookies in front of him. "Want a Coke?"

"Nah." He stood up. "I need to run. My shift starts early. If you need anything at all, you have my number."

Torres left, and Alex bolted the door. I yanked a burnt tray of cookies from the oven, tossed the last dozen in the trash, then put away the baking supplies while he carried our bags down the hall. Once the counters were wiped down, I headed for my bedroom. The thumping on my temples was nearing the point of unbearable.

He caught my hand. "I want to move the air mattress into your room. Is that okay?"

I leaned into him. "Please, will you hold me?"

"All night." He kissed the top of my head, which pounded with the weight of the decision left to me.

I pushed off his chest. "I've got to take something for my headache." I fished acetaminophen and pajamas out of my bag and stepped into the bathroom.

When I walked back into the bedroom, the lights were out. He was already under the covers. His phone lit a path to the bed.

I snuggled next to him, resting my head above his heart. "I don't know what to do."

If I chose to help, he'd go with me, and that put him in danger. That thought alone made me sick to my stomach.

He stroked my hair. "I'll support whatever you choose."

What he wanted me to do was no secret.

I pushed up to look him in the face. "If Jeff weren't involved or if . . . if I could think of another way, I wouldn't even consider it. I know you don't want me to go."

He met my gaze. "I'm going with you."

I laid back down. Arguing with him would get me nowhere. "When did you realize it was Rory?"

"When DJ said Agent Jacobson." His lips resting on my forehead, he spoke between kisses.

"He looked stunned when he saw you."

"I knew Rory before I met Ellie. We were friends. After she died, it was easier not to see or talk to her family. But it wasn't right."

"I know it was hard for you to see him. I'm sorry."

"Don't apologize, Kate."

I leaned on his chest listening to his heartbeat, wishing there was a way to reach inside and detach the pain from his memories of Ellie.

"You need to sleep." He patted my shoulder.

In my favorite place, temporarily safe from whoever wanted to hurt me, I closed my eyes. He trailed his fingers up and down my back. I focused on the thumping inside his chest, trying to forget about whatever tomorrow might bring.

After a while, his hand stopped moving, and he started to snore. I rolled onto my side, giving him my back. Within minutes, he spooned against me and draped an arm over me. I pulled his hand to my lips and kissed his knuckles. Soft snores sounded behind me. I whispered into the darkness what I'd been almost afraid to admit to myself. "I love you, Alex."

Sleep came, but only in short fits. How had seeing Rory affected Alex's walls? Although, given our current entanglement, it seemed to be a non-issue.

Pulled out of my light sleep when Alex rolled over, I shifted closer to him and snuggled my face between his shoulder blades. Even as he slept, he reached back and patted my hip. *I've let my guard way down. This isn't good.* But it felt good—hot-chocolate-with-marshmallows-on-a-cold-night good—and I chose to enjoy it.

Nestled against his back, his warm hand on my hip, I fell asleep again. After a while, my dreams started like a movie reel. LeAnn flipped through an album, then she waved her arms, holding up a photo. Like channels being flipped, my dream changed, and Alex was in Jeff's position. He turned to look at me from the backseat of a car as Keith drove away. I cried out, and Alex was next to me. Over and over, I kissed him, thankful that he hadn't been harmed. The dream faded, and I settled into a more restful sleep.

Beth-

If your sister asks, Sticks isn't sleeping here. He's asked more than once, but I told him I just couldn't. Don't worry. I didn't explain why. He doesn't know that I know. But I can't tell you how hard it is to let him walk out that door at the end of his visits with Scooter. I want him, Beth. I want him to want me. I want him to be a daddy to my kid all the time.

But I'm wise enough to know that he doesn't want me. He wants in my bed. That's all he wants.

I can't ask him to stop coming over. Scooter would be crushed.

Remember how I waffled about letting Scooter give Sticks that mug? Well, Sticks took the mug with him. I expected him to make up some excuse about why he should keep it at our house, but he left with it. I almost wish I had a picture of his face when he opened it. He beamed.

-M

May 1986

Beth-

Just when I think life can't get any worse, Scooter asked me if Sticks and his daughter could move in so we could all be a family. I need to talk to Sticks about telling this kid the truth.

I haven't heard from Brad in a few weeks. Some days I'm hopeful that we'll work it out. Other days, divorce seems inevitable.

-M

Chapter Fourteen

January 26, 2016 – 3:33 am

Alex woke up. Unsure of what pulled him out of sleep, he listened for floor creaks or footfalls. He reached behind him, for Kate, for reassurance that she was safe. When his hand met empty air, he sat up.

She lay on the opposite edge of the bed. He gazed at her, planning how to keep her safe.

"Alex." Stress raised the pitch of her voice.

He noticed her closed eyes and erratic breathing. *She's having a nightmare.* He shifted closer and spooned against her. She settled, her breathing more even. When she rolled onto her back, he laced his fingers with hers, and she smiled, her eyes still closed. He met those upturned lips with a kiss. She snaked her arms around his neck, pulling him close.

"You're safe." She never opened her eyes, her voice far away and dreamy.

It would've been so easy to let her dream continue and enjoy whatever happened, but he'd made a promise to himself and to her.

And right now, what he'd promised her meant more than anything else.

He stroked her face and pulled her head to his chest. She nestled against him with a sigh. When her breathing relaxed into a deep rhythm, he rolled her off his arm and slipped out of bed.

He trudged down the hall. Since he wasn't sleeping, he'd paint. In the laundry room, he gathered the paint supplies, then focused on the extra room. He laid plastic sheeting on the hardwood floors before pouring paint into the tray. When everything was prepped, he started rolling color onto the walls. Thankful he had his earbuds with him, he listened to classic country tunes as the mushroom color took over the white room.

An hour later, he dropped the roller into the pan and admired his work. *Hopefully, it still looks good in the morning light.* He grabbed the angled brush, climbed the step ladder, and cut in along the ceiling.

When he got down, ready to paint along the baseboards, a song he hadn't heard in ages played in his ear. He smiled as Eddie Rabbitt sang. When the song ended, he downloaded it, to have on his phone. Once all the craziness was behind them, he wanted to play it for Kate.

The soft glow of pre-dawn light filled the room. Kate could wake at any time. He knew what he wanted to do. How to do it was the question. After a quick shower, he dressed and closed her bedroom door.

CHAPTER FIFTEEN

January 26, 2016 – 7:27 am

An alarm clock went off in my head, and sleep ended. I didn't want it to be morning. I didn't want to make a decision. Keeping my eyes closed held back the inevitable. I reached for Alex but only found cold sheets.

I sat up. "Alex?" A dread swept over me like a hot wind in summer. "Alex!"

The door swung open partway. "What's wrong?"

"I'm okay. I shouldn't have panicked."

He stood next to the bed, arms crossed. "Listen, I . . ." He sat down on the edge of the bed and grabbed my hand.

"Are you okay, Alex?"

He shook his head, his gaze fixed on the colorful quilt. "I almost just left without saying anything, but I . . ."

I inhaled sharply, his words jumbled in my head. My heart pounded in my chest like it was trying to escape. My vision blurred. I tried to pull my hand from his, but he didn't let go.

He looked at me. Confusion etched in his brow, he dropped his gaze to our hands. His red-rimmed eyes made me want to cover my ears and run from the room.

As was becoming a regular happening for us, we were interrupted by a knock. People always knocked at the wrong time.

Alex jumped up and ran down the hall, leaving me to wonder about the rest of his sentence.

I curled up in a ball but didn't shed a tear. Rory's voice drifted up the hall, and I pulled the covers over my head. *I can't face him right now.*

Minutes later, Alex sat on the bed again. "He wants to talk to you. I dug the coffee pot out of the storage unit. Come have a cup."

"Why does it smell like paint?" Avoiding the conversation about leaving was my only hope of not dissolving into a puddle.

"Sorry. I had a window open for a little while." He walked out of the room.

Reaching deep inside for whatever strength I could muster, I marched down the hall. Jeff needed my help.

Rory eyed me, gripping his disposable coffee cup a bit too tightly. "Morning."

I jumped when Alex slid his arms around my waist. "Kate, I told Rory—" His voice was only loud enough for me to hear.

I rubbed my eyes, which knocked into place pieces of my brain, and my dream made sense. "What if you had a photo?"

Rory let out an impatient exhale. "If I had a photo, I probably wouldn't be asking for help."

I met his stare. "I think I have one."

Alex spun me around. "The gift?"

I nodded.

He yanked keys out of his pocket and hurried out the door. I stayed right behind him. By the time Rory joined us outside, we had the storage unit open. I tore into the last box packed, tucked near the cleaning supplies. I pulled out the apron and draped it over my shoulder. The card, which had been wrapped up in it, fell to the ground. Alex tucked it in his pocket. I lifted the album out of the box and stepped into the sunlight flipping through pages.

"Here. This is Keith." I pointed at a skinny, bookish-looking fellow that no one would have accused of kidnapping or any other crime for that matter.

"You're sure?" Rory hovered near my shoulder.

"That's the guy." Alex pressed his hand into the small of my back.

I slipped the page out of its sleeve and tore off the picture.

"This isn't a great picture." Rory studied it.

Alex wrapped his arms around me in that protective way. "As I told you, Rory, I'll go, but Kate stays."

"No." I stepped away from him and shook my head.

Rory sighed. "You sure you can identify him?"

"I've met him. I can identify him." Alex had made up his mind.

I turned my back to Rory and, facing Alex, glared at him, willing him to listen. "You can't go."

He nodded toward the house. "Give us a sec, Rory."

I followed him inside.

He didn't stop until he reached the far end of the hall. "Kate, please. Let me do this."

"I'm worried something might happen to you. Keith sounded like he hated you last night on the trails."

"I just need to identify him. The FBI will be with me. The security guard is out front, and Torres will be bringing my truck. You'll be safe here. Please."

"You have to come back." My plea was about more than leaving to identify Keith. The conversation in my bedroom played in my head.

He planted his hands on the wall, one to my left, the other to my right. Bent low, he made sure I met his gaze. I waited for him to answer me, to say anything to reassure me. His hands dropped to my waist, and he pinned me to the wall with a kiss, as much a promise of return as a goodbye.

My heart clung to the former, but thoughts of the latter soured my stomach. "You have to come back to me."

He squeezed my hand before walking back into the kitchen. Rory waited just inside the door.

Alex stopped in the kitchen. "You have Kate's phone?"

"Yeah. Just you?" Rory glanced down the hall.

"Let's get this over with."

As the back door closed, I sank to the floor, worried and alone.

After a few minutes, I pushed up, determined to do something else to pass the time other than stare at empty walls. Genealogy research would hopefully serve as a sufficient distraction.

It wouldn't, but I could pretend.

I settled on the bed and flipped through the photo album as the laptop booted up. Staring at the faces on the page, I ached to know them, to know my family. I buried myself in research, hoping the census records, birth certificates, and marriage licenses would paint me a picture of the family I didn't know.

Every time I thought about Alex, I reached for my phone, but it wasn't there. *Please, God, bring him back to me.* A low growl of panic rooted inside me. I couldn't shake the unsettled feeling that something was very wrong. *They should be at the cabin by now.* How long would Keith and his accomplice take to show up?

I jumped from research to worry, always forcing myself back to the hunt. Worrying wouldn't solve anything or bring Alex home.

A knock pulled me out of my researching. *Must be Torres.*

I hurried down the hall and peeked through the front window before opening the door. A woman with chestnut brown hair and a friendly smile waved at me. I opened the door. Before she spoke, when we made eye contact, I recognized her. Not that we'd ever met, but I'd seen a younger version of her face in the photo album.

"Hi. My name is Beth."

"The Aunt Beth Travis mentioned?"

She gave a quick nod. "May I come in?"

I yanked open the door. "Please. I don't have much here yet. We can sit at the table. Emma bought it for this room."

"I'm guessing you've seen the album I sent over." She stepped inside.

Nodding, I motioned to the table. "I'm so excited to meet you."

Beth-

I'm going to share something with you, but I'm not sure who knows, so please keep it quiet for now. Sticks stopped by last night, late. I've never seen him so broken up. His mom got bad news from the doctor. It doesn't look good.

I'm sure it makes me a horrible person, but my first thought was to ask if Scooter could meet his grandma before it was too late. I didn't ask. The question sounded too selfish.

I'm tired of keeping this secret, but keeping it ensures that Sticks visits Scooter. If I made it public, I'm not sure what that man would do.

I still feel so connected to that little town. As much as some of the people there drive me crazy, whispering everybody's secrets all over the place, Schatzenburg is home. I miss living there, but I can't. The first time Sticks showed up to hang out with Scooter, phone lines in that town would catch fire from overuse.

I miss seeing you. Let's try and have lunch soon.

-M

September 1986

Beth-

I feel horrible for Scott and Travis. Betty always seemed like such a sweet lady, not that I really knew her well. As much as I'd like to pay my respects, I can't attend that service. Please extend my condolences to the family, as an old friend.

-M

Beth-

Scooter was at Dad's, so I stopped in to grab a quick bite at The Drugstore. When I walked in, there was a low hum of murmuring, and I wondered what had every table in the room so intent on conversation. The waitress—I can't remember her name, but I went to school with her daughter, Maggie—poured me a cup of coffee and, out of the blue, says how shocking it is that Scott ran off with his kid. I nearly spit coffee everywhere. Before I'd even ordered my sandwich, I learned Scott was gone.

Here's something no one at the diner was talking about because I haven't told anyone (besides Scooter, but I'll get to that). Sticks/Scott—I don't even know what to call him anymore—stopped by my house that afternoon, said he wanted to take Scooter out for ice cream. The daughter was there. I'd have happily sent my boy out for a fun outing, but he wasn't home. He'd gone to play with a friend.

Scott stood on that porch looking like he was about to cry. He turned to leave, then spun back around and kissed me. Holding his daughter! It caught me completely off-guard. I pushed him back and told him I couldn't do that anymore. He swore that he'd never, as long as he lived, do it again.

I didn't have any clue he was leaving, not in the slightest. I swear it. He'd have taken my baby, too. If Scooter would've been home, I'd have lost him.

I ache for Scott's poor wife, your sister. I never thought Scott capable of something like this.

I made the mistake of telling Scooter that Sticks had dropped by before I heard what happened. How do I tell Scooter his dad—that he doesn't even know is his dad—isn't coming back? Please, if Patrick hears anything at work about Scott, please tell me. I want to know he's okay. What he did is horrible, but . . . please keep me posted.

-M

Chapter Sixteen

January 26, 2016 – 11:25 pm

Alex snapped back to reality when Rory spoke his name. "I'm sorry. I missed what you asked."

"It seems serious with Kate."

"We haven't known each other long." Alex had no interest in giving Rory a behind-the-scenes account of his relationship with Kate.

"Oh. I see." He raised an eyebrow, but before he could ask any other questions, his phone rang. "Jacobson." Rory's expression remained unchanged until he spoke again. "Great news. Let me know when they get there."

"What's up?"

"Jeff's been located." Rory tossed the phone in a cup holder.

"Alive?" Alex held his breath waiting for an answer.

"Thankfully. They found him in a small town near Amarillo. Someone drugged him heavily and dropped him off at a rural hospital."

Alex reached for his phone to text Kate the news, then remembered that her phone was with them in the car. "Drugged? I guess no one knew who he was?"

"Not until he woke up today." Rory glanced over at Alex. "I have men headed that way to talk to him and see if he can give us any more info."

"Kate will be very happy to hear he's okay."

The remainder of the car ride, Alex stayed quiet. For the better part of a week, he'd thought he and Kate needed space for their bond to deepen. Thirty miles away from her, he couldn't imagine needing her more. He knew what he wanted, and neither time nor distance wouldn't change that.

As they neared the cabin, Alex's thoughts jumped back to the task at hand. He calculated the expected wait time based on where Keith might be when Kate's phone got switched back on. The thought of waiting over an hour until he showed tortured Alex. He hoped Keith and that friend camped somewhere near the cabin.

Alex looked up just as a deer broke through the tree line. "Watch out!"

Rory swerved, the brakes screeching a deafening tune. When they hit the gravel, without traction, the car refused to stop and barreled toward an ancient oak. All they could do was brace for impact.

CHAPTER SEVENTEEN

January 26, 2016 – 11:53 pm

I dropped into a chair. "You sent me the album?"

While Beth didn't look like Emma, there was a sweet temperament about her, which from what others said of my mom, they had in common.

"I did. I almost showed up at your door the minute you arrived." She carried a stack of papers and journals.

"Why didn't you?"

The stack shifted as she set it on the table, creating a small pile of disarray. "There's so much to tell you. Your world had just flipped upside down so I hesitated. Gram insisted you'd want to know."

"I do. I want to hear everything."

Beth shuffled through the stack of envelopes, papers, and albums. "I forgot one. Let me run home and get it." She tapped the top of the pile. "I'll explain all of this."

"Can't it wait? We'll look through these first."

"No. I want to start with that other one. I had it out this morning. I know right where I left it. I'll only be a few minutes."

"Okay." I ran down the hall to get the album she'd sent over. "Just let yourself back in," I called out.

Beth rushed out the back door, and I sat down at the table and waited, but rather impatiently. *I have an aunt, a family. I can't wait to tell Alex.* Of course, thoughts of him brought worry.

What if all this danger and togetherness was too much? Maybe it would end as quickly as it began. I glanced down the hall. His good-bye kiss didn't feel like an ending. *Had they made it to the cabin? Had anyone taken the bait?*

A sharp knock startled me. *Why didn't she just come back in?* I opened the front door.

The security guard stood there, eyes cast downward. "Ma'am, they asked me to get you. On the way to the cabin, there was an accident."

I hesitated. There was no reason to distrust the security guard, but without a phone, I couldn't confirm the story. "Can I use your phone?"

"I'd gladly let you, but the guy's phone died at the end of the call."

"Who called?"

"Didn't catch the name."

"Were they both hurt?"

"Maybe. I thought he said something about a fatality. I'm sorry. We got cut off, so I don't have a lot of info."

The temperature in the room dropped about 30 degrees, and I wrapped my arms around myself. "Fatality? Is Alex okay?"

"Let me take you there."

I couldn't risk never seeing Alex again, so I picked up my tennis shoes and followed the guard toward his car, swinging the front door closed behind me. "Did they say what happened?"

He started the engine and pulled away from the curb as soon as I buckled in. "Just something about seeing him one last time."

He continued to talk, but I didn't hear him. My pulse beat on my eardrums. My worst fears unfolded before me. *This can't be happening. I need more time.*

Beth-

Can we just cancel Christmas this year? I already know it isn't going to be good. Scooter keeps saying that Sticks will come back because he always gives us Christmas presents. When I told him that Sticks went away and will be gone for a long time, he said that Sticks loved him and wouldn't miss Christmas.

I can't tell him that Scott never really loved anyone. Well, except his mom, he'd have died in her place if he could have. Scott loved Scott. But I think maybe, even at eight years old, Scooter knows that because he turned around and asked why Sticks was always so nice to him.

At that, I lost it. I broke down and told Scooter the truth. I'm not sure it was the right thing to do because now he's more convinced than ever that Scott will come back and bring his little sister to visit. That's what Scooter said.

So, you can see why I'm so excited about the holidays this year. They'll be filled with all kinds of happiness. Not!

Brad hasn't called in two months. The short separation he wanted has dragged on much longer than I expected. I'd file for divorce, but that cost money I don't have. What difference does it make anyway? No one's beating down my door.

Can we just get this year over with?

-M

Beth-

Christmas was hell. My eight-year-old spent more time alone in his room crying than he did with me. One of the few things he said to me during the holiday was that he doesn't believe in Santa anymore. He thinks if Santa Claus was real, he'd have brought his daddy home for Christmas.

If Scott ever shows up at my door again, he'll wish he hadn't. All those years he hung out with this kid, only to walk away. And for what? Was he afraid his wife would get custody? I assume something must have triggered the departure. Were they planning to divorce? She had grounds ages ago.

Whatever the case, keeping his little girl in his life was more important to him than seeing his little boy. He stood on my porch and made that decision. That man is a rotten beast, and I'm left to pick up the pieces.

How did I not see this way back then?

I apologize for my wallowing. I can't even imagine what Christmas must've been like for your sister. That poor woman.

-M

CHAPTER EIGHTEEN

January 26, 2016 – 12:18 pm

Alex blinked. "Rory? You okay?"

Rory mumbled a few expletives. "I'll live. Where the hell is my phone?" He slapped at his pockets.

Alex climbed out of the car and surveyed the damage. "You're gonna need a new car, but—good news is—Bambi's dad left unscathed." Alex winced as he let out a nervous chuckle. His chest burned.

Rory stood up, holding his phone, his face red, covered in powder and scratches from the airbag. A deep gash on his wrist bled down his arm as he raised the phone to his ear. "I'm calling the team. We aren't far, right?"

"Less than half a mile from the cabin."

Alex paced while Rory talked to one of his team. Hitting the tree only delayed the return to Kate. The thought of her alone made Alex nervous; although he was sure she was safer there. The wreck only convinced him he was right about that. He tapped out a quick text to DJ telling him what happened, then dialed Torres. "Ben, hey."

"I was just going to call you. Just finished putting air back in the tires. Until those guys are caught, instead of taking the truck back to you, maybe I should park it at my place. Then they won't know you are at Kate's."

"That's good. Listen, can you do me a favor?" Alex raked his fingers through his hair.

"Everything okay? You sound rattled."

"Rory and I hit a tree. We're okay, but would you go check on Kate and tell her what happened. She doesn't have her phone, but if wind of this gets back to her, she'll worry."

"Sure you're okay? Need me to drive her to meet you at the hospital or anything?" Worry pooled in Ben's voice.

Alex glanced up as a car approached. "I'm not injured. Airbag did its job."

"I'm leaving right now. I should be at her place in forty-five minutes."

"Thanks. I appreciate it." Shaken by the accident, Alex tried to maintain his calm. "I'm not sure how I can thank you for everything you've done."

"Maybe I'll need something one day. I know who to call." Ben's keys rattled. "I'll text when I get to Kate's."

Rory waved Alex over. "Ambulance will meet us at the cabin."

"I don't need medical attention. I'm fine." Alex slid into the backseat.

"You'll get it just the same." Rory untucked his shirt and pressed the fabric to his bleeding wrist. "Not risking you, too."

The ambulance arrived a few minutes later, and Alex let the EMTs check him over. Arguing would only delay things longer. Aside from a large bruise on Alex's chest, he'd come out mostly unscathed.

Rory, on the other hand, needed stiches on his wrist and had abrasions all over his face. "Just wrap it for now. As soon as we catch these guys, I'll go get the wrist sewn up."

No one argued with him, but his team wasn't happy with his decision. The ambulance pulled away, the wrecker scheduled for later, and then everyone got into place. Finally, Rory replaced the battery and turned on Kate's phone.

Alex sat in the backseat of an unmarked sedan and waited.

Forty-five minutes later, Alex jumped when his phone buzzed in his hand. No one had come anywhere near the cabin, but they were still in place, waiting. "Hello?"

"You said Kate was here." Ben sounded concerned.

"Isn't she?"

"No one is here. The front door was unlocked when I got here."

Alex's mind raced. None of what he'd just heard made any sense. "Ask the security guard."

"There isn't any security here. The car is gone."

"Is Kate's car gone?" Alex drummed on his leg trying to think of where she might've gone.

"Her car is here, same place as the other night."

"Rory, I gotta go back. Something's wrong." Alex didn't hide his panic.

Rory nodded at Agent Jordan, the one behind the wheel, and the engine roared to life. Rory informed his team that he was leaving. After he dropped the radio, he glanced back. "What's going on?"

"I don't know. Kate's gone." Alex clenched his jaw. "I'm on my way, Ben."

"I'll text if anything changes." Ben used the same voice he used when dealing with police matters, the same one Alex had heard last week during Kate's first ordeal.

The drive back to Schatzenburg seemed three times as long as the drive out to the cabin. Jordan drove the highway like it was a race track, but Alex's worry slowed time.

"It could be serious. With Kate, I mean. We just haven't known each other long." Sharing his hopes of a future with her kept him focused on the possibility that he wasn't too late.

Rory turned in his seat and met Alex's gaze. "We'll find her."

"We don't even know who took her or why." Alex clenched his fists, struggling with the guilt of leaving her alone.

"We don't know she was taken. Maybe she left for a bit, went to visit a friend." Rory's measured tone made it clear he didn't share in Alex's alarm.

"Then the security guard should be there to tell us that."

Rory's lack of response spoke volumes. They had nothing, except an empty house and an empty street where Kate and a security guard should have been.

"I have to tell Travis." Alex's stomach clenched at the thought.

"Why? Who is he?"

"Kate's dad. She's only just come back into his life. He trusted me to watch out for her." Alex stared out the window, the lane next to him a grey blur.

"You could wait until we know more."

"No. He'll want to know." Alex dialed Travis's number.

"Travis Bentley."

"Hi. It's Alex." He took a deep breath. "I think someone took Kate. I'm headed back to her place now."

A long silence heaped guilt on Alex.

"I'm so sorry, sir. I'd never have left her if I thought for a second she wouldn't be safe. Security was parked out front." Alex's relationship with Travis always felt off kilter, as if each was in the other's way. Alex had promised her dad she'd be safe. "Did you ever hear anything back about Justin?"

Travis paused several seconds before answering. "He's out of town."

"Could he have done this?"

"I'll meet you at Kate's." Travis ended the call.

Beth-

How's your sister? I think about her a lot. I sometimes have nightmares that I come home and find a note from Scooter saying that he went for ice cream with Sticks. Your sister can't wake up from her nightmare. I feel awful for her.

Scooter still isn't handling it well. I keep hoping that tomorrow will be better, but it's only getting worse. He's stopped visiting with friends. If he's not in school, he's in his room. Saturday I'm taking him out to Dad's to see the new puppy. Maybe that'll bring out a smile in Scooter. I'm hoping he won't fight me too hard about leaving the house.

How are you? Will you be around Saturday? If so, I may stop by.

-M

May 1987

Beth –

Scooter is getting harder to live with. He's pulled away from almost everything, but I asked him, begged really, to please play baseball one more season. I promised that if he didn't like it, after the season he could quit for good. He agreed. He's so good at it. I think he has a real possibility of going somewhere with his talent.

But I think my attempt to distract him from Sticks with baseball backfired. After the first game, we got home, and Scooter shut himself in his room. He didn't even want dinner. Baseball made him miss Scott more than before.

There was one tiny ray of sunshine. Brad showed up to Scooter's first game. Afterward, he came to the house. I was glad for the shoul-

171

der to cry on, but I'm not sure there's anything left of our marriage to salvage. He didn't even ask to stay the night.

-M

CHAPTER NINETEEN

Jan 26, 2016 – 1:30 pm

Leaning forward, I stared out the car window. "Where are we going? How long until we get there?" Fear of losing Alex gnawed at my insides. *An accident? Fatality?* I didn't want that for Rory, but I couldn't bear the thought that it might be Alex.

"We'll be there soon." The guard looked more like a banker delivering bad news than a security guard, not that I had any clue what a security guard should look like.

I glanced at him, my reflection staring back from his reflective lenses. The sunglasses set off alarm bells, but worry muddled my thoughts. I peered out the window trying to figure out where we were headed, but the landscape of dry grasses, juniper trees, and scrub oaks looked like a looping video feed.

He turned onto a narrow two-lane road. The car bumped along the weather-worn road, and he slowed to a crawl.

"Please hurry. I need to see him." If I'd had my phone, I could have at least been talking to Alex during the drive. "Why didn't they take him to a hospital?"

"He's important to you?"

I nodded. Opening my mouth to answer that question only invited sobs I'd so far managed to control. I held back tears, but the longer it took to get to Alex, the prospect of losing it became more likely.

The guard turned down a driveway. A nagging familiarity got brushed aside as the car approached the house. The farmhouse sat far back from the road, pastures all around it, with a barn near the edge of the property.

"They're here?" I looked around for any sign of Rory's car.

"Trying to keep him comfortable." He eased to a stop near the back door.

Then Alex is still alive. That means . . . Rory's poor parents.

As soon as the car stopped, I jumped out and ran to the door. Pounding on it, I yelled, "Alex!"

The guard hurried up next to me. "Go on in."

The back door opened into a kitchen. I rushed in calling out, "Alex." When I ran into the empty den, dread washed over me.

It's a trap.

I whipped around. Distracted by the thought that something had happened to Alex, intent on seeing him one more time, I'd let my guard down and raced headlong into danger. *Stupid.*

The guard leaned against the doorframe, a smug grin plastered on his face. "Good news is—as far as I know—your guy isn't hurt. Though I imagine he'll be all weepy and torn up inside when he finds out you're gone."

I glanced around scouring the room for an exit plan. "Why?"

"Sit down." He pointed to a wooden chair in front of the sofa. "And don't look so horrified. It's just a friendly family chat . . . for now."

Family?

I perched on the edge of the chair. "You're too young to be Justin."

"I have no idea who he is, but if you have more people after you, they'll have to get in line. Or, hmm, maybe I can line up everyone that wants something from you and charge admission."

"What are you going to do to me?"

"Stay put. I won't be but a second."

When he disappeared around the corner, I scanned the room looking for a way out. A single door on the far wall offered a glimmer of hope. I raced over to it. The cold knob wouldn't turn. I wrestled with the bolt, but it didn't move.

"Tsk, tsk, tsk." He laid a hand on my shoulder. "That hasn't been opened in years. Probably stuck."

He nodded toward the chair, and I returned to the seat. Given his size—bigger than me—I had little chance of succeeding if I tried to tackle him and run. I folded my hands in my lap, my legs pinched together at the knees.

He dangled a length of rope in front of me. "Guess I'll need this. Put your hands behind the chair."

"Please, don't." I blinked, determined not to let him see me cry.

He grabbed my wrists and stopped. He ran his finger along the remaining marks from my recent rope burns, a not-fully-healed reminder of being kidnapped less than three weeks before. "Oh. You were tied up not long ago. You and Alex playing games?" His head cocked to one side, he squatted in front of me. "No. This looks like it hurt. Maybe I wasn't the first in line. Damn. Second place. Again."

Second place?

I chewed my lip, retreating into my inner ivory tower. I didn't even have hope that my prince would find me. Even if Alex could read my mind, there was little chance he'd know where to look. I didn't know where I was or who'd kidnapped me. There wasn't any way Alex would figure it out.

"Just to show what kind of a guy I am, I'll make a compromise." The man wrapped the rope around my wrists as they lay in my lap. "I won't pull them behind you."

I froze when he yanked out a pocket knife. I held my breath as he moved it closer to my hands. When he got close, he pulled back, amused at my fear. After toying with me for several minutes—laying the blade against my wrist, touching the tip to the palm of my hand, then flipping it closed—he switched it open right in front of my nose. A quick slice and the extra rope fell away.

He sat back on his heels, that stupid smirk curling his lips, and rested his hands on my knees. "I can't expect you to just stay in the chair."

I focused on the gun dangling in its holster. "I'll stay put." *Until I find a way out.*

"Forgive me if I'm not ready to take your word for it." He forced my knees apart.

"No." My voice came out barely audible. I squirmed trying to pull them back together. "Don't do that."

"That's not why I brought you here. Relax." He tied my leg to the chair, then repeated the process with the other leg. "Although, Keith might feel differently."

I whipped my head back and forth expecting my neighbor to jump out any minute. My anxiety only humored my kidnapper.

"He tried to break into your apartment. Wanted to talk to you without your bodyguard around. Did you know that?"

I shook my head, nausea tying my stomach in knots.

"He was most unhappy when I mentioned that your friend was staying in your apartment." The fake guard's low chuckle sent shivers clawing up my spine.

He had to be a fake guard, but that made me wonder what had happened to the real security guard.

A hand-stitched *Home Sweet Home* sampler hung on the opposite wall. I focused my attention on the shape of each letter, the spacing.

"Poor Keith was disappointed in you. Didn't think you were that kind of girl."

"You were there?" I stared at the floor when the man shifted in front of me.

"Look at me." He pulled on a ball cap and sunglasses, then held his hand over his lower face.

I gasped. *Why didn't I recognize his voice when he came to the door?*

"I can't grow back the beard in an instant, so you'll have to use your imagination."

"Keith's friend. And you called me."

"Very good. Didn't think you'd catch that one."

"How did you get my number?"

The man flashed a twisted smile. "Truth is, Keith and I aren't friends. I met him when I stopped him from breaking into your place. He helped me after that." He patted my leg. "He can't pick a lock to save his life. When I saw what he was doing, I hurried up the stairs and warned him that your guy was in the apartment. He didn't believe me at first."

"He helped you kidnap Jeff?" I had trouble believing that my neighbor of two years could have done what he was being accused of. Then I remembered my unease that day I packed and cleaned.

"I needed help, and Keith agreed to do that if I didn't call the police or rat him out to your what's-his-name. Granted, he didn't know about the kidnapping when he said he'd help. That freaked him out a bit." The man rested his arms on my knees.

My chest ached. I wanted him to stop touching me, but nothing was going my way. The story kept getting worse. *If I can make it to the kitchen door . . .* How would I make that happen?

He slowly unlaced my shoes. "In case you do manage to get out of the house, you won't get far out there without these."

Don't cry. Stay calm. Helpless to prevent him from removing my shoes, I sat rigidly. "You broke into Alex's cabin?"

"Thought you'd be shacked up there with him. Keith went a little crazy making a mess, expressing his anger. I let him have his tantrum, but didn't let him break anything of real importance." He wanted praise for the limits he put on Keith. "You had no clue he was so smitten. Did you?"

I studied the room. *There has to be a way out of this.* I was new to the idea of extended family, but I was pretty sure family reunions didn't include being tied to a chair.

"Answer me." He threw my shoe across the room, grabbed my shoulders, and got nose to nose with me. His breath hot, his eyes red, he took issue with my silence. Through gritted teeth, his words escaped several decibels louder. "Don't ignore me."

"I didn't know." I maintained a calm, measured tone, refusing to let him see me rattled. Curtains drawn, the sunlight peeked around the edges and lit the small den. At least I had a connection to the outside world, could watch time pass with the sun. "How did you find the cabin?"

He spun me around so I faced the couch and dropped down in front of me. A satisfied smirk creased his face. "Keith felt just awful that he wasn't able to return your favorite book before you left."

"What book?"

"Yeah, I didn't think it would work either, but properly motivated, Keith makes a pretty good actor." The sneer widened on my abductor's face. "He talked to the lady in the office, and she gave him your forwarding address."

"Properly motivated?"

"I told him your bodyguard was forcing you to move away and convinced him that if we had the address, we could rescue you."

"Where is he?"

"If he was smart, he'd be well on his way back to Denver." He slipped off my other tennis shoe. "But he ain't smart. He became more a hindrance than a help, and it ended our partnership. Poor, misguided fool."

I tried to stifle my gasp, but his smirk told me he'd caught it.

He brushed hairs out of my face. "You don't remember me, do you? And I don't mean from Denver. Before that."

The playing field tilted in his favor. I had no clue who he was or why he'd kidnapped me. "Is Jeff okay?"

"Pretty sure. It's been a while since I've used, so hopefully I didn't give him too much, but we left him at a hospital."

"Hospital? What did you give him?"

My captor sat staring at me. "Listen to you, all concerned about Jeff when you are the one tied up. Perfect Claire. Aren't you even curious how I found you at the restaurant?"

Claire? Crap! Who is this? And why has he brought me here? I snapped back to the conversation, not wanting to delay my answer.

"My phone." I focused on the sampler, determined to find a way out of this just like I had the smelly closet. *Home.* Yanked away after only a nibble at a happy-ever-after, I needed sparkly red shoes.

"But you don't know *how,* do you? When you weren't at the cabin, I was a tad upset. Then I found that app. So glad you wanted your BFF to be able to find you." He held up a familiar jeweled case. "The worried texts you kept sending were sweet. Maybe when I'm finished, I'll leave the phone so she can see how much you cared." He pushed off the sofa. "Maybe I should send your Alex a message. He has your phone, I'm guessing."

That explained why LeAnn hadn't replied to my texts. *Why didn't anyone mention her phone was missing?*

He spun the chair back around again and paraded in front of it. The phone came to life as he pressed the power button. He opened a new message and tapped furiously. Shwoop. The message whisked through the air across the miles to my phone. He kept typing. After two more messages, he waved the phone in front of my face before swiping to power it off.

I made a mental note to delete that app when this was all over, but I resisted the urge to ask about what he'd sent. Based on the childish snickers, whatever he texted would send Alex reeling. *At least they'll know I'm missing and that he has LeAnn's phone.*

He jumped when someone knocked at the door. "Don't make a sound." To ensure I complied, he tied a rag around my mouth.

The knocking didn't stop.

"Jonathon?" A female voice called from outside the door.

Jonathon? Racing through names in the family tree and photos in the album, I came up empty. The name wasn't familiar. I had no clue who he was, but hope sprang up because I recognized the woman's voice.

He mumbled and walked out of the den. I strained against the ropes thinking my last chance at a rescue stood talking to Jonathon in the kitchen. *If I can just get loose . . .*

She knew him well, it seemed. "Hey. I got your message. When's your mom getting back from Chrissy's?"

He turned into a different person, warm and charming. "She'll be back in a few days. You didn't have to come over. I just wanted to chat with you about, you know."

Beth's tone changed with her next question. "You heard the news?"

The news? This was about me. I silently rooted for her to figure out that something was wrong.

"Yeah. Mom always said I could talk to you about the family secret. Want some coffee?" The door scraped against the floor. Footsteps followed.

"Sure. Sorry about your da—."

Thud.

I waited. The quiet made me uneasy. *What happened?* My question was answered as Jonathon dragged Beth into the den. He didn't even look at me as he bound her hands and feet. She lay on her side, twisted in an unnatural way.

He stepped behind me, and I winced when he pulled my hair.

"Sorry." He removed the gag from my mouth.

The apology bewildered me. It gave me a glint of hope that maybe there was someone softer inside the angry, guileful guy that relished seeing my fear.

"Why are you doing this?" I let my curiosity override my better judgment. Engaging him in conversation didn't help me.

"Have you ever wanted something so badly and waited so long only to find out it would never come?" The man stared at me.

The tears in his blue eyes surprised me. Maybe it did help. If I got him talking, could I convince him not to hurt me?

"What did you want?"

"He's never coming back." He rested his forehead against my arm. "I blame you."

I gulped down fear and stared at the floor. "Who is never coming back?"

"My original plan has gone all to hell. I don't much feel like talking right now." He stood and patted my head. "Don't go anywhere." He disappeared into the kitchen, then the back door opened and closed.

Beth-

Seems like every time I cross the city limits sign and go into Schatzenburg, I learn something new. This time it was from the clerk at the post office. Please, tell me what I heard isn't true.

That little girl isn't even his daughter? There's too much irony to know where to start. While I was sleeping with Scott, his wife was sleeping with his brother. Serves Scott right.

I hear your sister and Travis are together now. Not surprising. I'm glad she's not suffering alone. At least I still have my little boy, who knows nothing about Claire not being his sister. And I hope he never finds out.

Brad moved to upstate New York. He said it was temporary, and that he still wanted to work things out when he got back. I told him I'd still be here. Like I have any place to go.

-M

❧～❧

Beth-

Sorry I haven't written. I keep meaning to write. I don't know why I don't. I'm sorry. Things are about the same here. There's nothing new happening. I'm still alone, and Scooter is still mad, a little angrier if that's possible.

My sweet little boy has turned into someone I hardly recognize. He's angry at Scott but takes it out on me. Who else can he blame? Betrayed by the man he's supposed to keep a secret—what a sad story for my boy.

You'd let me know if you'd heard from Scott, right? For all his warts, I miss him. Makes me sound stupid, doesn't it?

-M

Chapter Twenty

January 26, 2016 – 2:03 pm

Alex clenched and opened his fists, willing the car to go faster. Why had he left her alone? Blinded by the desire to protect her, he hadn't given the situation enough thought. He'd put too much trust in that security guard.

Kate's phone beeped a flurry of notifications, and Alex picked it up off the center console before Rory could grab it.

Alex swallowed back the bile rising in his throat. "Dammit."

Three texts, all from LeAnn's phone filled the screen: *You shouldn't have left her alone.*

All I had to do was tell her Alex needed her, and she voluntarily came with me.

She's still alive, for now.

Alex's fingers hovered over the screen, battling the urge to respond. Who'd sent them? His gut said it wasn't Keith. Who was the other man with him at the restaurant that night?

Rory cast him a wary look. "What?"

"They've got Kate. Texts came from LeAnn's phone. He's had it this whole time." Alex read Rory the texts.

"Don't reply." He glanced at the driver, and the car sped up.

"If he hurts her . . ." Alex stared at the phone in his hand.

"Do *not* finish that sentence. I'm on a case. You threatening a suspect will only make life more complicated for both of us." Rory dropped his voice to a whisper. "But off the record . . . you won't be alone."

Alex prayed he'd wouldn't have to cash in that chip.

Rory pressed a button on his phone and after half a ring cut off the "hello" at the other end. "Walters, I need a location on a phone." He motioned to Alex, who called out LeAnn's phone number.

The line was quiet except for the sound of tapping on a keyboard. Agent Jordan, who'd barely spoken, kept his eyes on the road, speeding down the county road toward Schatzenburg. "Almost there."

"Sorry, sir. It doesn't appear to be on. I'll keep scanning. As soon as I have a location, I'll let you know." Walters repeated the number before ending the call.

Alex jumped out of the car as soon as they pulled along the curb. Ben met him on the front porch. "Both the front and back doors were unlocked when I got here."

"Not a good sign." Alex swallowed down panic.

"Maybe if we talk to the neighbors . . . Someone might've seen her." Rory pointed down the street.

"Her purse is inside." Ben kicked at the porch rail. "If only I'd gotten here sooner. I'm sorry."

Rory called his team as he walked down the street to the next house, Agent Jordan right beside him.

"It's not your fault." Alex walked across the yard to the neighbor's place. While he and Ben made their way toward the door, Alex told Ben about the texts that popped up on Kate's phone. "I should never have left her."

After thirty minutes of going door to door, discouragement

weighed heavily on them. No one had seen Kate or reported anyone strange hanging around town. At Gram's, Alex ran up to the door, and Ben hurried down the block to catch Rory.

Gram gave a promising tidbit. "Talk to Beth. I'm not supposed to say much. She wanted to tell Kate herself, and I saw Beth walking that way earlier."

"Where does Beth live?"

"Next street over. White rock house with blue trim, ranch-style."

Alex hugged Gram. "Thanks."

She didn't let go of him. "Travis know?"

"He's on his way."

She kept hold of his hand as he turned away. "You'll find her."

"I have to." Alex didn't dare look back before rushing off to meet up with Ben and Rory. He filled them in on what Gram had told him.

DJ pulled up and jumped out. "Jacobson called me. What can I do?"

"I need to talk to Beth."

"Maddox?"

Alex filed the name away, connecting the dots. "Next street over?"

"Yep. Get in." DJ floored it as soon as the door closed and had him at his destination in under a minute.

Alex knocked and waited. After a minute, he rang the bell. The knob jiggled and a familiar face opened the door.

Libby, the young waitress working at The Drugstore when they were there the first time, cocked her head in surprise. "I remember *you*. Where's your friend?"

"I need to speak with Beth. It's urgent."

"Mom's not here. I don't know where she is."

"Can you call her?"

"I have. It just rolls to voicemail." Libby shrugged, not seeming the least bit concerned. "Her phone probably died. She forgets to charge it all the time. I'm sure she'll be back after while."

Alex left her standing at the open door, cut through yards, and ran back to the house. He didn't take the time to get into the truck. Back at Kate's, room by room, he searched for any clue, anything out of place. From all appearances, Kate had walked out of the house of her own accord just like the text stated. There were no signs of a struggle that indicated she was taken by force. He scanned the floors. No blood.

He dropped into a chair at the dining room table. Forehead pressed to the tabletop, he imagined her next to him. *Where are you, Kate?* What had he missed? Tension built until it exploded as restlessness. He jumped up and paced up and down the hall.

Ben, DJ, and Rory pow-wowed on the porch, discussing what to do in hushed whispers.

Travis rushed in the back door. "Alex?"

Alex met him at the end of the hall.

"Any news?" The color gone from Travis's face, he looked like he might be sick at any moment.

"No. Gram sent me to Beth, but she's not there and not answering her phone." Alex stood in front of Travis, intensity clipping his words. "Would she hurt Kate?"

"Absolutely not. Beth is Emma's sister." Travis turned around, fingers laced together behind his head. When he reached the table, he pushed the stack of journals and papers to the side. "She has so much she wanted to tell Kate."

"What about Justin? I know he's Kate's uncle. We figured that out. But would he do this?"

"I don't think so. I don't know. I'll get Pat to contact him again."

"Pat?"

"Captain Maddox, Beth's husband."

Alex reached for the stack of papers and journals on the table. "What are these?" He flipped through the pages of the journal on top. "These weren't here when I left."

"They were here when I got here."

"What if Kate and Beth's disappearance has something to do with this?" Alex sat down and shuffled through the pile.

"We don't know for sure Beth is missing."

"I have to *do* something." Alex jumped up, and the chair skidded backward. "I feel so helpless."

"I know." Travis focused on the table. "I'm trying not to punch a hole in her wall."

Beth-

Brad showed up at my door today, flowers in hand, begging me to take him back. It's been two years, two long and difficult years. I said yes. I'm so tired of trying to do it all on my own.

I buried what he said about wanting his own kids and am trusting that he came back for Scooter as much as for me. I hope that's the case. Please let that be the case. Scooter needs that right now.

I want to be excited, but I've been disappointed so many times, I'm afraid excitement is just a curse. I'll try to be better about writing more often.

-M

❧

January 1989

Beth-

I wasn't foolish enough to believe having Brad back would fixed everything, but I had hoped it would improve with a man around again. I was wrong. Nothing has changed with Scooter.

The school counselor called. I explained that a good family friend moved away, and she gave suggestions about what to try. I feel like a failure as a mom. The school has more ideas about what to do than I do. Scooter's living in a cage of anger, and I don't have the key.

Brad has been wonderful. He really tries with Scooter. Hopefully, with a little more time, things will be better.

Dad says those boys of yours are growing like weeds. I'll try to get by there soon to see you.

-M

Chapter Twenty-one

January 26, 2016 – 2:45 pm

I flexed my wrists, trying to loosen the rope. Beth lay injured next to me, which made escaping way more complicated. Even if I managed to untie myself, I couldn't drag her with me but neither could I leave her behind.

I closed my eyes, remembering the road at the end of the driveway. One of the houses I'd committed to memory that first day Alex and I drove into town flashed in my head. *Just outside of town. I'm so close.*

My eyes squeezed shut, I pictured Alex and Travis combing the streets for me. *Will they come this far?* My heart ached thinking about their despair. Checking that Jonathon wasn't around, I allowed myself the tears I'd dammed up. Hope that I'd make it out unscathed withered with every teardrop.

When Beth had been still so long I feared he might have done more than hurt her, I nudged her with my toe, praying she'd wake up. *Please don't be dead.*

Her eyes flickered open. "What—?"

I leaned down as far as I could. "You okay?"

She rolled over and blinked at me. "Kate?"

"It's me."

"How'd you get here?" She squeezed her eyes closed.

"Stupidity. I don't want to talk about it." My gaze swept toward the doorway. "I think he left, but I'm not sure."

"What did he say?" She shifted around the floor, trying to sit up.

"He blames me."

"I had no idea."

"Who is he? Why is he calling me Claire?" My life went from being turned upside down to spinning like it was on a gyroscope, and I had no clue why. "What has him mad enough to kidnap me?"

Beth shuffled again, then moaned. "Sitting up hurts." She scooted until she rested against the sofa. "The light hurts."

"Why did you come here?" If she knew where to find me, hopefully, someone else did too.

Beth was quiet.

"Beth?" My voice sounded shrill, strained by the panic coursing through me.

"I got back to your place, and you were gone. I didn't know what to think. I went home, figuring I'd stop by again later."

"That doesn't explain how you found me so quickly."

"I had a message from Jonathon. He wanted to talk to me."

"Who is he?"

She sighed. "Perhaps I should start at the beginning."

"You have a captive audience."

"You even sound a little like her."

I didn't answer. Thinking about the mom I couldn't remember only brought me closer to tears, but I desperately struggled to keep them at bay.

"Give me a few minutes. My head hurts." Beth turned away and slouched even more.

"Don't go to sleep. You can't. Talk to me."

"I went to college in Austin. My roommate, Marla, was a sweet girl. She grew up here in Schatzenburg."

"How does this relate?"

"Emma came to visit me one summer. Our parents were sometimes hard to live with, and Patrick suggested I invite Emma to stay with us until she found her own place." Beth leaned forward, and blood was visible on the back of her head. "Not many husbands would do that, you know."

I worried that her rambling was evidence of head trauma so I backed off trying to get her to the point, hoping she'd wander that direction if she kept talking. "Do your parents live near here?"

"They're not alive anymore. They lived in a small town not far from Kerrville. Close enough to know some of Schatzenburg's gossip."

"Who's Patrick?"

"He sauntered up to me at a dance hall one night. A wiry cowboy. I didn't stand a chance. I fell hard that first night but didn't let him know. Mystery and the chase, and all that. But he knew. After that first dance, we saw each other all the time. On nights he didn't come over to study, he'd call, sometimes just to say goodnight."

"So Patrick is your husband?"

Beth tilted her head back again the couch, a faraway smile on her lips. "My Captain Maddox."

"Who is Jonathon?"

Beth acted like she hadn't even heard me. "You know how it is, at first you don't know how long something will last. Days turned into weeks, and he still came around. When our six-month anniversary came around, we started talking marriage. That's a big deal for a college sophomore and freshman. But we waited to walk the aisle 'til after his graduation."

"Beth? Can you get back to who this guy is?" I couldn't wait for her disjointed stories to circle around to what I needed to know.

"Sorry. That summer Emma met the Bentley boys. Funny to call them boys. They were both out of college by then. They had to have been. Emma was. No one knew she was my sister. It's not like we look alike or wore nametags. At first, I was happy about it, the Bentley boys, I mean. Travis and Emma seemed to really hit it off. Scott was never far away." Beth closed her eyes.

"You didn't like Scott?" When my redirecting didn't work, I reverted to asking whatever question popped in my head to just keep her talking.

Her eyelids snapped open. "My parents demanded that she stop spending time with *those Bentley boys.* Bad stock, they called them."

"Why?"

"Marla's parents said the same thing, but no one ever said why. Anyway, that's not part of this story." She turned away from me and stopped talking.

I wrestled with my rope, trying to free my hands so I could reach for her. "Come on, Beth. Stay awake."

"They wouldn't say. Emma hated being told what to do. I often wonder if that's part of the reason she finally said yes to Scott." Beth rubbed away tears with her bound fists. "They cut her out of their lives. Didn't attend the wedding. Threatened that if I had contact with her, they'd cut me off, too."

"You didn't have contact with her? Your sister? In the same small town?" Hurling accusations at an injured woman, who was barely coherent, was not my most compassionate move, but the pain and betrayal I imagined Emma felt weighed heavy on me.

"Poor Marla met her boy the same night. We'd begged her to come with us. To this day, I feel culpable in what happened. I mean, I didn't shove her into bed with him, but if they hadn't met, none of this would've happened."

I tried separating the names and storylines, hoping to string together a narrative that made sense. "What does Marla have to do with this Jonathon guy?"

"I snuck around to see Emma. To this day, I regret not standing up there as her matron of honor. Maybe I don't. I didn't want Emma to get married, not to Scott. I regret a lot of things."

Gram didn't like Scott for Emma, Beth didn't like Scott for Emma. Why did Emma marry Scott? Was she blind to his faults? *Everyone says I'm so much like my mother.*

"Why does Jonathon blame me?"

"Poor Marla raised her little boy all by herself. When she lived in Austin, my friends and I helped out as much as we could."

"Who?"

Letting her be quiet wasn't an option, but listening to her tell disconnected stories added to my stress.

"I was wrong, Kate. Forgive me." Beth hung her head. "The last year of her life, Emma and I saw each other often, nearly every day. She begged me not to tell our parents she was dying. I granted her that."

"What did they say after she died?"

"They were heartbroken. Consumed with regret. They both died within a few months, but they tried to make amends in the only way they could think of."

I made an awful mistake and looked down at her. Grief showed in the lines of her face. Tears washed over mine.

"They left you everything as a tribute to Emma's legacy. Held it in trust until you were found. My brother, suffice it to say, wasn't happy about it."

"Justin." Some of the pieces started to fit together.

"He'll probably call you trying to get you to split the inheritance with him. He doesn't need it, so don't do it."

Outside the sun faded, changing the room into a cage of shadows. I had to keep Beth alive through the night. Without a clue about what Jonathon was up to, I pushed Beth to give me more information. "You still haven't explained who this man is."

"I had so much I wanted to tell you." Beth sighed. "I'm sorry. This headache makes it so hard, but I'm getting to it."

I just hoped we'd both live long enough to get to the end of her story.

Beth-

I miscarried again, but Brad didn't leave me this time. He's not perfect, but he's mine.

As if dealing with losing another baby wasn't enough, Scooter got picked up for damaging someone's truck. He took a crowbar to someone's pickup! He won't say why. No explanation. But I'm afraid I know why, and the reason scares me. The truck looked just like Scott's.

He hasn't mentioned Scott in ages, not a whisper. I wasn't so delusional as to think he'd forgotten about him. But why now? After so long?

-M

March 1990

Beth-

The hard part about keeping secrets is sometimes you forget who you've told what to and who still doesn't know. I think I discovered why Scooter was so upset with Scott.

Dad doesn't know who Scooter's dad is. I've been very careful about that. I almost spit out my ice tea when Dad started talking about Scott and Travis the other day and recounted an interesting story.

He and Scooter had lunch at The Drugstore a few weeks back. A couple at the next table talked about the Bentleys. Dad learned the rumor for the first time. I hadn't told him because—never mind the why—I hadn't told him.

Anyway, Dad tells me everything the couple said at the next table, and Scooter heard it all. He knows that Scott left with someone else's kid.

I haven't talked to Scooter about it. I'll just see if he brings it up. Poor kid.

-M

❧～❧

May 1990

Beth-

Please pray. I'm expecting again. I haven't told anyone else.

-M

❧～❧

August 1990

Beth-

The more time that passes, the more excited I get. Brad wears a smile constantly. I think I might be falling in love with my husband. (You do burn these letters, right?)

Scooter isn't happy about it, but he isn't happy about much. I'm not sure he cares what happens to the rest of us. I'm struggling with that. He looks like me, except for those blue eyes, those Bentley blue eyes. Sometimes he looks at me, and it isn't my kid that I see. It's Scott. Scooter's turning out to be like his dad, thinking only of himself, and I can't change it.

-M

February 1991

Beth-

A baby girl! Chrissy arrived healthy and beautiful. Brad is over the moon. Hopefully, I can get Scooter to look at her, maybe even hold her. He refused to come up to the hospital.

But now is the time to be happy.

I heard about Patrick's promotion. You must be so proud of him.

-M

November 1991

Beth-

I forgot how much work it was taking care of a baby! Brad is such a great dad. He gets up with her at night, changes her diaper, and gets her back to sleep. If I ignore the fact that my teen is perpetually grumpy, I'm living a fairy tale.

But every fairy tale has a dark twist. There's something I need to tell you, but promise that you will not share it with anyone. Cleaning out one of the closets, making more room for baby stuff, I stumbled on one of Scooter's notebooks. He'd written *Death to baby sister.* I don't know when he wrote it. There was a drawing next to it that I cannot bring myself to describe. It was horrid.

The crib got moved into my room. I gave Brad some fake excuse about why I wanted her in the master bedroom with us. I'm worried for my baby girl.

When I handed the notebook to Scooter, I didn't say anything. He looked at it, laughed, and asked me where I'd found it. He said he drew it a long time ago. Why lie about something like that?

I didn't show it to Brad. I probably should have, but I didn't want him thinking Scooter was a horrible kid. He's not. He's just angry, and I hope he grows out of it.

-M

Chapter Twenty-two

January 26, 2016 – 5:48 pm

Alex drummed his fingers on the counter as a pot of coffee brewed. Waiting for information from Rory and DJ left him antsy. Hoping a clue to Kate's disappearance lay buried in the pile of letters and journals, he'd poured over them. Carrying two cups to the table, Alex shook his head. "Poor Kate. Her family was a mess."

Travis gave a humorless chuckle. "Indeed."

"No offense." Alex set a mug of coffee in front of Travis.

"None taken." Though clearly stressed, Travis hadn't lashed out or laid a guilt trip on Alex.

He felt enough guilt on his own, but wallowing in it wouldn't help find Kate. "Let's see what else is in this pile."

The sound of shuffling papers filled the otherwise quiet house. Rory and DJ had both left, working the kidnapping through law enforcement channels. Ben had been called away on a police matter and reluctantly left, promising to check in later.

Becca texted: *Any news?*

Alex responded: *Not yet.*

A stack of envelopes rubber-banded together caught his attention. The elastic band snapped as soon as he touched it. He opened the top envelope. The letter to Beth said nothing that aided in finding Kate, but something in the secrets and scandal hinted at in the letter tugged at Alex.

He handed the letter to Travis. "Read this."

"What do these have to do with anything? Beth's roommate got pregnant and dropped out of college. So what?"

"I'm grasping at straws. Whoever brought them over—I'm guessing it was Beth—wanted Kate to see these. Why? I'm hoping there's a connection."

"So, who is M?"

Alex shrugged. "All of them are signed that way."

After reading through the letters, they laid them out on the dining room table, arranging them in chronological order. Working from the beginning, they skimmed through each one again.

"Girl gets pregnant . . ." Alex stepped through the life story etched out in the letters. "When the kid is two, the dad shows up again, but they only call him a friend."

Travis shook his head. "He's a piece of work."

"A piece of something else, I'd say." Alex swallowed down a swig of coffee before continuing. "There are gaps between some of these. Maybe some letters are missing."

Travis riffled through the pile of papers. "Don't see any others."

"Guy stays with her for a summer, but goes back to his wife." Alex paused, rereading to be sure he hadn't made a mistake. He scanned the next several letters. "Then the guy up and leaves, taking his daughter with him."

Travis grunted like he'd been punched in the gut. "Scott."

"Says that he stopped by to take the kid for ice cream, but he wasn't home."

"I had no idea he had any other kids."

Alex raked his fingers through his hair. "Scott left a kid behind when he took off?"

"This is shocking, but is there anything here that helps us now?" Hands laced behind his head, Travis paced.

For the next couple hours, Alex poured over the remaining letters, praying for a lead. "In these letters, I see a heartbroken woman and an angry, angry kid." He glanced at his phone when it buzzed.

Ben texted asking for an update. After a quick reply, Alex ran down the hall. He picked up Kate's laptop and hurried back to the table.

"Look at this." He shoved a letter toward Travis and pointed at the sentence he wanted him to read. "Here."

"Death to baby sister?"

"What if that wasn't about his little sister? What if he meant Claire?"

"That was *years* ago. Besides, what are you going to search?"

"If there is a kid, there's a paper trail."

"Okay?"

"Angry kids sometimes grow up to be angry adults. What if he never got over it? What if he saw Claire on the news?"

"How do we find him? I have no idea who it might be."

"I watched Kate and learned a thing or two." Alex opened a browser window and navigated to a genealogy search site. "What do we know?"

Travis scanned the letters. "The mom calls him Scooter."

"Not helpful. What else?" Alex scribbled on the back of a receipt.

Travis read through the first letter again. "The kid is older than Kate. Born—let me see—1978."

Travis and Alex got along more comfortably without Kate around. Both wanting her attention—for different reasons—they were in each other's way when she was with them.

Alex typed in the birth year and started a search. "I wonder if Scott was listed as the father."

Travis shrugged. "Wait, yes. She says something about the clerk knowing the father's name. It must be on the birth certificate. And the mother knew this town, lived here at one time, based on what she wrote."

"This is where you and Scott grew up?"

Travis nodded. "I rarely gave Scott a moment's thought until he married Emma. After that, I was jealous of my brother. That devolved into hate when he stole away with my daughter."

"We have to stay focused."

"Hating him was something to do. He's dead. How can I hate a dead man?" Travis stared down the empty hall, looking back in time.

"Please." Alex tapped his arm. "We'll find her."

"I carried her down that hall the day he took her. She kissed Emma before she disappeared through the back door." Travis covered his face, holding the floodgates in place.

"Please, Travis. I'm barely hanging on. If you lose it, I won't be far behind. I need to find her."

They both started when a knock sounded.

Alex jumped up and pulled open the door. A man about Travis's age, with his hands in his pockets, gave a quick nod.

"Pat? Any word from Beth?" Travis waved him in. "Alex, this is Pat Maddox, Beth's husband."

After shaking Alex's hand, Pat stuck his hands back in his pockets. "I was hoping y'all might be able to tell me something. Last I heard from her, she was headed over here to talk to Kate."

"Coffee?" Alex held up the coffee pot and pointed to a mug. "Is it possible both of them were kidnapped?"

Pat dropped into a chair. "No. I have no reason to think that. Beth's tougher than she looks and twice as feisty. No coffee. I won't be here long. I want to be home when she gets back."

"I wish I had more to tell you." Alex sat down in front of the laptop. "I'm looking for anything that might give us a clue, but haven't turned up anything so far."

Restless and worried, Maddox walked back to the door. "Keep me posted."

"Wait. Have you talked to Justin? Are we sure he's not mixed up in this somehow?" Travis asked.

"He's a greedy fool, not a kidnapper. Besides, he's out of town. I talked to his wife yesterday." Pat grabbed the doorknob. "Any other questions?"

"Do you know anything about these letters?" Alex pointed at the covered table. "They are all signed M."

"Beth wrote to lots of folks. It isn't like her to leave without telling me where she's headed. Something's really wrong."

"Beth is smart. They'll be okay." Travis sounded almost sure enough to convince the rest of them.

"We don't even know they are together. Kate's been kidnapped, maybe Beth hasn't." Pat double tapped the doorframe before stepping into the night. "I'll talk to DJ."

Travis closed the door. "I've never seen him that distracted or upset."

"He might know something."

"He won't be much help right now. He's been head over heels for Beth since before I knew him. He wouldn't know how to live without her." Travis wiped his eyes. "Keep searching."

Alex resumed his hunt. Getting his head back on track, he filled in the search screen. Entering the father's name and limiting results to Kendall County, he clicked search. The results surprised him. "And you're sure your brother never said anything about other kids?"

"Never."

Kate's phone rang, and Travis rolled his eyes.

Alex braced himself as he answered Meg's call. "Hello."

"You screening her calls now? Let me talk to Kate." Meg didn't know the first thing about being polite, at least to him.

Rubbing his temple, he closed his eyes. "She's not here." He wasn't about to tell her Kate had been kidnapped yet again, not until he knew more.

"She conveniently left without her phone? You afraid that if I talk to her, she might wake up and realize you aren't any good for her?" Meg's words spoke volumes about her deluded state. She hadn't listened to her sister at all.

"As soon as she gets back, I'll let her know you called." He exuded a calm he didn't feel inside.

"You can't stop me from talking to her." Meg's accusations landed like a dropped glove, declaring a duel.

"Listen, Meg, I get that Kate's big revelation is hard to accept, but from where I sit, you only care about you in this whole thing. I want what's best for Kate." He swallowed words he wouldn't say aloud until he could tell Kate himself. "But I am not trying to keep you away from her. You are doing that all on your own."

The phone clicked.

Alex laid the phone on the table. "I shouldn't have lost my temper with her, but ugh . . . that woman."

"I'm convinced you are serious about Kate. Otherwise, that wouldn't be worth it."

"I am, sir, I mean, Travis. Meg is so blinded by her own denial, she won't even listen. The irony is, I'm the one who encouraged Kate to keep trying."

Travis patted Alex on the shoulder. "Enough about Meg. Search. Find our girl, find Kate."

Alex turned the screen so Travis could see the results.

"Maybe there is another Scott Bentley in this area? There are seven children listed with that as the father's name."

"Who's listed as the mother?" Travis jumped out of his chair as he finished the question to answer a knock at the door.

"Five different moms for the seven kids." Alex jotted down the list of names.

When Travis opened the door, Becca held up a bag of tacos. "You both need to eat."

"Come in." Travis carried the tacos to the table.

"Thanks, Becca, but I don't have any news." Alex tried to sound hopeful despite the worry clouding every thought.

"I was going crazy at home, so I came to paint. It's something to do while I wait for news."

Alex smiled. "That's why Kate likes you. Painting supplies are in there."

Travis dug into the bag while Alex helped Becca lug supplies down the hall. Once she had all she needed, she closed the door to the master bedroom. He joined Travis at the table and took the proffered taco.

"These two have the same mom, and these two, here." Alex pointed at the list of moms. "We have Mary, Marla, Melanie, Misty, and Cassandra."

"How could Scott not mention something like having other kids?"

"The letters talked about a boy. Five of these are boys." Alex refused to get sidetracked talking about Scott's motivation for keeping secrets. "And I think we can eliminate Cassandra. The letters are signed M."

"He never said a word."

"Why Scott kept secrets doesn't help us right now. All I care about is finding Kate."

Beth-

I don't mean for these letters to be this far apart. Life is just passing by crazy fast right now. Chrissy is walking. All I do is cook, clean, and chase her. At least that's how it feels. I'm home now, not working anymore. When Brad asked if I wanted to do that, I thought he was joking. He wasn't. Being home with my kids is a dream come true.

I thought I'd have at least a few years left before Scooter moved out, but he asked to live with his grandpa in Schatzenburg. As a mom, I don't want my boy to leave home, but I can't stop thinking about what he wrote and what he drew. I need to protect my baby girl.

In my heart, I don't think he'd hurt anyone, but I can't get that picture out of my head.

Dad was agreeable to the idea. With more misgivings than I can count, I'm letting Scooter move in with my dad. I told Scooter that he could go to you for anything and even talk to you about the secret.

Thanks for being my friend.

-M

⬦⬯⬦

August 1992

Beth-

I'm so embarrassed. Please let Patrick know how grateful I am. Hopefully having a deputy haul Scooter home will brand the error in his memory. Dad called me late last night to tell me. What is that boy thinking? What's a 14-year-old doing out in a field drinking with friends?

I miss having Scooter here, but life is so much easier. Guilt sours my stomach even admitting it. I hoped being away from me would help Scooter move past all that happened with Scott.

Blind hope was all I had left in that regard.

But, now, after finding out what he's doing, I talked to Brad about having Scooter move back home. My husband wasn't happy about the idea, but he didn't say no outright. He left the decision to me.

I talked to Scooter, but like everything else lately, what I want doesn't matter. He didn't move back home. He even threatened to run away if I forced him. He's better living with my dad than on the streets.

-M

December 1997

Beth-

I haven't gotten over there in a while. Now that Chrissy's in school, I'm working part time. I miss seeing you. When I got your letter, I had to read it twice. What a surprise! You'll have lots of helping hands around when this baby comes along. Are the boys excited?

I hope your family has a great holiday.

-M

Chapter Twenty-three

January 27, 2016 – 12:30 am

I arched my back, sore from sitting upright so long. My hands tied in front of me, I contemplated throwing myself forward and scooting to the door on my knees and elbows, the chair still attached. But I didn't trust Jonathon not to hurt Beth if I managed to escape. It wasn't worth the risk.

"Beth, I need you to tell me about Jonathon."

"I can't believe he's doing this. It doesn't make sense. When he was tiny, my friends and I took turns watching him while his mom worked. She lived in Austin, but only for a while. Moved out to Kerrville, a quieter place to raise kids."

"Who is he to me? Why does he blame me? And for what?"

She rested her head on her knees and sighed. "All I knew at the time was that the guy was from her small town. Later after the wedding, years after, I figured out the two guys were one and the same. I shoulda guessed. He was the same pain in the ass to both of them."

My stomach sank. The pieces only fit one way. "Scott had a kid?"

"Who told you he had a kid? Who have you been talking to? No one knows that." Her coherency weaved like a drunk on the road, sometimes right on track, other times, way over the line.

"Did you tell her?"

"Emma? How could I? Besides, I figured it out when things were rough in her marriage. Didn't exactly seem like the best time."

"Marla was from Schatzenburg?"

"Patrick was nervous that night, asking me to dance. At the end of the evening, he didn't even ask for a kiss. Secretly, I was a little disappointed. He thanked me for dancing with him and strolled away. I was halfway to my car when he came running out asking for my number. I gave him mine, but I got his, too—just in case."

"What about Marla?"

"You know how when someone with warm hands touches you, but when they let go, you feel cold in that spot? That's the way I felt when we parted that first night."

"Can we talk about Patrick later?"

"I'm not sure what Emma guessed about Scott and his string of broken hearts, but the bottom line was, he wanted her. That meant something to her. And the way she was, once he'd talked her into bed, getting her to the altar was easy."

"Was Scott married before Emma?"

"Oh no. Poor Marla. They were just friends. She hated that she had a sweet spot for Scott. No matter how resolved she was to send him away, he'd show up and she'd go weak in the knees."

"Did she know where he took me?"

"No. She would never have kept that a secret. He stopped by her house that day but didn't tell her he was leaving."

"Why did he stop?"

"After Scott left, I vowed to keep all this other stuff from Emma. She'd been dealt enough hurt."

"Marla saw Scott the day he took me?"

"He wanted to take Scooter for ice cream. That's what Scott called Jonathon."

"She didn't let him go?"

"Patrick will be so worried. I didn't tell anyone where I was headed. He knew I planned to talk to you, but we aren't there."

"Do you think he'll look for you here?"

"Captain Maddox won't stop until he finds me, but my Patrick will be sick with worry."

"Patrick is in law enforcement?"

"Scooter wasn't home."

Shuffling that tidbit into the right storyline took a second, but then it dawned on me. The idea that I could've grown up with Jonathon as my older brother sent chills over me. "Talk to me about my mom." I stared across the room, knowing the sampler hung on the wall, though it was nearly impossible to see.

As the hours passed, complete darkness cloaked the room. Beth recounted memories of Emma and Patrick and Marla and Jonathon. "I kept journals. Anything Emma shared or I heard through the grapevine I wrote down. I don't even know why. It helped me feel closer to Emma."

I closed my eyes, my feelings about Scott more conflicted than ever. Overwhelmed, I wanted quiet, but Beth's tales continued, which in its own way was a blessing. It kept her awake.

"Marla sent me letters. I still have 'em all. Took them to your house for you to see."

"I'm not sure I want to read them."

"This is a nice little town, but it's got some secrets. Secrets are like bandages trying to cover old wounds. If the wounds aren't cleaned out, they fester, bandaged or not."

"Please don't let there be any more secrets that involve me."

"We'd been dating seven months and three days. Patrick picked me up, said he had a surprise. He drove me out to a friend's place—land south of Austin. I waited in the truck while he set up his surprise. And I didn't peek."

"Was it your birthday?"

"Nope. He'd strung up a piñata, a heart-shaped one. He handed me one of those colorfully wrapped sticks and told me to hit it."

"Blindfolded?"

"Love isn't blind. I didn't want to break the heart, and I told Patrick that. He said just matter of fact like, 'You can't get to what's inside unless you break the heart.' Well, I walloped on that thing. When it cracked open all my favorite candies showered onto the ground. He handed me a big bucket."

"How fun."

"Not just candy, though, in the grass lay a small velvet box. When I picked it up, Patrick dropped to one knee. I said yes, of course. But we didn't get married until after he graduated. Long engagement."

"Patrick sounds like a wonderful man."

"Uncle Patrick. He's your uncle. But most people call him Pat. Maybe you should call him Uncle Pat."

"I still don't understand why Jonathon blames me."

"When Chrissy was born, he wanted nothing to do with her. Moved out not too long after. He missed Scott. Probably a case of the grass is greener. Marla and Scooter didn't have the easiest time of things."

"Chrissy?"

"Marla's daughter. Jonathon's sister."

"Where's she now?"

"Northeast. Moved with her dad after the divorce." Beth fell silent.

In the dark room, the wind could be heard whipping against the side of the house. "I'm afraid." I barely whispered the words.

"Me, too." Beth shifted again, muffling her yelp of pain. "Kate, I've talked your ear off. You sleep for a bit. I'll wake you if he comes back in."

"Sleep is out of the question, and you shouldn't either until someone checks that bump on your head. Keep talking. Tell me more about Emma."

"There were always rumors about Scott. He had a reputation in certain circles, but I had nothing solid to offer as evidence. I didn't know until after he'd gone home that he'd been at Marla's that summer."

"Did you know Scott wasn't my dad?"

"Emma didn't tell me. When you were born early, I had my suspicions. She and Travis spent a lot of time together at the beginning of the summer, then nothing. I rarely saw them together until after Scott returned home, even then, never just the two of them."

I took advantage of her sudden clarity. "Does everyone know Jonathon was Scott's kid?" I wanted the answer to be yes.

"No. I knew. Marla begged me not to tell anyone. She didn't want people hounding her son about Scott."

"But she told him?"

"Jonathon found out after Scott left." Beth's voice sounded weaker, weary.

I kept pressing her with questions, trying to keep her awake. "How long had he been gone?"

"Not that long."

"They kept that secret all this time?"

"Keeping secrets is a way of life in this town."

I failed at measuring time in the dark room. Darkness continued much longer than I thought it should have. Beth got quiet, and I worried about her falling asleep.

"Tell me about you. Do you and Patrick—I mean Uncle Pat—have any kids?"

"Yes. I have three, two sons and a daughter. You've met her."

"Have I?"

"Libby. She works at The Drugstore."

"I remember her. Nice girl. Are your sons older?" I had to think up new questions to keep her talking.

"Yes. The oldest is just a bit older than you. My boys were only 20 months apart."

"Are they married?" When she didn't answer, I inched my toes her direction until they connected with something. "Beth, stay awake."

"Sorry. Yes. They're both married. I have five grandchildren. What about you?"

"We can talk about me later."

"No. Tell me about Alex."

"Does everyone in town know his name?"

She laughed, and for the briefest moment, worry and stress vanished. It returned with a force.

"Libby came home after work that day gushing about this couple that shared a menu. Pretty sure she could've told me what brand of jeans your man was wearing."

Wrangler. I closed my eyes, reliving the moment at the end of the hall. Pinned to the wall by his kiss, I'd feared for his safety. But now, somewhere, not far away, he feared for mine.

Beth giggled in the dark. "She went on about how he looked at you, talked to you. I already feel like I know him."

"He helped me when I needed it most, but we haven't had a chance to slow down enough to see if it might actually lead somewhere. I want it to, but . . ." I didn't finish the sentence because the thought that Jonathon might be listening from somewhere inside the house flashed in my head.

"Our fellas will find us."

"I hope so. Tell me about when Emma lived with you."

Beth continued her stories. Whenever she paused too long, I nudged her. Hopefully, she'd be willing to repeat the stories when life returned to normal because my brain, too busy trying to figure a way out, didn't listen well.

Beth-

I'm sure Patrick told you. Dad found Scooter unconscious. He's been taking drugs. That explains why he's been fired from his last two jobs. He can't blame Scott for his anger. Scooter isn't a kid anymore. He needs to make something of his life. I'm not sure he wants to, and anger is just an excuse.

I'd never say that to him. Or maybe I should. I think I need to see a therapist.

-M

❦∼❦

August 1998

Beth-

I'm thrilled for you. The guys in your house must be melting over that new baby girl. I'm finishing up the gift and will be coming by soon to deliver it. I want to hold that sweet baby bundle.

With everything going on with Scooter, I quit my job. Between getting Chrissy to school and dance lessons and keeping Scooter alive, I hardly have time to clean my house, but I'll make time to come see you. I need that.

Some people get to live in a big, happy bubble. I only get happiness bubbles. They're small, and they pop easily.

-M

CHAPTER TWENTY-FOUR

January 27, 2016 – 4:18 am

Alex lifted his head off the table with a start. He'd drifted off to sleep. He jumped up from the chair and walked to the counter. Rubbing his fingers along the keyboard indentations in his cheek, he brewed another pot of coffee. He stared out into the darkness, the door in his head labeled *what if* still closed, but even so, the stench of despair and heartbreak seeped out. *Don't even think about it.* He ran his thumb down the cleft in his chin and smiled. *Her second favorite part.* He couldn't even worry like he used to without thinking of her.

Mug in hand, he dropped back into his chair, a fresh determination driving him. Kate made searching look easy. Figuring out what to search proved to be the hardest part. He'd searched the names of each of the boys, hoping for a way to prove or disprove that their dad was the Scott related to Travis.

A rap at the door pulled Alex's attention away from the screen. DJ waved at him through the window in the back door.

Alex wiped his face as he opened the door. "Hey. Becca's painting the den."

DJ ran his fingers through his hair, staring at the floor.

"Any update?" Alex swung the door closed.

"The security company reported their guard missing. No one's heard from him."

"The car?"

"No sign of it. I'm so sorry, Alex."

Alex shook his head. Pity wasn't what he wanted. "Help yourself to coffee." He returned to his search. "Travis is down the hall somewhere."

"Sleeping?"

"Not likely."

Alex read the names of the kids again. One of them used Bentley as the last name. All were born around 1978. Surely they weren't all his.

Travis and DJ talked somewhere down the hall while Becca painted.

Alex walked to the sink and splashed water on his face. He didn't have time to be sleepy. He sat down at the computer again and studied the three names. "Is it one of you three? Did one of you take my Kate?"

He brought up the birth certificate for the one that used the name Bentley. The address listed was in Comfort. Alex searched the Kendall County tax appraisal records for the same address. According to the records, the Bentley family still resided there. Alex drew a line through the name on his list and moved on to the one above it.

Checking the same information, he discovered the certificate listed a Kerrville address. After searching the address and learning nothing new, he Googled the child. He couldn't connect him to Scott, but he also couldn't rule anything out.

Checking the name of the other child on his list, Jonathon, Alex hit the same dead end. *There has to be something else I can search.* He opened another browser tab and brought up Google. If he couldn't connect the kid to Scott, maybe Alex could connect the mother to Scott. What could Alex find out about the two women?

He started with Jonathon's mother. After typing her name in the search bar, pages of results popped onto the screen.

"Alex, go sleep for a while. We'll wake you up if we get any news." DJ dropped into the chair next to him.

"Not now." Alex clicked on the first link and quickly dismissed it as the wrong person. "I'll sleep after we find her. You and Becca go sleep for a bit. Please. I need it quiet to hunt."

DJ nodded and headed into the den.

Alex opened the link to an obituary. J. W. Miller, of Schatzenburg, Texas, had died five years earlier. One of the letters mentioned growing up in Schatzenburg. He read through the obituary. The short write-up referred to Mr. Miller's late wife, his only surviving daughter, Marla, and his grandchildren: Jonathon and Chrissy.

Alex jumped out of his chair. "DJ, I think I found something."

Beth-

Brad was late getting home from work, but I didn't think much of it at first. I'd made dinner instead of picking something up from a restaurant. Dinner was so quiet. I thought something was wrong at work. After we cleaned up the kitchen, he served me with papers.

He's leaving me. There was no talk of separation or trying to work it out. It's hard to blame him. I'm spending half my time chasing down Scooter when he's using. I can't just let my kid die. It's my fault his life is such a wreck. I chose poorly. He suffered for it.

We'll tell Chrissy when she gets back from camp. She's such a daddy's girl. She'll be devastated.

-M

❧

August 2007

Beth-

I need—I don't know what I need. My heart hurts so much, I'm not sure how to breathe. Chrissy chose Brad. We let her decide where she wanted to live, either with Brad, in upstate New York, or with me, here. My baby is leaving me. In a week, they'll get on a plane and leave Texas.

I want to curl in a ball and shut out the world, but dad called a few minutes ago and said that Scooter showed up high as a kite. I need to go help.

Does life have a reset button?

-M

Beth-

I begged Scooter to get clean, laid a little bit of a guilt trip on him. He ran my husband off, chased his sister off, embarrassed his family—those things matter. Something I said made a difference, I guess. He went into rehab and has been clean sixty-five days.

I'm sure laying guilt on him makes me a horrible mother, but I didn't know what else to do. I lost my job because of him, and if it weren't for Dad giving me money, I'd have been evicted.

Scooter is all I have left, and I need him. You can imagine how thrilled I was when he asked to move back in with me. To take care of me, he said. He's doing really well. Got a job, is going to meetings. I'm so proud of him.

I'm working again. Found a really great job. Dare I say that things are good?

Chrissy calls me nearly every night. She likes it up there. The snow is still a novelty. We'll see what she thinks when it's 80 here and still snowing there. But just hearing her voice makes each day brighter.

I'm trying to find the sunshine in every day, focus on the good things. At least there are more good things in my life now than there were two months ago.

-M

CHAPTER TWENTY-FIVE

January 27, 2016 – 5:30 am

I froze at the sound of footsteps in the kitchen.

Beth prattled on about what Patrick did every year on their anniversary. "Every year he brings me a heart of some sort. The first year, it was a heart-shaped box of chocolates. Another year he made a small piñata by hand. The year our son was born, he gave me a heart-shaped locket. The note read: *You have to crack it open to see what's inside.* He'd tucked a tiny picture of our baby boy in it. Never a doubt that—"

"Shut up already." Jonathon, who had returned to the house hours ago, staggered into the den for the first time since he'd dropped Beth in a heap on the floor. "You two have been yapping for hours. I didn't intend this to be old home week." He lifted Beth to her feet. "I think it's best if I separate y'all for a while. Don't want you trying to cook up a plan to leave."

"No, Jonathon, please. Let me stay and talk with her. I haven't seen her in so long." Beth tried to wriggle free.

Her pleas were met with an angry stare. "It's all about Claire, isn't it?" He dragged her out of the room, and she argued the entire time.

When everything fell quiet, I guessed that he'd gagged her. *Stay awake Beth. Please don't sleep.* I had to believe she was still alive, but penetrating fear wormed its way under my skin. The anger in his eyes scared me.

When he returned, he knelt in front of me, close enough that I could smell the alcohol on his breath. He'd changed out of the guard uniform into jeans and a fitted tee shirt. Nothing about his appearance indicated crazy kidnapper. He whispered, "I heard everything, even that part about Alex."

Determined not to show him how afraid I was, I met his gaze. "What are you going to do to me?"

"I've been thinking about that all night." He stretched with his fingers interlaced, knuckles crackling. "Drunk isn't the best way to plan things. Originally, my plan was to make you miss someone as much as I did. Take him away from you forever. Like you did to me. It would've been so fitting. Maggie gushed about him almost as much as she talked about you. Alex this. Alex that. But that plan went awry."

I swallowed the lump in my throat.

"He left you alone. I didn't plan on that. He complicated things."

"Where's the security guard?"

"Barn, with Keith. Don't worry. I gave them blankets." Jonathon stood up and paced, the butt of a gun sticking out of his pocket. "Tell me about him."

"Who?" I wasn't sure if he was asking about Alex or Scott.

"You know who."

"My dad?" I needed to turn the conversation away from Alex.

Immediately, Jonathon was in my face, raging. "*Do not* call him that!"

I cringed. "Okay."

He knelt next to me, resting back on his haunches. Using a slurred version of the charm he'd exuded when Beth arrived, he spoke softly. "He brought me matchbox cars sometimes, when he visited on the weekends. Sometimes we'd go fishing."

When he jumped up, I winced, thinking he was lunging for me.

Jonathon sat down on the sofa directly behind me, but didn't bother to turn me around. "Then one summer, he was there all the time. Every morning, he'd sit with me and read the comics as I ate my cereal."

"How old were you?"

"Five, maybe six."

"He wouldn't want you to do this."

"Mom cared about keeping secrets and finding her happily-ever-after. Dad cared about you." He gave a low humorless chuckle. "And, well, Dad's dead. Mom won't like it, but as long as it's all a tidy secret in the end, I'm golden."

Scott only cared about Scott. That's what I'd learned in the last couple weeks. I didn't like Jonathon out of my line of sight. My neck couldn't turn far enough to see him.

"No one cared about me. Not really. What I wanted didn't matter. He left when I was eight."

"Jonathon, I'm sorry. He hurt a lot of people."

"He chose you."

If I had any chance of this ending peacefully, I needed to change the direction of the conversation. "That makes us cousins."

He grunted in agreement. "He missed my games. I was a star player, and he didn't come see me. Eventually, I quit the team. No reason to keep playing."

"I'm sure he thought of you."

Jonathon's hot breath on my neck preceded his response. "Shut up. You don't know that."

I'd been awake too long to think clearly. What could I say to talk Jonathon out of whatever he'd planned?

"You haven't told me about him."

My mind raced. Heaping negatives on Scott would only make Jonathon more agitated. I struggled to remember good things. "He liked to fish. He'd pack his tackle box and go off by himself, sometimes for a week."

"We used to fish together."

"And he read the comics on Saturday morning, sipping coffee out of his favorite mug." Worried that I'd set Jonathon off saying the wrong thing, I danced through a minefield of words, hoping for the right ones.

"What did it look like?"

"What did what look like?"

"The mug."

"It had 'I heart Sticks' on it. I don't even know what it meant."

"Blue lettering and a red heart."

"You know about his mug?"

"I gave him that mug for Christmas one year. Sticks was what I called him." Jonathon gulped. "I remember his blue eyes."

"Very much like yours." I wiggled my feet, trying to loosen the rope. Jonathon's depressed state concerned me as much as, or even more than, his slurred words. Impaired judgment and a handgun were a dangerous combination.

"I wanted my dad to come back." The words squeaked out like he was a young child.

I froze when he rested his chin on my shoulder.

"Mom told me the truth after he left, about him being my dad. What she doesn't know—to this day, because I faked it well when she did tell me—is that Scott had told me long before that, just after you were born. He picked me up one afternoon and had you with him. We went to a fast food place, and he let me hold you." Jonathon dropped back onto the sofa. "I told him I'd always wanted a little sister. That's when he said I already had one."

No. My mind painted a picture of the scene, the happy little picture of Scott admiring his sweet little darlings.

"At first, I didn't believe him, but he swore he was my dad. Mom never talked about it, and even as a kid, I knew not to bring it up. But he told me details, little things he couldn't have known unless it were true. Finally, I believed him. That day was like Christmas." He leaned forward again and dropped his voice to a whisper. "Wasn't until years later that I learned I wasn't your big brother. Overheard it eating dinner with my grandpa. My dad left me so he could keep you when he knew—he *knew*—you were his brother's child."

"Did you talk to your mom about it?"

"Never. She wasn't the only one good at keeping secrets." Jonathon's breath reeked even more.

Has he been sitting there drinking? The flask hit the floor, my question answered.

"I don't know what to do." He grabbed my chair.

"You could let us go."

His inebriated state worried me more than I allowed myself to feel.

"I went to The Drugstore for lunch. On Tuesday. Maggie was thrilled for an audience to proclaim the big news. I barely made it out of that restaurant without completely losing it." He leaned his head on mine. "I came here, to mom's, turned on the news. There you were. All smiles. The happy story of the little, lost child finally found. I hated you, despised you. My dad would never come home. You were the reason he left me." He pulled back but kept a hand resting on my shoulder. "As my tequila bottle emptied that day, a plan came together."

"Please, Jonathon. Just let us go."

"The Captain won't be happy that I knocked his wife on the head. Since he hasn't shown up, I guess she didn't mention she was coming to see me. That helps, means no one has to know about any of this."

"We can keep quiet. I'll help Beth walk back to her house. We can say that a car dropped us off at the edge of town. No one has to know the truth."

"You're only right about that last part. I may be drunk, but I'm not stupid."

I have to think of something. Escape wasn't possible, not without leaving Beth, which I refused to do. Rescue—I needed to be rescued.

A lightbulb, all decked out in pink rhinestones, flashed in my head. "Would you like to see a picture of your dad?"

Jonathon stumbled around the chair, holding onto my shoulder for balance. His eyes wide, his words slurred, he asked, "How? Is this a trick?"

"LeAnn has pictures on her phone. Lots of them. There is one of Scott and me." I was careful not to call him Dad. That would only inflame Jonathon more.

After wrestling the phone out of his pocket, he held down the power button, while cursing about how long it took to come on. When the screen came to life, he opened the photos. He scrolled, sliding backward through time. I prayed that scrolling through fifteen years of pictures would give Rory or DJ or whoever was searching for me enough time to locate the phone.

June 2008

Beth-

I'm sitting on my porch, sipping a glass of ice tea and for the first time in nearly as long as I can remember, I'm not fighting back tears or raging inside as I write to you. Life's not perfect. June has been a little too warm for my taste, but all in all, I'd call life good right now.

Scooter is doing so well. He's working during the day and attending night classes. The manager at a dealership gave Scooter a business card and told him to call. Says he might have a future selling cars. The dealership is closer into town, not far from Schatzenburg. Scooter really misses living in that small town and wants to move back. I may move with him. Dad has room.

It'd be nice to be closer to you. I feel like I never see you. Your little girl turns ten soon. How is that even possible? Time speeds up the older I get.

I miss my little girl. I so desperately want to fly out and go visit her, but I'm afraid if I leave Scooter, something will snap. I don't want him to return to the angry, drug-using kid I had to drag home and nurse back to health.

I'll pop in after I move. Imagine being able to talk over a cup of coffee. I can't wait.

-M

Chapter Twenty-six

January 27, 2016 – 6:12 am

Alex called Rory, speaking so quickly he had to repeat himself to be understood. "I don't know how much you know about Kate's story. Her uncle kidnapped her when she was two. Turns out he also had another child. That kid was angry that his dad ran off with Kate. May have even blamed her, based on some letters his mom wrote."

"That was a long time ago. What does that have to do with anything?"

"Maybe he stayed angry. It's all we have. Do *you* have any clue where she is? Hold on. Someone's here." Alex opened the back door. "Pat, come in."

Captain Maddox dropped into a chair, eyes red, jaw set. "Any leads? And before you ask about Justin, I talked to him. He's on a *business trip* in Vegas. His wife thinks he's in Phoenix. And the lady that answered his phone wasn't happy about being awakened at two in the morning."

"Rory, head this way. I'll call you back." Alex tucked the phone in his pocket and slid one of the letters toward Pat. "Marla had a son, Jonathon. He was Scott's kid, wasn't he?"

Maddox stared at him. "No one knows that."

"Would Jonathon hurt anyone?" Alex paced near the table.

"Don't think so. No, he wouldn't. Why?" Pat rubbed his face. "But . . ."

Travis grabbed Pat's arm. "But what?"

Pat shook free of Travis. "He left Beth a message yesterday morning."

"You should have said something!" Alex waved off Travis' scolding look but lowered his voice. "If you knew, why not say anything?"

"Beth babysat Jonathon. He wouldn't hurt her. Marla and Beth were roommates in college. It doesn't seem possible."

Alex sat across from Pat. "Where does Jonathon live? Or Marla?"

"I don't know where Jonathon lives these days. Marla moved into her dad's place out on Flat Rock Road after her ex left. That place just before you get into town." Pat jumped out of his chair. "Tell the FBI to meet us there."

Alex called Rory.

"You know where she is?" Rory's voice crackled with the spotty signal.

"Maybe." Alex gave him the address. "How quickly can you get there?"

"We're ten minutes out."

Alex had Rory repeat the address back before he stuffed the phone in his pocket.

DJ ran into the den. "Becca, we'll be back."

"Where are y'all going? Give me a second, and I'll go with you." Her voice pitched with excitement.

"No. Stay here, please." He hesitated. "But lock the door behind us."

"Keep me posted." Becca wiped her hands as she met them in the kitchen.

DJ gave her a peck on the cheek. "I will."

They piled into DJ's Tahoe and raced the few blocks to Flat Rock Road. As the house came into view, DJ switched off his headlights and pulled off into the grass. From their position, they had a full view of the barn and a partial view of the house.

"I'll check the barn. If Jonathon has them here, the guard's car can't be far away." Maddox motioned to DJ as he got out.

DJ tapped Alex's arm. "Stay here."

Alex complied, at least until the two men were across the street. Eager to get inside that house but unwilling to put Kate at risk, he got out but hung back near the Tahoe. He pulled Kate's phone out of his pocket and turned it on. Scanning the apps, he tried to determine how the Jonathon guy had used LeAnn's phone to track Kate.

Maddox and DJ darted through the grass, hunched low, in the early morning light.

As soon as Alex swiped to the second screen, he saw the offending app—Find My BFF. He glanced up to see the guys pull open the barn door. Maddox stepped in with DJ right behind.

Alex opened the app and clicked on LeAnn's name. *Where are they?* A dot flashed on the map. He hurried across the street toward DJ.

He met Alex in the grass. "I thought I told you to stay put."

"She's in there. Look."

"Car, the missing guard, and your old friend Keith are all in the barn. We'll wait for Rory's team before we go inside."

Alex pounded out a text to Rory: *She's here.*

Rory's number appeared on the screen and Alex swiped to answer. "Hello." He risked barely a whisper and rushed behind the Tahoe.

"I underestimated you. You were right. The guy turned on his phone. His location? The address you gave me. Be there in two minutes."

"Yeah, I just used Kate's phone to find him."

Alex met DJ near the front of the Tahoe. "They'll be here in two minutes."

DJ patted him on the back. "You did it. You found her."

Alex quietly walked to where he had a better view of the house, the first house Kate noticed when they visited Schatzenburg. She'd been less than a mile away all night.

Rory and his team arrived less than two minutes later and silently poured out of their vehicles. While they approached the place, Alex hung back as agents peeked in windows and motioned to each other.

Agents gestured and nodded. Rory pointed to the back door. They rushed up to it, guns drawn, and hunkered down waiting for directions. Rory tried the door. It opened with a quick turn of the knob. His team followed him in. Ignoring DJ's whisper to stay put, Alex quietly ran up and slipped into the house behind them, stepping back against the wall in response to Rory's reproachful glare.

Two agents moved down the hall, and others filled the kitchen. Voices wafted from the den. Alex closed his eyes and whispered a silent "thank you." Kate was alive.

CHAPTER TWENTY-SEVEN

January 27, 2016 – 6:38 am

I spied motion through the tiny gap between the curtain and the window frame and hoped Jonathon was too drunk or too distracted by the photo to notice.

Still holding the phone, he started pacing. "My mom wasn't a happy sort. It was my fault. She wasn't ready for a baby."

Blame Scott. "That wasn't your fault. She loved you." Shooting from the hip, making up whatever sounded right, I'd do anything to live.

He shoved the phone in my face. "This him? The man with the blue, blue eyes?"

"Yes. That's your dad."

"Everyone said how horrible he was. The whole town hated him for what he did to Emma and Travis."

I cringed at the desperate tone in his voice. "Jonathon, he wasn't horrible." *He was horrible, the worst kind of person.*

The springs on the couch squeaked. "I used to imagine my dad was a hero, that he was away saving people. How silly is that?"

"I didn't know the awful person everyone talks about. He wasn't like that to me." Defending the man that spent years lying to me and hurting others felt wrong. But I'd told Jonathon the truth. The Scott that stole a child and kept such a dark secret wasn't the man I knew as my father. He wasn't perfect, but he wasn't anything resembling a monster, either. *How did I not see the other side of him?*

"Did he ever save you?"

Jonathon's question surprised me and triggered a memory I'd never shared with anyone. "What?"

"Heroes save people. Did he save you?"

"Once, but . . ." My voice cracked, which I hated.

He stepped in front of me and leaned in close, the smell of alcohol burning my sinuses. "Tell me." He tapped the butt of the gun, a desperate pleading in his eyes. "You understand? I *need* to know."

My head bounced up and down in a terrified nod, incapable of hiding my fear any longer.

He squatted in front of me, resting his hands on my knees, which made it harder to recount the story.

"I was in high school. One Saturday, I invited a guy to the house to study. When he got there and saw that no one else was home, he thought the invitation meant something completely different." I tried to steady my voice and not show emotion.

"Get to the part about my dad." He glanced from the picture back to me.

"Dad walked in my room and found the guy on top of me, pulling off my—"

"Did he get there in time?" Jonathon pressed down on my legs, eager to hear how his dad acted the hero.

In time? Jonathon wanted to hear that Scott had arrived before any damage was done, but I couldn't bring myself to lie to him. Physically, I was unharmed, but emotionally . . .

"What'd my dad do?"

"He grabbed the boy by the collar, ripped him off me, and dragged him out of the room." Images I hated remembering flashed in my head.

"And?"

"I don't know. I never saw the guy again."

"You think he killed him?"

"No. Probably not. I don't know." Worries I'd stuffed for years threatened to explode their holding cell. "Why would you ask that?"

"I would have. I'd have killed him. Bang! Shot him right through the head." Jonathon staggered back to the couch and sat behind me. "I'm sorry, Claire."

"Why don't you let us go?"

"My dad was a hero. Too bad I didn't grow up to be more like him." He leaned forward, his breath stinging my neck.

"Untie me." Spurred by either desperation or courage, I didn't beg. I demanded. "Now! Get these ropes off me."

Right behind me, he whispered, "I can't."

Click.

I swallowed back a scream and squeezed my eyes closed. "No. Jonathon, no. Please don't. Please don't shoo—"

CHAPTER TWENTY-EIGHT

January 27, 2016 – 6:45 am

Alex listened as Kate told her story. Her voice barely wavered, even though reliving the memory must've torn her apart. He clenched his fists, remembering that day on her bed. All of it made sense now—the hesitation, the pulling away.

Staying in place took every bit of willpower he could muster. Barreling into that room would only put her life in more danger. He had to trust Rory to do his job. He was trained for these situations.

Kate demanded to be let go.

Every agent in the room tensed before rushing into the den. Alex pressed his back to the wall and listened, holding his breath. Time clicked by in slow motion.

She pleaded with Jonathon.

A gun discharged.

No. This can't be happening. Alex raced to the doorway, but DJ blocked the path.

He struggled against Alex's attempts to get around him. "You can't go in there."

Alex leaned to the side, trying to catch a glimpse of Kate.

"Stay back." Rory knelt next to a toppled chair, a pool of dark red spreading around it.

CHAPTER TWENTY-NINE

January 27, 2016 – 6:52 am

Voices surrounded me, but in my haze, I couldn't make out the words. I lay on my side, my head pounding. *Where did he shoot me?* I mentally inventoried what hurt: my head, my wrists, and the tender skin on my ankles.

The rope shifted. My eyes popped open.

"Sorry." A man knelt next to me, working the knots in the rope.

Straight, light brown hair came into focus as I strained to put a face with the voice. "Rory?"

He loosened the rope. "Hope I didn't hurt you when I knocked you over."

I stared at the blood pooled around me. "He's . . .?"

"Yeah." He gently turned my head away from the couch. "You don't want to look that way. Are you hurt?"

The last knot gave way, releasing me from the chair.

"I don't think so." Instinctively, I surveyed my body with my hands to be sure. After touching my side, blood covered my hand. I gasped.

"I don't think it's yours." He waved over an officer and whispered to him.

"He didn't shoot me." Waves of relief buried me. I stood up, clutching Rory's shoulder for balance when the room started spinning.

"Be careful and watch your step. EMTs are coming to check you out."

"Beth is in the other room. He hit her on the head."

Rory held out his hand to steady me. "We found her."

"Is she okay?" I purposefully kept my eyes on the doorway.

He nodded. "They are taking her to the hospital as a precaution."

The other officer returned, a blanket draped over his arm. "Here ya go, ma'am." He wrapped it around my shoulders.

"Thank you."

"Don't leave the house just yet. I want to get your statement." Rory pointed toward the kitchen. "Alex is in there."

I yanked off my socks, the only clothing I was willing to shed in the house buzzing with officers. Inside me, something shifted. Rory wanted my statement. Jonathon wanted me to pay for his years without a dad. The guy from high school wanted what wasn't his. I trudged into the kitchen, battling dark emotions that sprang out of the shadows.

Alex was bent over the sink. The unmistakable reek of vomit hung in the air. I slipped one hand out of the blanket and gingerly touched his back.

He stiffened.

"Alex?"

He whipped around, dragging a rag across his face. Pale, he swayed but steadied himself on the counter. "I thought—" The words caught in his throat. "Are you okay?"

He pulled open the blanket, sliding his hands over my body.

I yanked the blanket back around me and mumbled, "I'm not hurt."

He pulled me to his chest, but his hands felt cold, foreign.

"Jonathon's dead." I stepped back.

"I thought I was too late. Again."

DJ rushed up the hall. "Kate? You okay?" He patted Alex's shoulder, grinning. "I thought I heard her."

"How did you find us?" I stepped out of Alex's reach as he extended a hand toward me.

DJ hugged me. "You've gotten into this guy's head. He researched until he stumbled on a lead."

"Really?" I spun back toward Alex. "You discovered he was—"

"Scott's son. Beth left letters at the house. Only, in the letters, his mom called him Scooter, so we had to figure out his real name." He stepped toward me but shoved his hands in his pockets. "And you got him to turn on the phone, didn't you?"

I nodded.

"Excuse me." A young medic smiled. "I'd like to check you out, make sure you aren't hurt."

Arguing would only be met by insistence from Alex and DJ.

Alex's eyes raked over me, and he never left my side. He pulled his hands out of his pockets, and if he wasn't grasping my hand, his fingers massaged my neck. His actions spoke volumes. He wanted more in the relationship.

I added him to the list of people who wanted something from me.

Chapter Thirty

January 27, 2016 – 7:48 am

Alex rested a hand on Kate's shoulder as she was checked over, and she didn't pull away. He stayed by her side, stepping away only when the tech needed more room.

Travis rushed through the back door. "She's okay?"

"I am." Kate stood up.

"Your dad helped me search." Alex moved out of the way as Travis folded her into his arms.

He didn't hold back tears as he repeatedly kissed her head. "I didn't know he had other kids. I'm so sorry."

"I don't want to talk about any of that." Kate returned to her chair. "Has anyone talked to Beth?"

"Pat called from the hospital. She's got a pretty severe concussion and is being admitted. He told me to thank you for keeping her awake." DJ tucked his phone in his pocket. "And Becca's crawling out of her skin waiting for you to get home. If Rory doesn't let you go soon, she may start painting the outside of your house, too."

"He said Keith and the security guard were in the barn." Kate stayed focused on DJ, not even glancing at Alex.

"Found 'em both." DJ ran his fingers through his hair. "Keith is madder than a fire ant in a rain storm, and that poor security guard just wants to go home. Jonathon snuck up on him just before dawn, not long after the shift change."

"He's okay?" Kate hadn't shed a tear since walking out of the den, which was worrisome.

DJ nodded. "They both are."

"I feel awful for her." Kate uncrossed her legs as the technician took her blood pressure.

"Who?" Alex squatted next to her chair.

Kate stared at her feet. "Jonathon's mom. Who's going to tell her?"

"Pat said they'd handle it." DJ motioned toward the door with his thumb. "I should let Gram know you're okay. I'll meet y'all at the house."

After nearly an hour of chaos and questions, Rory sent Kate and Alex home.

Kate beelined for the shower as soon as she walked inside.

Becca set the table, preparing for the food Ben was bringing. "Is she really okay?"

"Don't know. Something's off." Alex shrugged. "But given what happened, that's understandable."

"He died right next to her." Becca shuddered. "I can't even imagine."

He wanted Kate to need him, to find safety in his arms. But at that house, when she'd found him in the kitchen, something had changed. "Maybe she just needs time." Alex trudged down the hall to clean up.

Locked in the bathroom, Alex pulled off his shirt. Darkening red marks covered his chest. Pain stabbed at him every time he moved, but he did his best to hide it. He only wanted to focus on Kate. If she knew he'd been hurt, she'd worry.

After his much-needed shower, when he walked into the dining room, she was sitting in a chair, her head resting on the table. She flinched when he ran his fingers through her hair. A different kind of pain shot through him.

"Sorry." He sat down next to her. "You can go back to the bedroom and sleep."

She shook her head. "No. Right now I need people around me."

"They found Jeff. He's okay."

Kate picked up her phone. "I need to call LeAnn." Her hand shook.

"It can wait, Kate." He wanted to hold her, but she'd surrounded herself with an invisible wall, climbed back into her ivory tower, and blocked the stone staircase. "Meg called while you—just call her at some point. She thinks I'm screening your calls, keeping you away from her."

Kate didn't even crack a smile. Since they'd gotten back to her place, she'd kept her distance and hardly touched Alex, which unnerved him.

Ben arrived with pizza rolls, and everyone sat down around the table. Alex stayed next to her. She nibbled on one piece while everyone around them ate their fill. He worried about her, afraid the ordeal was too much. She'd come too close to death, and she'd faced it alone.

The thought made him ill, and he dropped his half-eaten pizza roll on the plate. "Kate? What can I get you?"

"Have you heard anything more about Beth?" She reached for his arm but pulled her hand back as soon as she touched him, almost as if it burned.

"They'll keep her overnight. She'll take a few weeks to fully recover." Alex clasped his hands together to avoid reaching for her.

Once everyone finished eating, Becca started cleaning up. "I'll stick these last two pieces in the fridge." She wiped off the table. "After I'm finished in the kitchen, we should empty the storage unit. Make use of all these guys. If that's okay with you, Kate."

"Uh, yeah. Just don't put anything in the den. That room still needs new carpet." Kate sank into a chair at the dining room table and dialed Meg's number.

Alex fished the keys out of his pocket and unlocked the storage unit. Becca took charge, directing, as furniture and boxes got unloaded.

Headed toward the back door, his arms loaded with boxes, Alex stopped when he spotted Gram walking toward the house. She was exactly who Kate needed to talk to. He passed the boxes off to Ben and ran out to meet the neighbor.

Alex offered his arm, and she accepted, patting his hand.

"You found her."

"Kate's inside. I'm glad you came." He didn't hide the worry in his voice, not that it was even possible to hide emotions from Gram.

"What's wrong? I heard she wasn't hurt." Concern filled her soft brown eyes.

"Not injured, but traumatized. What worries me is that she won't talk about it. I don't think she's even cried. Will you talk to her?"

"Me? I'm happy to visit with her, but she hardly knows me."

He slowed his pace as they walked up the front steps. "You always seem to know what needs to be said."

The door swung open with a slight push, and they stepped inside.

Gram clapped at the sight of everyone carrying boxes. "She's moving in."

"Yeah." Kate smiled as Gram sat down next to her. "Thanks for coming."

"How'd your call go?" Alex reached toward her shoulder and breathed a little easier when she didn't lean away.

"I left a message." Kate nodded toward the phone. "She'll call back when she feels like it."

Alex hurried out the back door and passed the word to leave Gram and Kate alone. He hoped Gram could inject whatever magic serum was needed to bring Kate back.

Until late afternoon, the house was a buzz. After Alex stacked the last box in the master bedroom, he dropped onto the edge of the bed and buried his face in his hands. He hadn't slowed down enough to plow through the sundry emotions thrown at him since she'd disappeared. When the others left, maybe then she'd open up, and together, they could deal with the muck she'd just lived through.

After a solitary five minutes, he headed back into the kitchen. Gram stood as he joined them at the table.

"I need to head back to the house. DJ, be a dear and walk me home." She patted Kate on the shoulder. "Don't forget what I said. Come by whenever you want to talk."

DJ stopped Becca from unpacking boxes. "Kate needs a quiet house. You can come help her tomorrow or the next day."

"You're right." Becca grabbed her purse and gave Kate a quick hug.

Ben glanced from Kate to Alex, then shook hands with him. "I'm going to go. You have my number."

Travis stood next to Kate's chair, rubbing her back. "I don't want to leave, but you don't need me hanging around."

Kate patted his hand. "Go home and sleep. You must be exhausted after being awake most of the night with Alex."

Travis wiped his eyes and hugged Alex. "You're staying, right?"

"She'll be fine." He couldn't make promises but didn't want her dad to worry.

As soon as Travis stepped out the door, Alex squatted next to Kate's chair. "I've been waiting all day to sit and talk with you."

"Can it wait until tomorrow?" Her body stiff, her eyes dark, her demeanor distressed him.

"Sure. What do you need from me?"

"I need you to go home. Just let me crawl in bed and forget this ever happened." She leaned on the table, head resting on her arms.

"I thought you wanted people around you." He rubbed her back and glanced down the hall. More than anything, he wanted to slide under the covers with her clutched to his chest, to hear her breath and watch her chest rise and fall. But he couldn't.

"I'd like to be alone."

Concerned that the trauma would replay when she closed her eyes, he slipped an arm around her. "Will you be okay here by yourself?"

"I'm not a child. I'll be fine." She stood and stepped away. "Go home, Alex."

Feeling like he'd been punched in the gut, he stepped back. "I'll call when I get to the cabin." He stuck his hands in his pockets. "You sure you're all right?"

"Go. I'm okay." She flashed him a smile, her eyes dark but not teary.

She wants you to leave. Alex reluctantly walked out the back door.

He mused about her behavior all the way home. The last few weeks had been a series of scares and shocks. He couldn't fault her for being overwhelmed and wanting to withdraw, but the switch from hot to cold had been so abrupt. She'd walled herself off from everyone around her, even him. *Why the sudden change?*

The story she'd told replayed in his head. He'd made her feel unsafe when he triggered those memories. Had reliving the past changed the way she felt about him?

He walked into the cabin and tossed his bag near the door. DJ had picked up the books and cleaned up part of the kitchen, out of the kindness of his heart, but so much still needed to be done. Before Alex began to put everything back in order, he called Kate.

She didn't answer. She'd had the phone with her at the table. It was in her possession. Convinced there was an explanation, he held back worry and tapped out a quick text: *Call me.*

He wandered into the kitchen and spent the next half hour wiping counters and cleaning floors. His phone buzzed.

Kate replied: *Glad you made it home safe.*

He called her again, but she didn't answer.

Frustrated, he worked his way through the cabin putting flotsam and jetsam back in its place. Far from finished, he dropped into the recliner and called her. The call rolled to voicemail after only two rings, so he texted her: *Why aren't you picking up?*

Her reply didn't answer his question: *I'm fine.*

Something was wrong. She wasn't okay. He hurried to the truck and drove back to Schatzenburg.

Chapter Thirty-one
January 27, 2016 – 7:30 pm

Even after a third shower, the memory of my ordeal clung to my skin. I slipped a night shirt over my head and burrowed under the covers. I'd lied to Alex, telling him I was fine. Hounded by the fear that Scott had killed that boy and the sound of that click every time I closed my eyes, I was anything but. After only a few minutes, I jumped back out of bed.

I picked up the phone but suppressed the impulse to call Alex. I wouldn't admit to being scared because it would only open up a conversation I didn't want to have. After checking the windows and doors for the third time since he'd left to make sure they were locked, I sat down at my kitchen table and opened the laptop. Applications filled the screen, and the open tabs on the browser brought tears to my eyes. I wiped the teardrops away before they could spawn more.

He'd searched all night to find me. I shivered at the thought of being alone when the gun went off. I wanted Alex in my life, to invest time in what could be, but no matter how much I tried to rationalize with myself, I couldn't give him what I was sure he wanted. Eventually, he'd leave just like the others after hearing "no" too many times.

I needed to be okay by myself. I glanced around at my home, The Castle, full of my furniture.

My phone lit up. Alex called again. If I answered, words I didn't want to admit would escape. I texted him a lie: *I'm fine.*

Opening a new tab because I wouldn't close the pages he'd used to search, I searched for the kid from high school. I prayed an obituary or unsolved case wouldn't pop up in the results. Page after page, I read about men with that name. One sounded like the right person, but the article had no photo, so I wasn't sure.

On Facebook, I entered his name. A list of people filled the screen. His picture was half-way down the page. Older, he still looked much like he did in high school, only with a little less hair and extra weight around the middle. Married, with three daughters, he'd lived long past that day at my house.

Long-held worries dissipated as foolishness.

I wouldn't be able to sleep so I opened Ancestry and added the new information I'd learned from Beth to my family tree. Little green leaves dotted the tree, plenty of leads to keep me researching all night.

A knock at the back door pulled me away from my hunt. *Who's bothering me?*

My phone lit up with a text notification from Alex, just as he waved at me through the window in the back door.

I really need curtains for that window. Only feet from the back door, I couldn't ignore him. I left my phone on the table and tugged at the hem of my nightie as I opened the door. "Did you forget something?"

"You didn't answer your phone." He stepped in and closed the door behind him. After flipping the bolt, he dropped a bag onto the kitchen table.

"I texted you." I didn't want to explain the whys of ignoring his calls and replying with messages. I masked emotions better in texts.

"I can't hear if you're okay in a text."

"Well, I'm fine. See." I put my arms out and spun around.

"You aren't fine." He shook his head. "You want to leave Texas because strange men keep kidnapping you? I get it. Tell me so I can pack my stuff."

Arms still dangling out to the side, I stared at him. "Leave Texas? That's not it." I wasn't at all prepared for him to offer to pick up and move.

"And if you don't want to talk about it, okay." He puts his hands up in a defensive position, then lowered his voice. "But there are things I need to say *tonight* before I walk back out that door." He pleaded more than demanded.

"Fine." I nodded without looking up. "Give me a minute." If we were going to sit and talk, I needed to at least be wearing pants.

His eyes on me, I hurried down the hall in my nightshirt, which felt shorter with every step. After slipping on yoga pants under my nightie, I trudged into the living room. I couldn't say yes to what I thought he might ask of me. I sank into the far end of the sofa, wrapped my arms around my legs, and rested my head on my knees.

He sat down next to me. "Kate? Please tell me what's wrong. You won't even look at me."

I glanced up, my emotions betrayed by the tears pooled in my eyes. "Everyone wants something from me. Jonathon wanted revenge. Justin wants money. Beth wants her sister back. Becca wants me to be careful with your heart. Travis wants a daughter. Meg wants me to act like none of this happened. It's overwhelming."

"Rainy . . ." He opened his arms. "Come here."

I melted inside when he called me Rainy. Such a silly nickname, but to me it meant safety. But I couldn't be in his arms and say what needed to be said. I shook my head.

He grabbed a throw pillow and squeezed it, unmistakable hurt in his eyes. "What did Gram say?"

"That I shouldn't let that horrid, black cloud cast shadows on the glimmers of goodness around me. And that not all men are like Scott."

He leaned back against the cushions. Without looking up, he asked, "What do I want, Kate?" A heavy sadness hung in his question.

I gathered my nerve, my mind racing as I tried to formulate sentences. "The other day . . . I wasn't completely honest with you when I said that my boyfriend just quit calling. He quit calling for a reason—because I wouldn't sleep with him. Most other guys left after the first 'no.' He just stuck around longer, hoping I'd change my mind." I glanced up and met his gaze. "You want what they all want." My words sounded harsh, even to me.

Alex launched off the sofa, rubbing his face. Like a wounded animal, back and forth across the kitchen, he paced.

I waited, hoping he'd at least say something before walking out the door.

He stopped, an awful, suffocating quiet settling in the house. As he stared at the floor, his shoulders sagged. "You really think . . .?" His question escaped in a ragged breath, a whisper of accusation.

When he slipped his hand in his pocket, and I heard the rattle of keys, my throat tightened. It was over.

Without even a last glance backward, he left through the back door. The truck engine roared to life, louder, angrier than I'd ever heard it before.

What have I done? His reaction made me question my assumptions. *What if I was wrong about what he wanted?* I tore out to the front porch as he cut the corner in front of the house, kicking up rocks. Taillights disappeared behind trees as he drove farther away from me.

The porch rail held me up. My accusation pounded in my head. *I can't let those be the last words I ever say to him.*

I ran back to my phone, fat fingering more words than I got right. After correcting my errors, I sent him a text I prayed he'd at least read: *You said you didn't expect it. And I know you wouldn't force yourself on me or anything.*

Honesty came easier with my heart cracked open. I followed with the truth: *But, what happens later when you tire of me not— when you get tired of just me?*

My phone on the kitchen table, I stared at the screen, hoping for a reply. I shifted the brown bag out of the way to rest my head on the table, but the chill radiating through the brown paper caught my attention. Curious, I peeked inside. A Cherry Coke and a chocolate bar were tucked inside. I tore open the wrapper, inhaled the sweet of the milk chocolate, and then popped a chunk into my mouth. I'd never needed chocolate more.

Frustrated, I jumped out of my chair. *Will he respond? Is it really over?* I checked my messages again while pacing around the great room. I'd been so busy typing out my thoughts, I'd forgotten that he'd sent me one when he arrived at the house. I scrolled up to his text and clicked the YouTube link.

I shouldn't have read the song title standing up. I collapsed in a heap on the floor and sobbed as Eddie Rabbit sang "I Love a Rainy Night." Alex had come back, pleading to be heard, but I let the dark cloud cast shadows, making the gold around me appear black.

CHAPTER THIRTY-TWO

January 27, 2016 – 8:42 pm

Alex skidded to a stop a mile down the road when his phone alerted him of new texts. He pulled off to the shoulder, wiped his eyes with the cuff of his sleeve, and tried to read the notifications.

Both Travis and Kate had sent messages. What could Kate possibly have to add to what she'd already said? He skipped over hers and opened Travis's message: *How's Kate?*

"Mr. Bentley, sir, you need to text your daughter directly. I'm not your message boy anymore." Alex texted back: *Not with Kate.*

He tossed the phone in the passenger seat. He didn't even know where he was headed. Not only was the cabin still a wreck, reminders of Kate lingered in every room, definitely not what he needed. He couldn't go to DJ's house. Becca would want to needle her way into the mess, determined to fix it.

He threw the truck in drive, and without a destination, drove toward the highway. Pain stung his eyes. Anger burned in his chest. The outrage wasn't directed at Kate, but to some sniveling rake, probably living somewhere in the world, happily unaware that he'd locked her away so many years ago.

Alex understood Travis's frustration with hating a dead man. Alex hated a faceless teen, who wasn't even a teen anymore, and Jonathon, for what they'd done to Kate.

When Alex reached the interstate, he headed away from the cabin, toward town. For the first time in a long time, he didn't want to be alone with his pain. When he hit the outskirts of San Antonio, he exited and pulled into a hotel.

Standing at the front desk, Kate's words replayed in his head. *You want what they all want.*

The desk clerk waved her hand in front of Alex to get his attention. "Here's your key. And we have a mixer here in the lobby until ten. Wine and snacks, just over there."

He glanced where she pointed and was met with waves from a table of ladies who were staring at him. He nodded before hurrying off to the elevator. In the hotel room, Alex dropped into the swivel chair at the desk and looked around the empty room. He didn't want to be alone. The silence hurt. He needed noise and people to distract him from Kate's accusation bouncing around in his head. A quick glance at the time reminded him that people would be socializing downstairs for another forty-five minutes. Based on the waves from that one table, he'd be warmly welcomed at the mixer.

He picked up his phone and walked out the door. As it closed with a thud behind him, he changed his mind. Socializing with the ladies downstairs wasn't what he wanted to do. Going to the mixer didn't have to be the solution to not being alone. He reached into his pocket for the key but shook his head when he pictured the key card laying on the desk, right where he'd left it.

As he boarded the elevator, he typed out a message: *Free tonight? Meet at BJ's? It's been a rough night.* He sent it to Ben. He sent the same message to DJ but added: *Come alone.*

Downstairs, the clerk's face lit up as he made his way to the desk. "I wasn't sure you'd come back down."

"I locked myself out of the room."

"Oh. Let me get you another key."

While she typed and swiped, he turned his back to the mixer and stared out the double doors. His phone buzzed, and he smiled at the response from Ben: *Almost done here. 10 pm too late?*

Alex replied: *See you then.*

He hadn't yet tucked the phone in his pocket when DJ responded: *On my way.*

"Your girlfriend?" The clerk handed him a new key card.

"What?" Alex shoved it in his pocket.

"The picture? On your phone."

He stared at the background pic on his phone, the photo of Kate and Cuddle Bunny. "Not sure anymore. Thanks for the key."

An hour later, Alex, Ben, and DJ sat in a round booth at the brew house, sporting events on every screen in the room. Alex's friends didn't spout off a series of questions about what happened or why he was there alone.

Tempted to read Kate's texts, Alex slid his phone in his pocket. "Thanks for coming. What did you tell Becca?"

"Said I was meeting a friend." DJ tapped out a text to Becca as he spoke. "But she knows something is up. The woman has radar. I told her not to bother you and Kate."

Ben laughed. "Nobody cares when I come and go."

"I don't want to discuss what happened. That wouldn't be fair to Kate. But . . ." Alex shrugged.

Ben slapped his menu. "Ribs. I'm having ribs."

"Pizza for me. And one of their handcrafted sodas." DJ scanned the room trying to get the waiter's attention.

Alex surveyed the menu. "Spurs win?"

"Beat the Rockets by more than 30 points." Ben smiled at the blonde waitress that hurried toward the table. "Hey there."

"Did y'all figure out what you want?" She tapped on her ordering pad.

DJ looked at Alex. "Do you know what you want?"

"I know exactly what I want." Alex's tension eased.

Ben raised his eyebrows. "You even going to order?"

Alex rattled off his choice to the waitress. "Not going back tonight."

The waitress trotted away.

DJ chuckled. "Is that about cooling off or absence making the heart do whatever?"

"Free marriage advice from the married guy, what every single guy needs." Ben rubbed his buzzed hair, laughing.

After a third text from Becca, DJ headed home. Alex pitied DJ the slightest bit, knowing he wouldn't be sleeping anytime soon, not until Becca ran out of questions—questions he didn't have answers to.

Ben shook Alex's hand. "I'm glad you texted me. Let's do it again. But under different circumstances."

"I'd like that. Thanks for coming."

Alex drove back to the hotel. The elevator—empty every other time he'd ridden it—filled with the waving ladies from the table headed upstairs after a swim. Kate's face smiled at him from his phone.

When the elevator opened on the third floor—his floor—the group exited. He hung back, letting them get off first. Thankfully, his room was at the opposite end of the hall.

In the hotel room, as he peeled off his clothes, he winced at the bruising on his chest. In the chaos, little had been discussed about the accident. With everything else going on, he was glad for that. After he and Kate reconciled and he made sure she was okay, he'd tell her all about the deer and the tree and the bruises.

Once he'd tucked in bed, he read her texts. Her honesty tugged at his heart. Pain and love were more than bedfellows, they were soulmates, forever connected.

After setting an alarm, he rolled onto his side and succumbed to much-needed sleep.

CHAPTER THIRTY-THREE

January 28, 2016 – 1:23 am

I woke up on the floor, my cheek pressed to a buzzing phone. I swiped the screen without looking to see who was calling. "Alex? I'm sorry."

"It's me, Kate. LeAnn. I'm calling from Jeff's phone."

"Oh, sorry. How is he?"

"He's okay, but you need to talk to me. Now."

In halted, disjointed snippets, I told her what had happened, what I said, how Alex had driven away, visibly upset.

After forty-five minutes on the phone listening to LeAnn tell me what I already knew, I crawled in bed, but not before setting an alarm. I didn't exactly sleep. I cried laying on my left side, rolled to my back and blubbered some more, then settled on my right side. I finally dozed laying on my right.

When my alarm screamed at me, I was still very short on sleep. After brushing my teeth, I pulled on tennis shoes. I grabbed my purse and keys off the counter and climbed into my car. Unsure if the home improvement store in Kerrville or San Antonio was closer, I opted for San Antonio because I didn't run the risk of bumping into Becca. As much as I liked her, I didn't want to see her for fear that I'd have to admit to her what'd happened. Granted, the sun wasn't even up, so the risk was low, but I wasn't going to take any chances.

I drove toward San Antonio and made it to the store just as it opened. Most people were shopping for lumber and other materials needed for job sites. I stood out in that crowd. In my yoga pants and Aggie sweatshirt, I didn't look ready to build a house. I only needed one item, but I need a clerk to help me.

I'd spent the better part of the night in tears, and my face looked it. When the clerk turned around, alarm registered on his face. *It's like he's never seen a woman cry before.* I wasn't actively crying— well, not much. The poor clerk barely made eye contact. He motioned me toward what I needed. I made my choice, and he flipped a switch. The machine screamed to life. As the grinder carved out its mastery, I checked my phone again, hoping for a message from Alex. *He's probably sound asleep. Or did he sleep at all?*

I'd done exactly what Becca feared—I'd broken his heart. But I refused to be like Scott, leaving a trail of wounded people. I had a list of people to call, but Alex's name took up the first ten slots.

I made my purchase. On the way home, classic country tunes played on the radio. When I heard the snapping in the intro of "I Love a Rainy Night" I started crying all over again.

Showing up to the cabin before the sun crested the horizon didn't strike me as the best idea. Waiting on the sun gave me time to make myself a bit more presentable. After I made myself less a fright, I'd drive out to Alex's and apologize.

My foot rested heavy on the accelerator as I made my way home to The Castle.

CHAPTER THIRTY-FOUR

January 28, 2016 – 6:45 am

Alex set the gift bag on the floorboard before buckling his seatbelt. Words popped around in his head like little white spheres in a bingo ball cage. Lack of sleep wouldn't play in his favor when it came to stringing coherent sentences together. He pulled through the drive-thru and ordered a Venti black coffee, the first of many caffeine installments.

He hopped on the interstate and headed west. *What if she's still in bed?* The thought made him laugh. *Not a chance.* She hadn't slept much, if at all. That was his guess. He expected red puffy eyes to greet him at the back door and almost felt bad for not going back last night.

While the roads into town were crowded, the lanes going his direction had very few cars. He made it to her exit in under a half-hour. After navigating the back roads and driving past the crime scene tape on Flat Rock Road, he pulled up to Kate's house.

Pamela Humphrey

His phone beeped. Ben had texted and included DJ on the message: *Have fun storming the castle.*

DJ replied: *Funny. You know that's what she calls her place, right?*

Ben responded: *Calls it what?*

Alex typed out an answer: *Just pulled up to The Castle.*

Before he slipped the phone in his pocket, two texts popped on his screen simultaneously, both the same: *Took you long enough.*

CHAPTER THIRTY-FIVE
January 28, 2016 – 7:03 am

I snagged a couple cookies before running back to the bathroom. Hopefully, hot water had magic powers to reduce swollen eyes.

After stepping out of the shower, when I saw myself in the mirror, my hope in magic hot water withered. If anything, my eyes looked worse. I pulled on a clean pair of yoga pants and Alex's sweatshirt. I dug through my bags, trying to find the tee shirt he'd given me. Every item of clothing looked like it'd been tied in knots, but that one was the worst. Somewhere in the house, buried in a box, hid my iron. But I didn't have time to find it.

Inspiration hit. I spread my clothes out on the hardwood floor in the living room. If I set heavy boxes on them, hopefully by the time my makeup looked presentable, the clothes would be somewhat flattened, even if not completely wrinkle-free. I hoisted a box of books onto my shirt, then picked up another box—of rocks, it felt like. Almost to the jeans, I nearly dropped the heavy load when someone knocked. I spun around still holding the container full of books. That was my mistake. When I caught sight of Alex at the back door, my hands flew to my mouth. The box hit the floor, missing my toes by a fraction of a millimeter. Alex pressed his face to the pane in the back-door window, a look of alarm engraved around his eyes.

I dashed across the room and pulled open the door. "I'm so sorry. Forget about what I said last night." I reached to hug him, but he put his hand out.

He walked to the sofa, stopping briefly at the box covering my shirt. Did he recognize the shirt? Did he notice the bottom of the heart and the word *Me* peeking out from under the box? "We need to talk."

Probably not, because those words never preceded happy conversations. Never. I wasn't good at relationships, and even I knew that. But I refused to give up without at least talking his ear off. Before launching into a monologue, I chose to avoid the mistake I made last night—not listening first.

"Sure." I sat at the opposite end of the couch.

Instead of a comfortable quiet, awkward silence sat like an elephant between us. Just when I'd nearly lost the battle of holding my tongue to let him speak first, he shifted so that he looked me in the eye. "Is that what you think, Kate? Really? You think I drove to Denver, hid with you under a bridge, and stayed up all night searching for clues so that I could earn time in your bed?"

I reached out to touch him, but he jumped up and moved away from me.

"In your apartment . . ." He raked his fingers through his hair. "I wasn't trying to—Is that what this is all about? What did I do to destroy your trust?"

"You didn't. Let's leave it alone. Please forgive me."

"No. You are not brushing this away. Be honest with me, please, Kate. I deserve at least that."

I hugged a throw pillow, my shield while I lobbed my fears at him. "You talked about leaving . . . and the way you looked at me in that kitchen."

"Leaving? I was talking about leaving with Rory to identify Keith without telling you, sneaking out while you slept." He waved an arm toward the bedroom. "But leaving a note on your pillow seemed in bad taste."

"I'd have been furious with you."

"Yeah. That's why I said something. I tried to protect you, but leaving turned out to be a bad idea." He shoved his hands in his pockets.

"It wasn't." I regretted my comment immediately and hoped he wouldn't ask for any explanation. Giving voice to what might've happened had he stayed required more anything that I had in my tank.

"I shouldn't have left you alone." He dropped back onto the couch, his face buried in his hands. "And, in the kitchen . . ." His voice cracked as he lifted his head. "I thought you were dead, Kate. Dead. That I'd never see you again—then you were there in front of me. And the way I *looked* at you? Unbridled desire, maybe. I wanted you, but not in the way you're talking about."

"Alex, please, forgive me." I grabbed his arm as he started to get up again.

His shoulders taut, he stayed seated but didn't look at me. "Why do you assume the worst of me? More than that, why do assume that's the only reason someone would want to be with you?"

I answered with tears, the big sloppy, not-gonna-make-my-eyes-look-better kind of tears. I leaned forward, trying to control my quiet sobs, sure that I'd ended what I so desperately wanted.

"I didn't mean to make you cry." A warm hand moved up and down my back. "And I'm sorry, too. I shouldn't have stormed out last night."

That simple, gentle touch was my invitation. I wiped my tears and buried my face in the curve of his neck.

He wrapped his arms around me, resting his chin on my head. "I give you my word. I'm not hanging around just waiting for you to change your mind. But—I can't—"

"Can't what?" I pulled away. Confusion swirled in my head. "What are you saying?"

"Can't isn't the right word." He slid his hand down my arm, barely grazing my skin. Goosebumps rose to meet his fingertips. "I *won't*, not until—but sharing a bed with you, *that* I can't do."

My heart raced. "I won't ask you to do that anymore."

Tenderness swirled in those green pools. He gazed at me, glancing a knuckle on my cheek. I met his kiss, supple and soft.

He pulled back and brushed hairs out of my face. "I love you, Kate."

I stared at him, the words repeating in my head. I'd accused him of being a letch. *Clearly, I'm a master at this relationship stuff.* "I listened to the song. More than once. Lying on the floor right over there. That's what you came back to say last night?"

"Something like that."

I laid my hand on his cheek. "Tell me, *please.*"

He pressed into my hand, then kissed my palm. "That was the main point. I wanted you to know that even though we haven't known each other long, I know how I feel. It's not a passing fancy. I decided."

"When?"

"This morning, yesterday morning, several days before that. Mostly, anytime I think about you."

"Go on." I wanted to hear all about how he loved me.

"While I searched, I wouldn't let myself even contemplate the what-ifs. But when I heard that shot—I'm not going to give you the I-thought-my-life-was-over-too bit because, sadly, that's not how it works. The sun would've risen the next day, just like before. But my life is better with you in it, because of you. I want it to stay that way. I love you."

I pulled him to my lips, and he pressed his mouth to mine, restrained passion burbling out of every pore. Snaking my arms around his neck, I responded to his hands wandering my back. "Mmm."

My soft moan sparked a low chuckle from Alex. "You're a lot more relaxed when you don't think me some rake."

"I let how those other guys behaved color my opinion of you. I'm sorry. Really, I am."

"The wrong kind." He tilted his head back against the couch and gazed at me several seconds. "I forgive you."

I felt like I'd won the lottery, but that nagging voice that whispers to double-check the numbers hounded me. "You're really okay with not sleeping together?" *Okay with me?* That was the question my heart wanted answered.

He tucked a hair behind my ear, focusing his green eyes on me. "Yes."

I craved his understanding but doubted he could begin to know how reliving the incident had shaded everything around me, how my trust evaporated when I told the story to Jonathon, seeing it play out in my head all over again. It frightened me to open my mind to the wound again, but I wanted him to know. "The reason I can't . . ." My heart thumped in my chest.

"Kate, I heard."

"What I told Jonathon?"

Alex nodded and rested his forehead on mine. His quiet presence acted as a protective sentry anchoring me to the present while I opened the door to the past.

"He didn't even—" I shook my head. "I tried to forget."

"You don't need to think about it anymore. Ever." Maybe he did understand. "Let's talk about something else."

"Thank you for the chocolate."

"I wasn't exactly sure what was wrong so I stopped at the corner store by the highway for a chocolate bar on my way over. Clearly, I underestimated what was bothering you."

"But you bought a Cherry Coke, too. You know me well."

"I want to, more than anything."

I ran my finger down the cleft in his chin. "Who painted the den?"

"Becca needed something to do. She painted the master, too."

"Maybe I overreacted to her meddling."

"I think you *should* be careful with my heart." He winked.

"She didn't want me to sleep with you until I was sure about how I felt. She said you were in love with me."

"That obvious, was it?"

"I did what she thought I might, too. Her implication irritated me so much, but I did break your heart."

"Not broken, only a small crack. It'll heal." His eyes closed, he pressed his lips to my temple. When he pulled back, he added, "So will yours."

I'd never felt more naked, fully dressed. "If you crack the heart open, you see what's inside."

"That's beautiful, Kate."

"Pat said it to Beth about a piñata."

"I think I'd like to hear the rest of that story."

"Becca painted the extra room, too?"

"I painted it while I was *not* sleeping in your bed."

"What happened? Why did you leave?"

"I kissed you while you were sleeping. You kissed back." He raised his eyebrows, a sparkle in his eyes.

My cheeks burned with embarrassment. "I thought that was all part of my dream."

"Dreaming about me, huh?" He played with a lock of my hair. "This is what I wanted, Kate. After everyone cleared out yesterday, I wanted to hold you, make sure you were okay. I just wanted to be near you."

"I chased you away."

"Seeing you, touching you reminded me that I wasn't dreaming. The night you were missing was a long night, for you and for me. Researching kept me sane. Worry kept me awake most of the night. Though I refused to entertain the thoughts, I wondered if I'd ever see you again."

I leaned back against him, pulled his arms around me, and rested my head on his chest. He inhaled sharply as if in pain.

I whipped around and faced him. "You're hurt." Without a second thought, I grabbed at his tee shirt and lifted the hem.

Purple splotches covered his chest.

"Alex? What happened to you?" I glanced my fingers over the bruising. Darker shades covered the area where a seatbelt would've been. "A car accident?"

"Rory and I collided with a tree on the way out to the cabin. I'm okay."

"All the bandages on his face. I noticed, but I was too shaken to ask about it. Why didn't you tell me?"

"Before or after you asked me to leave?" Alex tugged his shirt down and pulled me back against him, letting his bicep serve as a pillow. "I planned to tell you, but we had other stuff to sort out first."

"I could've lost you."

"That's why I didn't bring it up earlier. You didn't lose me. I'm here."

"Tied to that chair, before Beth came to, I sobbed. Not just because I'd been kidnapped *again*, but I knew how horrid it must be for you and for Travis. Then, later, when I heard the gun click, I didn't think about anyone else. I thought it was over, my life gone. Oddly, I don't even remember the gun going off, just that horrible click. When I got up afterward, blood everywhere, darkness and anger climbed inside me. Jonathon was full of anger and hate. It was as if I absorbed what he felt."

Alex kissed the side of my head and tightened his embrace.

I trailed my fingertips up and down his arm. "Jonathon kept calling me Claire, but that's not who I am. I haven't been Claire since Scott pulled away from the yellow house for the last time. I'm Kate. No matter where I got the name, that's who I am."

Alex didn't fill the quiet spaces, his breath in my ear the encouragement for me to continue.

"But I *am* a Bentley. I'm going to change my name, legally."

"Kate Bentley. I like how that sounds. I'm sure Travis will happily set his lawyers on it immediately."

"I'll need lawyers for more than that. According to Beth, her parents left everything to me, as penance."

"Let me guess. Justin is unhappy with that?"

I nodded. "Before you showed up last night, I searched for that guy from high school, to make sure Scott didn't ki—hurt him."

"I'm guessing he threatened to if that guy ever touched you again. What did you find?"

"He's a mayor in some town out west."

"Not dead." The small hitch in Alex's voice gave me pause. "Feel better now?"

I shrugged. "I never saw the guy again, and Scott never mentioned it. Ever. He acted as if it never happened."

"Are you really okay?"

"Mostly. Trying to make Scott sound like a good guy irritated me. He doesn't deserve it. I want to hate him for what he did—to me, to Jonathon, to everyone—but then I remember my dad, Gavin Westfall—driving us on road trips, making kolaches with me. It's hard to hate *that* man. How is it possible they were the same person?"

"Give yourself time to sort through feelings." In words soft and low, he added, "I'll be here whenever you need me."

"Thank you." I patted his hand. "Want me to make you breakfast?"

"I'm not done talking." He shifted me out of his lap and crossed his arms. "There are a couple other things I need to say."

My smile shriveled at his sudden seriousness. "What?"

"First of all, please delete the Find My BFF app. Just in case lightning strikes twice."

I pulled out my phone and swiped through the screens, letting him see. "I did that as soon as I got my phone back. What else?"

"All my life I thought love took a long time to develop. With you, I've learned that's not true." He put his hand up when I leaned in to hug him. Again. "But if this relationship has a real future, I need you . . . to consider—and I mean seriously consider—" He looked down, covering his face with his hand for a moment before locking eyes with me. "Will you watch Star Wars with me? All of them?" His eyes dazzled with mischief.

I wrinkled my nose. "How many?"

"Seven. Eighth comes out in December."

I shifted into his lap, careful of his bruising, and slipped my arms around his neck. "That's a lot of hours."

"It'll be worth whatever time it takes. I promise."

"I love you, Alex." I dotted kisses along his unshaven jawline. When he didn't answer immediately, I tilted my head back to see his reaction.

"I know." His grin made me wonder what I was missing.

Chapter Thirty-six

January 28, 2016 – 7:45 am

Alex patted her hip. "Wait here."

"Where are you going?

"I brought you something. Gotta get it out of the truck." He darted out the back door as soon as she hopped out of his lap.

She stood in the doorway, watching, while he unlocked the truck and opened the passenger side door. When he pulled out the large gift bag, delight exploded on her face.

He sauntered toward the door, amused at her reaction.

"Pretty bag. And big." She reached for the gift.

He pulled it behind his back, deciding to drag out her anticipation a little longer. "You mentioned something about breakfast?"

"I've got sausage, eggs, cheese, and tortillas. I can whip up some breakfast tacos."

"That's Texan for *I love you.* You know that, right?"

She crossed her arms and pursed her lips, giving an unconvincing pout. "You're going to make me wait to open it?"

"Yep." He chuckled and set the colorful sack in the den. "I'll make coffee."

She cut open a tube of sausage and dumped it in the skillet. "I talked to LeAnn late last night. She's with Jeff."

"He's back in Denver?" Alex set the table, waiting for the pot to finish brewing.

"She's in Texas, in whatever little town he's in. He'll be released tomorrow."

"But he's okay?"

"They don't expect any lasting issues from whatever they gave him."

"I'm glad that all turned out okay."

"They'll be here to visit in a few days." Kate added eggs to the pan. "And Travis texted me early this morning. Patrick talked to Justin. Travis said I wouldn't have any problems with all of that. Oh, and he's making an appointment for me to meet with lawyers tomorrow."

"What did he say when you told him about changing your name?"

"I haven't told him. I'll call him later, have him come over, and tell him in person." She pinched the edge of the tortilla and flipped it. "Did you spend the night cleaning the cabin?"

"Cabin is still a disaster zone. Too many reminders of you at my place. Last night I needed to be someplace I could think."

"You didn't want to think about me?" She asked her question without turning around.

"You're about to burn that tortilla." He kissed her on the cheek before pouring them each a mug of coffee, then sat at the table.

"Don't you have oodles of work waiting on you?"

"Yeah. If I wait too long between jobs, leads dry up, so I accepted three new projects."

"Now that life isn't crazy, I'll get cash to pay you for everything you've spent on me."

"No. You won't. It's not necessary." He shifted. "I may not get over here tomorrow. I have to get the cabin in order before I can work."

She surprised him by dropping into his lap. "I require kisses in advance for scheduled absences." Her arms draped over his shoulders, she stared at him, laughter glinting in her dark eyes.

He loved this side of her. Playful and confident, she relished his affections and acted as if they were deserved.

"Let's double it just in case I can't get over here on Saturday either." He made advance payment until his stomach growled.

"Okay, I'll feed you." She hopped out of his lap and set food on the table. "Dig in."

Before she sat down, her phone lit up with Meg's face. "Start eating. I won't be long." Kate picked up the phone and disappeared down the hall.

He obeyed, so he'd be well-fed and ready to listen when she came back out in tears.

Part-way through his second taco, his phone rang. He swallowed down his mouthful and swiped the screen. "Hey, Rory."

"Just calling with an update and to check on y'all. How is she?"

Alex glanced down the hall. "She's doing much better today."

"Good to hear. Listen, Keith's in custody and talking. Based on what I've heard, I'm not sure he would've hurt Kate. You, on the other hand—that's a different story. I'm only sort of joking."

"Yeah. He wasn't my biggest fan."

"Alex," Rory hesitated. "DJ filled me in a little. I'm glad you've returned to the land of the living."

"Me, too. And I don't even begin to know how to thank you for saving Kate."

"I didn't, Alex." Rory paused, leaving Alex wondering if he'd get more explanation. "Jonathon went to a lot of trouble to end his own life. I can't imagine it was his original intent. None of that really makes sense to me. Maybe something she said changed his mind."

"But I saw the chair knocked over."

"He was right next to her. I wasn't sure where he was aiming from outside that door. I reacted. Protecting her . . . it's what I'm trained to do. No one on my team discharged a weapon."

"I had no idea. She thinks . . ."

"I'll let you tell her what happened."

"I will. And, Rory, about your parents . . ."

"Email them when you're ready. They'd be thrilled to hear from you. You're family, Alex. Always."

Alex rubbed his face. "How can I thank you? You have no idea . . ."

"Yeah, I do. It's obvious you love her. As far as thanks, you can invite me over for tamales at Christmas. You still make them?"

"Every year. But I won't wait until Christmas to call."

"Deal."

Pricked with regret about the choices he'd made after Ellie's death, Alex hung up the phone, but he needed more time before he was ready to email the Jacobsons. He would. They needed him to reach out, to be a connection to memories of Ellie. He wouldn't deny them that, but it would take him time. Hopefully, life in his circle of the world would settle down a little first.

Alex was on his third cup of coffee when Kate came strolling back into the kitchen.

"Sorry I took so long." She pulled the clip out of her hair, letting it fall around her shoulders.

"You don't look upset. Things are good?"

"No. She's still furious, but I can't change that. All I can do is be honest with her." Her voice caught at the word honest, and she looked away. "Not completely honest. I did leave out the part about her half-brother kidnapping me and dying next to me."

"Probably wise. She might not be ready for that, yet. When I talked to her, I might've been a bit harsh."

"She didn't say anything to that effect. Didn't mention you at all, actually." Kate leaned on the counter. "I told her that learning about my past didn't change the way I felt about her and that when she was ready she could call me."

"I'm proud of you, Kate."

"Thanks." She dropped into his lap. "I'm not hungry."

"Not hungry? There's plenty left. It's delicious, by the way. Want me to get you a fresh cup of coffee?" He peppered her with comments and questions, seeing how long she'd wait before asking about the gift. "You sure you don't want at least a small taco?"

She brushed her lips along his jaw. "Can I open it now?"

"As you wish."

Anticipation lit up her face.

"It's a house-warming present. It sat in my truck all night, but I got the gift bag this morning. I've never dated an heir to a fortune, so I wasn't sure what to get you."

"Very funny." She poked him in the arm. After removing handfuls of tissue, she stared into the bag. "Oh, Alex."

"You like it?"

She wrapped his grandmother's quilt around her. "I love it. Thank you." She tapped the cleft in his chin. "Stay right here."

She ran down the hall, the quilt flapping behind her. He leaned on the counter and fished the small envelope out of his pocket, just as excited about the anticipated reaction to his other gift. He tucked it away when she came up the hall.

"Close your eyes." She ran up to him and touched his arm. "And open your hand."

He obeyed, reaching for her with his other hand.

She inched closer. "I laid awake part of the night rehearsing what to say to you, but all the poetic words I thought of before the sun rose, disappeared with the darkness. So, bear with me. I'm making it up as I go."

Standing with his eyes closed, he wasn't in charge. There wasn't anyone else in the world he'd do this for without an argument. While he waited for her to continue, he smoothed the wrinkles on her sweatshirt under his hand. His sweatshirt.

"Meeting you has changed my life and probably saved it more than once. There's no way to thank you properly."

"I don't expect—"

She put a finger to his lips. "I was wrong to say what I said last night. You aren't that kind of guy. I'm safe with you."

"I want you to believe that, Kate."

"I do." She laid her hand on his, between their palms a cold, metal key. "A key to my castle."

He swallowed back a swell of emotion as he pulled out his keyring and slipped the key on the loop. "When did you have time for this?" He stared at the brass key. It meant as much to him as the words she'd whispered only a few nights ago and repeated this morning.

"The home improvement store opens early. I drove into San Antonio and made sure to get there as soon as it did."

He slid a small envelope out of his pocket. "I must've just missed you. I went to the same store." He opened her hand and let the key fall into her palm. "A cabin key."

"It's purple! I love it."

"I spent fifteen minutes looking through the rack of coated, patterned keys. This one will be easy to find on your keyring."

She pulled his arms around her. "I'm happy. I can't think of anything else I need."

"You need to unpack. And you need a red sectional and coffee table for the den."

"And popcorn."

"Exactly. For the movies you're going to watch with me."

"But not today."

"Right. Today I'm taking you to the Riverwalk." He traced his knuckle along her neckline. "That is, if you *want* to go."

"Give me a few minutes to get dressed. The box should've flattened the wrinkles out of my shirt by now." She ran across the room and picked up her jeans.

He lifted the box and blew her a kiss when he saw the *Someone in Texas* ♥*s Me* shirt. "You are by far the craziest woman I've ever decided to love."

"But good crazy, right?" Kate scrunched up her nose as she inspected the flat, wrinkled tee shirt.

"The best kind."

Epilogue

February 1, 2016 – 2:17 pm

Patrick set a mug of tea on the nightstand. "How are you feeling, love?"

Beth squinted at him. "Wonderful. Just a small headache." She tapped the bed next to her. "Come sit."

He slid in next to her. "You got a letter from Marla. She mailed it before everything happened." He laid the envelope on the blanket between them.

"Will you read it to me?"

He fumbled with the seal until it tore open, then patted his pockets.

"Your readers are probably on the top of your head." Even with her eyes closed, Beth took care of him.

After planting a soft kiss on the side of her head, he pulled on his cheaters and unfolded the letter.

Beth-

You may have already heard the news from Jonathon. I called him Monday night to tell him. It wasn't what I intended when I left, but let me explain.

When Brad and Chrissy left, I lived day to day barely feeling, struggling to keep Jonathon from killing himself using those horrible drugs. It wasn't what I wanted, but he needed my help.

For many years, I was afraid to leave Jonathon long enough to fly out and visit Chrissy. Afraid that he'd start using again. When I flew out to see her five years ago, I almost didn't come home. I missed my little girl. But as you know, I returned home.

Not this time. I'm choosing what I want. My little girl isn't so little anymore, and I want as much time with her as I can get. And Brad asked me to stay. He said that away from Texas—I know he meant away from Jonathon—maybe we could find our happily-ever-after.

I'll be back in a month to clean out the old place. I pray that Jonathon will be okay with my decision. He didn't say much last night.

-Marla

Beth wiped at tears.

Patrick tossed the letter aside and wrapped his arms around her. "Marla's timing couldn't have been worse. Jonathon was a powder keg. Hearing about finding Claire lit the fuse."

"Finding Kate didn't bring him closure. Thankfully, he wasn't like Scott after all. He didn't take what wasn't his."

ACKNOWLEDGMENTS

Without support and encouragement from others, I wouldn't have finished this book. I'm overwhelmed with gratitude for those that read *Finding Claire* and fell in love with Kate and Alex in the same way I did. Thanks goes out to my mom and sister (who is nothing like Meg) and the awesome members of the 10 Minute Novelists group on Facebook, where I found helpful beta readers and much needed encouragement.

Special thanks go to Shannyn, Lisa, and Pamela for listening when I ramble and being encouraging, and Glenda (and her "Darlin'") for answering my every question and making sure the law enforcement details were believable. If they're not, the error is mine.

And a huge thank you to my family. Without their understanding and patience, I couldn't write.

About the Author

Pamela Humphrey was inspired to write after researching her genealogy. Intending to create a booklet for her mom and immediate family, she set about gathering stories and pictures of the Ramirez family. She ended up writing her first book, *Researching Ramirez: On the Trail of the Jesus Ramirez Family*, a family history of her great great grandfather's family. During that research, she found a christening record that ignited her imagination. Using the documentation she'd found as a backbone for the story, she imagined what life was like for her ancestors and wrote *The Blue Rebozo*, a fictional account of her great grand aunt's life.

On a road trip, when driving through the Texas Hill Country, the landscape sparked the idea for a romantic suspense series. Weaving mystery, genealogy, and romance, she wrote *Finding Claire* (Book One) and *Finding Kate* (Book Two). She is currently writing the next installments in the Hill Country Secrets series.

Pamela is a stay-at-home, homeschooling mom who enjoys many creative outlets: sewing, paper-crafting, jewelry-making, practicing her bass guitar, reading, and conversing with imaginary characters (what most call writing). She lives in San Antonio, Texas, with her husband, sons, black cats, and leopard gecko.

CONNECT ONLINE

Website: www.phreypress.com
Facebook: http://www.facebook.com/phreypress
Twitter: @phreypress

If you want to read more about the town of Schatzenburg, TX, or the characters who frequent that little town, check out the website for extras and short stories.